The Salvation of Perception

Lesley Precilla

The Salvation of Perception

First Printing June 2017

ISBN-13: 978-1546853671

ISBN-10: 1546853677

Cover Design by radeXP

Printed in the United Kingdom

Distributed by Amazon.com

For a prince and a princess, without whom, the desire to shape a nurturing future may not have been born. For Reece and for Maisen.

For all offspring. The future is yours, wake up. Be all you can be.

∞

Was fear the apple that Eve picked? Lesley Precilla

It was raining that evening as I recall, the last Friday of the Xmas term, everyone rushing about, trying to get home; in from the downpour. I remember it so well because in five minutes, three hundred seconds, life paths changed. For the better or the worse, I wasn't sure, but after the rampage passed, life was permanently changed.

It was at the bus stop on Homerton High Street, just before the junction with Chatsworth Road. Rain had been pouring consistently for the past few hours, and the streets were comparatively empty of pedestrians. The few people that were about, seemed intent on getting to their destination in as quick a time as possible. They clung to their coats, the shelter of bus stops and shop fronts, anxiously peering into the oncoming headlights, trying to make out the number of the bus that would take them to the warmth and security of their homes. The evenings were getting colder as winter embraced its' season, but it didn't seem to bother everyone in quite the same way.

At the far end of the bus shelter, Micha and her girlfriends imposed their presence in the way only familiarity and youth could express. "Eh eh!, what the fuck is that ugly bitch looking at!' announced a heavily made-up teenager who interrupted her lip glossing to glare at her alleged usurper. It was around 9pm and the shelter heaved with the cacophony of teenaged girls, preening and posing into their collective idea of independence, sex appeal and most importantly, post pubescence. Jogging bottoms, trainers and hoodies, evidently a must, sported the sought after logos of Nike, Timberland and Adidas.

Hearing the shrill statement of their girlfriend, they quietened, turning half-cocked heads in the direction of the potential offender. Fifteen feet away stood an adjoining bus shelter for the Clapton run. Empty in comparison, the shelter contained just two girls. The first, Tasha, about sixteen years old, wore blue skinny jeans and a fitted baby blue shirt under a black mack. Eyebrows sculpted, hair let down and secured with an alice band, lipstick perfect, she appeared to be unaffected by the encroaching cold or the open distaste of Micha and her friends. Her companion, a younger girl, decked out in open toed high heels, calf length fitted black jeans and an off the shoulder black jersey with a peg sleeved short black jacket was clearly uncomfortable with the attention, but held in any fear, imitating the nonchalance of the older girl. Tasha looked back at the raucous group with boredom and distaste, smiling to herself at their apparent lack of the 'nu nu' style, confident in herself, she ignored them.

By now Micha's girls fanned out for a better look at the transgressors. Openly eyeing them from top to bottom, arrogant in the familiarity of their manor and their click. They spat audible sounds and animated gestures of disgust and intimidation, aimed at reducing the receivers to submission, should they dare try to retain self-respect by responding. Their feisty friend, adorned in the latest Nike trainers, bottoms and fleece jacket, now preening and full of pomp, continued her accusations, seemingly encouraged by the lack of response. At five feet nothing, Micha was full figured and blessed with the lumps and bumps of a full grown woman, assets which gave her most things she wanted, most of the time. "What! What!...what the fuck you looking at?...do you know me...you best mine girl! I'll mash you up and send you home to your man looking like a facie hole!" Micha ended her speech with a long kiss of her teeth and slapped her own arse. With no response forthcoming, she retreated to the end of the shelter where she leaned and glared at Tasha almost daring her to respond. As could be expected, her girlfriends burst into raucous fits of laughter. "Micha man, you give me too much joke!" they exclaimed, eyeing up their girlfriend's prey for any signs of retaliation.

"What!" recoiled Tasha, tired of Micha's insolence, "Who da fuck do you think you're talking to, you greasy bitch!' Tasha stood defiantly to approach the adjoining shelter, only to be physically stopped by her companion. "Fuck them Tasha, what you railing up yourself for?" Tasha kissed her teeth as loudly as her front gap would allow her. 'I ain't having that from that greasy fucking sket! What?!..if she wants it she can have it you know!..please believe me!' she spat in the direction of the now attentive girls, whilst animatedly removing the loop earrings from her lobes.

As Tasha stood, so did Micha.

"This is the same reason I don't even like to come down these ends you know! See how the tramp just start on me though!...I weren't even looking at her, fucking cretin!" Her companion exhaled and kissed her teeth, 'Just leave them Tasha, I ain't got time, and I ain't looking no drama!' She grabbed on to Tasha's arm as she stepped towards the adjoining shelter. "You got a problem?" Tasha continued, eyeing her adversary. Not getting a suitable response, she walked closer. "Is there something you want to say to me?" she continued animating her arms. Micha kissed her teeth as she bounded the remaining distance towards Tasha, carefully not straying too far from her girls.

"Listen bitch, you don't know me you know, I ain't from these ends but I'm repping my own t-w-e-n-t-y-four-O!, if you wanna step up on me, just step! Less of the long talk cause I ain't got time!" spat Tasha, noticing her antagonist's weakness of not wanting to come straight over to her. Perhaps she let her guard down, perhaps not, but after that brief exchange of words, Micha arrived at the adjoining stop. By now, the girls were face to face, and although Tasha knew her sister had her back, she also knew they were outnumbered, but it was too late to do anything about that. 'Let's play' she whispered to herself, and before Micha could say another word, Tasha grabbed a bunch of her long black weave and twisted it round her fist so that Micha's head ended up parallel to her crotch. 'You want dis bitch, don't you!' she hissed and began punching Micha's face to the immobilising shock of her girlfriends. They were taken by surprise, sure that their sheer numbers would stop any attempt to retaliate. Their momentary delay meant a black eye and split lip for their girl, but seconds later, as the initial shock passed, her friends finally made it to Micha's aid, and so began the beating of the two girls who awaited the bus to Clapton.

∞

Hot Baths

Nothing can happen - I say to you, nothing can occur - in your life which is not a precisely perfect opportunity for you to heal something, create something, or experience something that you wish to heal, create, or experience in order to be who you really are. Abraham Hicks

18 Months Earlier

Wayne grinned uncontrollably as he made his way to the steps of the 747 aircraft, almost holding his breath until he was directed to his seat by the window he specifically requested. His mother and Andy couldn't see his face, and he was glad. He wanted them to think him mature, but at that moment, all he could think about was going to England, and how great everything would be from then on. He'd spent the last three years with his grandparents in Trinidad, whilst his mother went ahead to carve out a life for them in London. He adored his grandparents. They raised him with the wisdom, love and patience only old age and contentment could offer. The opportunity of living in London with his mother though, could not be rejected regardless of the cost. The Cheshire cat grin would not move itself from his face no matter how much he tried.

The plane landed at Heathrow on a mild June morning. Wayne couldn't wait to step on to English soil, and was the first person in line as the doors were pushed open, and the gust of morning air entered the temperature controlled cabin. He felt the cold air enter his entire being, finally settling in his bones, causing a ripple of goose bumps on his sun kissed skin. "You alright babe, it's cold isn't it?" Ivy asked huddling closer to her son as she saw him catch his breath, bracing his body against the wind. "Cold? this isn't cold!" interrupted Andy catching up to them, "just wait till winter and you'll really be wondering what you doing in England!" The trio laughed as they made their way to collect their suitcases. Wayne didn't care that he was cold, he was in England, everything was just fine. He thought briefly about his grandmother, and the hunting trip he'd miss with his grandfather, but was too excited to dwell on them for long, as he took in the expanse and technology of Gatwick Airport.

The train arrived at their transit change destination in Victoria. Crowds bustled to the opening doors, seemingly irritated by the two large suitcases sitting on either side. Wayne followed his mother, gathering his suitcase and bags, ready to ascend the escalators to street level. He wondered why he hadn't heard the customary 'good mornings' from the masses of people walking past him, all in a hurry to come in or go out. By the time they made it up the escalators and he showed his ticket to the attendant, he wasn't surprised to be ignored when he greeted him. He suddenly felt very aware that he was indeed, not in Trinidad anymore, and as the trio made their way to the number thirty-eight bus stop, the cold finally began to eat away at his eagerness to be there.

At the bus stop though, he was heartened once again at the sight of the red double decker buses and black taxi cabs. The sullen, self-absorbed faces around him suddenly faded into the background as his preconceived ideas - drawn mostly from old television programmes - once again came to the fore. As they boarded the bus, the smiling driver, noticing the POS tags on their suitcases greeted them warmly, briefly reminiscing over his youth on the tiny island. The bus made it's way past Hyde Park, down Tottenham Court Road, and on to the border between Hackney and Islington. Wayne, positioned on the front seat of the top deck, soaked in the people and places he passed.

"Babes, the next stop is ours!" his mother Ivy shouted from half way up the staircase. The bus stopped on a main road full of businesses, whose shop fronts would not have looked out of place on any main road in Trinidad. They were an eclectic mix of the very old to the nearly new, all of which were bustling with activity. They disembarked in front of a dishevelled row of shops offering sweets, burgers and legal advice at the top of Dalston Lane. "Is it far from here mum?" Wayne asked dragging his suitcase behind him, trying to look like he didn't just land, as he caught the stares of a group of boys noisily making their way past him. Ivy responded gleefully, happy to have her son in London as she stepped out into the road, pointing in the direction of their home.

The road was alive with Saturday morning traffic. Wayne followed the sound of his mother's rambling suitcase as she turned off the main road on to a row of identical red brick houses. He walked on to the housing development his mother proudly declared as home, reassuring him that he was just a few minutes away from sitting down and releasing his feet from the pressurized squeeze of his new shoes. He smiled heartily at her as he dragged his suitcase behind him. Making his way to their front door, Wayne became acutely aware of the attention that his arrival was causing amongst the youths of the estate. Heads turned and conversations appeared to stop as they sized up the 'new kid on the block' without even the slightest welcoming smile or gesture. He felt inadequate as he noticed under hooded lids, the seemingly expensive attire of the children who were clearly no older than he was. He pulled himself up even straighter, silently cursing his new shoes as they pinched the corners of his toes, and steadfastly completed the final meters to number thirteen.

The house looked smaller than Wayne expected, and definitely not what he'd imagined on his ten- hour flight. It was joined to another two houses on either side, and they were joined to another two completing a row of ten. Each house was separated by a red brick wall and enclosed with a little wooden gate. As he looked left and right, his heart sunk as images of English grandeur melted away and were replaced with a contrasting reality. Ivy proudly showed her son his new home. Knowing he was probably thinking as she did two years earlier, she was quick to point out it's positive features. "It's just twenty minutes to your new school and if you look out your bedroom window, there's a small swing park right behind us!" Number thirteen Cronos Walk had two bedrooms, a kitchen, a front room and to its' redemption, and Wayne's delight, a bath.

Ivy smiled at her son as she put the kettle on in the kitchen. "So glad you're here babes! Go check out your room, it's at the top of the stairs at the back. While you unpack I'll make us something to eat." Wayne smiled and embraced his mother "I'm glad I'm here too mum" he returned, before eagerly climbing the flight of stairs to his bedroom. Painted blue and furnished with a cd player, bed, desk and chair, and a wardrobe filled with new clothes, it too was smaller than he was expecting, but he smiled as he threw himself across the bed and closed his eyes.

A scream from outside drew his attention to the window in the single room. Twenty feet away was a brick enclosed area containing three swings, a seesaw and a climbing frame where a few younger children played and a few older children congregated. 'Funny' Wayne thought to himself, 'no trees or grass, not even mud. Just concrete.' Some boys looked directly up at his window and Wayne smiled eagerly, raising his hand in acknowledgement. They didn't return his gesture. Instead, the boys looked at each other, laughed and turned away. He felt foolish and backed away from the window, rifling through his back pack to find his cds. He found them, chose one specially made for him by his best friend Semp, put it on, and lay back on his bed listening to a Courtney Melody mix. It wasn't what he'd been expecting, not at all, but it was England, and he had arrived, he was with his mums, and this was just the beginning of the fantastic life everyone was sure he was going to have. The Cheshire cat grin returned to his sun kissed face as he drifted off to sleep.

By the time Wayne awoke, it was dark outside and cold air blowing in from the open window, consumed his room. Closing it, he wiped the sleep from his eyes as he made his way down stairs to the sound of a television. In the living room, Andy was fast asleep on the couch, snoring so loudly Wayne wondered how he himself could possibly sleep through it. Following the pangs of hunger coming from his belly, he made his way down to the kitchen expecting to find his mother but instead found a plate of food and a note. It was from Ivy, she had gone to work and would not return till morning, but she prepared him some food and hoped he would be ok without her. Wayne lifted the lid covering the plate and found chips, vegetables and sausages that were stone cold. He yearned for Isobel's coconut bake as he followed the instructions and placed the plate in the microwave to reheat it.

The instant the timer went off, he ravenously placed the plate on the table before pouring a glass of grape flavoured KA from the fridge. Despite his hunger, the overcooked food was the most inedible dish he had ever eaten, and after a few bites, he pushed the plate away from him. Instead he searched the kitchen's cupboards for something that would satisfy the increasing growling from his belly. After countless hours spent helping his grandmother prepare their meals, he was confident in his abilities with the simplest of provisions. Half an hour later, Wayne sat down to his meal of tuna fish and bake and wondered what his grandparents thought he was doing.

By his third weekend, Wayne's days went from eager anticipation to all consuming, friendless solitude and boredom, as he settled into the practicalities of London life. Ivy worked most nights and as much as she wanted to introduce her son to his new world, she was asleep till late afternoons, leaving Wayne alone to explore his new territory. At fourteen, his world had completely changed. Most days he sat alone in his bedroom, reading or listening to his cds and wondering what had possessed him to leave his much loved island. Then he would hear his grandmother's words, warning his mother against her decision to take him, and as tears rolled down his cheeks, he would remember wanting his grandmother to shut up.

His new home was nothing like Tamana. There was no liming, barbequing, foraging, storytelling, hunting or even gathering. Even if there was it didn't matter, he wasn't invited and was on no guest list. For the last two days he sat on the swings hoping someone would come over to him, or at the very least, that the football would be accidentally kicked in his direction, but neither happened. As the days passed, he began dreaming at night and sometimes in the day, of running wildly through the dense Tamana bush, screaming as loudly as his vocal chords would allow, naked. He longed to feel the rain on his skin, to sit with his best friends Semp and Robin in their tamarind tree, to reason with his elders, for sports day in the Savannah, for drying cocoa, but most of all for the warmth and scents of his grandmother's kitchen.

Andy, his mother's partner, wasn't much help either. He was either at work, or asleep. He liked Wayne though, and tried to protect him from getting hurt by 'trickster London' the only way he knew how, by ensuring he knew what he must not do, could not do or should not do. But from Wayne's perspective, Andy was a presence to be avoided, and a usurper of his mother's time. Time that could have been spent with him.

By week four, he'd devoured Lord of the Flies, To Kill a Mockingbird and Animal Farm. Reading became his release, and his vicarious life as he became consumed with the lives of the characters on the pages he read. Temporarily relieved of the tedium and monotony of his own life, he soon saw no reason to get out of bed apart from food and bathroom calls. Freedom and privacy were suddenly thrust upon him like treats he hadn't been aware of, but there was no-one to explore them with and so he didn't. The days slipped by, one into the other with no interruption. He'd read his books and listen to his cds but somehow the distraction they offered no longer compelled him as he realised that was all he did. He felt loneliness creep into his system, as easily as the wind did when he left a window open.

∞

"You bored darling?" Ivy asked her son as he sat on the kitchen stoop surveying the trail of black ants unwittingly making their way to the line of poisonous white powder she'd laid down. "I ok" he replied, feeling every bit of the boredom his mother suggested. She had observed her son since his arrival and her heart ached at the loneliness she could see in his eyes. Suddenly Ivy jumped to her feet, "I have an idea. Come with me!" she demanded with a grin that made Wayne obey her without another word. Two minutes later they stood outside number twenty-two as she gently rattled the letterbox flap. Within seconds, the door opened releasing a blast of music and a tall boy, beaming a welcoming smile at the pair. "Hi Ivy, come in, mum's in the kitchen. Is that your son?" he asked inquisitively eyeing Wayne from head to toe. "Yes sweetheart, this is Wayne, Wayne this is Cavell" Wayne had seen Cavell on the estate before. He was always in a loud crowd, making animated gestures. Cavell was about a year or two older than him, with a lot more gold jewellery. The boys said hello to each other and followed the sound of lovers' rock coming from the kitchen at the back of the house.

"Eh eh, so Ivy, you finally decide to bring your prize possession out for people to see girl!?" As they entered the room full of women, a skinny girl sitting on a cushion on the floor, looked up from underneath a mass of hair. Her stylist, a gold toothed, plump woman with a red weave rushed over to take Wayne by the hand. "Uhhm, but he handsome ee!", she declared after eyeing him from head to toe. "Hello darling, I'm Angela, Cavell's mum, how are you finding England? you like it?" she asked between hugging him and rushing back to an incomplete plait. "Yeh, it's ok, not at all what I was expecting though." Wayne responded timidly, conscious of all the stares he was receiving. "Yes, I think they call that an 'anti-climax', I am very familiar with them myself!" The room burst into laughter as Wayne steadily kept his eyes on the floor. "You lot are embarrassing the boy man!", Cavell butted in, signalling Wayne to follow him upstairs. "You want something to drink?" he continued. "No thanks, I'm good", Wayne replied, eager to leave the room behind. "HHmph, somebody have manners too!" came another voice. He felt his face heat up as the women erupted again.

The boys made their way to Cavell's bedroom on the third floor, bumping in to his sister Keisha coming out of the bathroom. "Ppssttppss! What the...can you watch where you're going please!" she screamed as she dashed back into the bathroom and locked the door. "Like anyone wants to see your bee stings!" Cavell replied kissing his teeth. "Don't watch that Wayne, she's probably on her period or something" he added leading the way to his room before locking the door behind them.

In the room was another boy who Cavell introduced as his brethren Marcus, a face Wayne also recognised from the estate. He was offered a chair sitting in front of a music system, whilst Cavell threw himself across his bed, un-pausing a Nintendo console to resume play on his game. A few minutes later Marcus sprang up from his seat, throwing the controller on to the bed. "I told you cuz, you mustn't try fuck about wit de dan dada! How much times do you want me to show you man!" he teased, stretching his legs. "So who's dis?" he asked Cavell as he eyed Wayne from head to toe. "Did you just land bruv?" he continued flicking through Cavell's cd collection. "What?" Wayne asked quizzically, not fully understanding each word but painfully aware that he was being ridiculed. "What, can't you hear me, I'm standing right in front of you bro?!" Marcus replied with more animated gestures. "Ah silence your lip man!" Cavell intervened. "He's from Trinidad innit! Just cool man!

So what's it like dere bruv. I used to always here your mums talking about you and how much she missed you and couldn't wait for you to come and shit." Cavell teased effeminately. "It's real cool boy, different, everything's just different." Wayne answered coyly. "Like how?" Marcus added, drawing a hip hop mix cd from the stack. "Much more space, much greener, but I like London, I just need to get to know it better." "For true, for true!" added Cavell, "and don't worry, you're under our wing now, we'll show you London!" "How old are you?" Marcus enquired. "almost fifteen, how old are you?" Wayne returned, "Sixteen. What school are you going to?" "Upton Secondary" Wayne answered beginning to relax "Yeh, same as us, alright cool, you need to fix up first though bruv, because you ain't really going nowhere with those!" Marcus pointed at Wayne's footwear releasing his laughter as Cavell continued. "Creps, creps, creps!! Lord the boy need some crepes, please Lord!" The duo continued, animating their request with dancehall gestures until Wayne himself had to laugh at his shoes, even though they were his best pair.

"So what music are you into? who's your favourite DJ?" Cavell asked removing the cd Marcus selected before putting on his current favourite, Jay-z's Kingdom Come. "Reggae, pop..." "Pop! oh my days man!" Marcus interjected dramatically falling to his knees in front of Wayne. "What?" Wayne asked, unsure of what he'd said wrong. "Say it ain't so man!" Marcus continued as he and Cavell held in their obvious disdain. "What? you guys don't like dat ?, that's cool music man", Wayne continued bare facedly holding his ground. "Not here boss, you're in Hackney now, man's listen to hiphop, bashment, grime, house and rnb! Which DJ you follow?" Marcus added standing in front of Wayne, resting his chin between his thumb and index fingers. Wayne felt both pairs of eyes on him and frantically searched his brain for the names of popular DJs, wishing he had Semp by his side, "...I like ...Chinese Laundry, Nyah Binghi...!" he answered finally, acutely aware that he needn't have bothered. "Bro, it's best you just say you don't know any, cause who the fuck is 'Chinese Laundry' blood, and what kinda name is that? You need to school yourself dread. You sound like you from foreign...and best believe that ain't a good thing!" Marcus added, intentionally jerking the chair Wayne sat on, as he made his way to the window sill.

"So you got a girl in Trinidad then, matter of fact what's the females saying over there?" enquired Cavell slicking his eyebrows flat. "No, but the girls are real sweet, I just never really had time for that." Wayne replied trying to sound as nonchalant as he could, while fretting that he sounded too nonchalant. Marcus jumped off the window sill laughing. He kissed his teeth. "Man's a virgin...he nah taste de pu-nahnah yet! About he never really had time for that!....what da fuck!" Cavell and Marcus bumped fists as Cavell patted Wayne on his shoulder. Wayne flushed under his skin, earnestly searching for an adequate response. Nothing came. "So, have you?" was all he could muster. "Of course man! What you ah chat say!! Listen C, you best educate this yout yuh know! Man's is de O-riginal dan dada!"

Cavell stopped the cd and looked at Marcus. "After me you mean, the mother fucking blueprint! I don't want you to forget about Jessica you know!" Cavell grinned resuming play on the cd before moving in between Marcus and the full length mirror. Marcus kissed his teeth and swiftly spun around, grabbing Cavell in a head lock, forcing him to the floor. As the pair struggled in front of him, Wayne felt uncomfortable. He was unsure of the seriousness of the scene, four weeks' experience had taught him the 'British way' was different to what he'd known, but before panic dawned upon him, Cavell sat triumphantly on Marcus's back and farted. The trio laughed until their bellies ached and Cavell's sister Keshia was sent to order them to stop the noise. Forcing open the door, she eyed them with obvious contempt. "Cavell, mummy said not to make her have to come upstairs, so if I was you,

I would control myself, and my friends, and try to act like I have some kind of behav..!" Before she could complete her sentence Cavell dug into his trainers perched precariously on the window ledge, retrieved his socks and flung them in the direction of his sister. The boys burst into more laughter as she returned downstairs vowing to report the incident to their mother.

"Yeh, what you saying now my friend, so what do you do in Trinidad?" Cavell continued. "Anything...like what do you mean...I live in the country in a place call Tamana with my grandparents..." "What do you do for fun I mean, ok like say we play computer games, rave, chirps gyal, hang out..." the older boy explained. "Ok no, I don't have any computer stuff or anything like dat, but in Tamana, I's fish, lime with my friends, play cricket, pick fruits, bathe by the spring, go up by de river, make a cook out in de bush, anything really, it's real cool boy, and it have a lot more space, a lot more bush and you don't need a coat!" Marcus and Cavell looked at each other and grinned.

"Ok country boy, so what's your manor like and please don't tell me your house is a cardboard box on the side of a mud slide?" Marcus continued, not quite sure what to make of the 'new kid on the block', and not appreciating Cavell's willingness to bring him in to their click. "No!" Wayne replied indignantly. "Why do you say that. My house was concrete with a driveway and my grandparent's house is concrete with a longer driveway and endless land!" "Listen darg, don't get on your back foot with me, I don't know do I, that's why I is asking you, I ain't never been innit! Whenever I see 'back home' on telly my yout, that's what I see. I definitely don't see what you're talking about?" "Easy, easy!" Cavell interjected, irritated at his friend's line of questioning. "For real Marcs, you're just showing your ignorance my friend." "Listen I'm just saying, da yout is making out like back home is so sweet, what's he doing here den? I'm just trying to keep it real!, look at the brother's clothes, does it look like he lives in a yard with a driveway!" Marcus replied animating his words as he eyed Wayne from head to toe once more. "I came here to be with my mum, to get a good education and to have a good life, life is supposed to be so great here, but to be honest, I've been here four weeks and it ain't all that it's made out to be." Silence fell over the trio as each pondered their own thoughts. Wayne ached for the ease of friendships in Tamana, and wondered how it was that a black boy could not know what 'back home' was.

Cavell skipped to his favourite track, 'Do u wanna ride' and looked at Marcus and Wayne. "Ok so who's going to kiss who first?" he concluded feeling the obvious tension. "PPsssttsps, I'm cool you know fam!" Marcus answered. "I cool." Wayne added. "Yeh, you both look cool too, so I guess my vibe is just fucking itself up then!" Cavell grinned, "but brethren nah fe worry, cah me have de most righteous ting right here now!" Opening the door of his bedroom, Cavell poked his head through, "let me just check little miss umpalumpa ain't eaves dropping as per usual." The corridor was clear and he closed the door, pushed the bolt across the top and proceeded to stuff a t-shirt into the already tight gap between the floor and the door's edge. Wayne wondered what he was doing but said nothing.

"Alrighty then!" Cavell teased as he shook some talcum powder in front of the door. "Now let me introduce you to my little friend!", he continued, producing a shoe box from under his bed. "Yes I, just what man needs right now...wait let me check...You do smoke don't you?" Marcus asked Wayne as he greedily retrieved the rizla from the bottom of the box. "Nah not really." Wayne replied sorry for the first time that he didn't. "Ah for fuck sake man, either you do, or you don't!...what da...cha fuck you, I can't deal with your breeze right now.!" Marcus continued building an ital spliff. "Easy! Easy! Dis shit don't grow in my garden yuh know, and you done know you owe me from dat last ting we got, so check yourself brethren I beg you do, and pass dat shit back over here please." Cavell interrupted menacingly. "So how come you don't smoke? you lot probably get da real deal over there as well?" Cavell enquired, laying out a sheet of rizla. "No reason, I just don't like it. I tried it and it didn't do anything for me so I don't, ain't no big ting!" Wayne answered wondering how in hell they could even dream of doing something like that with their mothers in the same house, but he knew better than to say anything.

The boys smoked the spliffs, blowing the smoke out the window, in the direction the wind blew. "Can I try your game?" Wayne asked not sure what to do with himself but not wanting to go back to the boredom and solitude of his house. "Course blood!" Cavell replied. "What do you wanna play?" "Anything, what games have you got?" "I have ALL games!" Cavell grinned, opening his bottom drawer to reveal row upon row of games. "Give him Mortal Kombat and when I finish this, I'll come and show him how we do it here in Hackney! You up for that rude boy?" Marcus asked, glad for the opportunity to beat his arse even if it was on a computer game. "Ok cool." Wayne replied, wishing Semp was there to play it with instead. "A, what you doing tomorrow?" Cavell asked returning to his half of the window perch. "Who me?" Wayne answered "Yes blood, who do you think he's talking to?" Marcus answered, hoping Cavell wasn't about to ask Wayne to tag along. "Nothing, why?" "We're going up to my girl's birthday party, do you want to come?" Cavell replied, pushing smoke out the window with his palm. "Yeh, but I have to check with my moms first, where is it?"

Marcus and Cavell looked at each other and burst into laughter, forcing them to fall on the floor. "Oh my days, you have to check with mummy first, do you tell your mummy every little thing you do?" Marcus teased. "No!" Wayne answered regretting speaking the words out loud "you do don't you, I bet he does?" Marcus asked feigning concern. Wayne kissed his teeth and carried on playing the game, he wasn't about to get drawn into another drama with Marcus. "All I'm saying is, don't bust the programme with them clothes yeah!" Marcus added touching Cavell's waiting fist. The remainder of the evening flew by in a blur of computer games, jokes, fights and taunting but by it's end, the boys were cool. Wayne and his mother left for their house promising that Wayne would come out the following day to be introduced to the rest of the True Hackney Millitants. That night as he lay in his bed waiting for sleep to quieten his mind, Wayne felt as though maybe, just maybe England was not so bad after all. His last thoughts were filled with images of shoes and his decision to ask his mother for a new pair as he drifted off to sleep.

∞

He awoke as usual to an empty house, but it didn't matter as much today, normally it would have emphasised his loneliness and caused him to feel home sick, but today he hardly even noticed his mother's absence. Today, instead of lingering in his bed daydreaming of Tamana, he woke with a smile on his face and immediately rummaged through his wardrobe for his coolest clothes. Two minutes later the smile disappeared as he surveyed the extent of his collection. There was nothing with a label, and what was new, looked like 'church'. After the grilling he took from Marcus the night before, for the first time in his life, Wayne felt only as good as the clothes he wore. He arranged and rearranged, and after rearranging his selection one last time, the good mood he fell asleep with vanished. He felt worse than he did before he went to number twenty-two. By the time Ivy came home, his enthusiasm, fully expressed the night before, was replaced by a quiet acceptance of rejection.

"You alright baby!" she greeted hoping to see his smiles of the night before. "How your face looking long so? what time are you going out with Cavell?" "I ain't bothering to go again." he responded woefully. "Why?" Ivy asked surprised. She was glad he'd made friends with Cavell, she knew he needed a companion to lime with, and Cavell was as good as any and she knew his mother. "I don't really have anything to wear mum but it's ok, I don't really feel like going anyway." "Boy, what rubbish you talking, come and show me your clothes!" she insisted, pulling him up out of the chair and marching him up to his bedroom. She entered the room and saw his entire wardrobe spread across the room in full outfits. Hiding a smile, she picked up the shirt he came to London in. "So what's wrong with this? and this?... and what about these, she asked eagerly holding up his favourite Levi jeans. "That's not the style here mum, none of these are, especially those shoes!" Wayne replied unable to stop himself grinning, pointing to his 'best shoes'. "What's wrong with them?" she asked feigning shock. "Mum, have you seen what they wear here? because it's not any of this!" Wayne replied gesturing to every item of clothing. Ivy surveyed the collection, hugged her son and smiled.

Last night was the first time she saw his eyes light up since he arrived. He needed friends. "You're right honey, we'll have to get you some clothes, but for now, you just suck it up you hear me! The boy I brought into this world, after eleven and three quarter hours of labour, without anaesthetic as you may recall, certainly wouldn't allow clothes to speak for him, I mean, what would his father say!" Ivy teased, caressing the small of his neck, pretending to look woefully into his eyes. "Mums, you sounding more and more like Granny!" Wayne laughed "Or, you could always stay home and help me cook? I have two chickens that need cutting up and a cabbage that needs grating..." she groaned. "It's ok mums, I going to the party!" Wayne replied hastily retreating to the bathroom. "That's my boy!" Ivy answered, feeling a rush of love for her child.

By the time Cavell knocked on his door, Wayne was ready. Decked out in his faithful Converses, worn blue jeans and oversized black Polo shirt, he eagerly made his way to the front door. "Yes blood" Cavell greeted him as he opened the door. Wayne stepped outside, conscious of his appearance. "Yo yo yo! This is my new junior, "Wayne-just-land", Wayne this is Babs, Sherrise, Marcus you know, Monique, Magique and Diggy. Standing just outside the gate were more faces Wayne had seen before, from the estate. He nodded his head in their direction as he closed his door, acutely aware of their stares on his back. The squad noisily made their way to the bus stop, both ignoring but fully observing their new companion. Catching the number thirty-eight, they clambered up the stairs taking up their usual position at the back of the bus.

"Did anybody bring a present?" one of the girls asked. "Present! What present? she's not my friend, I'm just coming with you!" came Magique's reply. "Yeah, we'll see! Anyways I got her that top we was talking about" Monique answered, admiring her face in a compact mirror. "Well, I got her me, and she's getting it hand delivered dread!" Babs replied, trying to squeeze in between Monique and her friend. "You look good you know

Sherrise, I find your body is just developing so nicely!" he teased, talking to her breasts. "Oh shut your hole Babs, can't you see the girl is just not interested in you!" Magique answered scornfully. "Was anybody talking to you though, and anyway, Monique done show me the real truth…." Babs returned, screwing up his face in disgust. "What, what you going on about!?" Monique asked, closing her compact. "You got some fluff on your lip!" he replied trying to reach towards her face. She kissed her teeth and knocked his hand away. "Just ignore him Sherrise, I ain't told him shit!" Monique swore adamantly. "Rare! don't lie!" Babs continued sitting on Sherrise's lap. "Ow, boy move your boney bum off me!" she screamed pushing him towards the floor.

"Listen, all I'm saying is that my girl told me that you rated me eleven out of ten dough! which makes me feel say somebody's feeling my smooth black ass!" The group burst into laughter as he attempted to kiss her cheek only to be pushed to the floor once again. "Don't worry, I know you secretly want to meet my little friend, so don't be shy, me will do it to you, like only I could…" he continued gyrating his hips and thrusting his pelvis in her direction. Sherrise kissed her teeth and turned her body away from Babs. "Oh whatever, so how are you liking London? Are you here for good?" she asked Wayne, ignoring Babs' attempts to regain her attention. "Yeh I like it, it's cool." Wayne replied, not sure what else to say but wishing he could think of something funny. "I see you changed your crepes." Marcus commented, diverting all eyes to Wayne's footwear.

"Oh my word, my man's pant's look like he's expecting a flood, but it's all good cos he's come prepared with them two boats!" Babs interjected. Wayne felt heat rise up to his face as the crew crumbled in laughter. His mind raced for a response but nothing came. Instead, he silently looked out of his window praying the topic would change, or at least that he would think of something worthy to say. It didn't, and he couldn't. The more he thought, the more his mind was a confusion of sounds and blank spaces. After what seemed like too long to Wayne, Sherrise finally stopped the laughter, "Don't worry, I'm sure the boys will hook a brother up" she stated looking directly at the THM boys. "Yeh after you drop and give me ten across my dick!" Marcus replied pulling Sherrise by the curl carelessly caressing the side of her face. "My man catches chickens and shit for his dinner you know!" he added, not appreciating her concern for the foreigner. "Errgh! what, do you kill them Wayne, how the hell do you do that?" she asked, disgusted at the prospect of eating anything she'd killed. "Easy, just catch it, cut the throat, put it in a pan of boiling water, pluck it, season it, then cook it!" The group listened intently with obvious signs of disgust on their faces. "Oh my God, how could you do that? that's making me feel sick yow!" Sherrise declared holding her hand over her mouth.

"Are you poor then, is that why your jeans don't fit and you have to hunt for food?" Magique asked feigning concern. "Oh my word, Babs you better tell your dumb broad to just occupy herself with your cockey and stop opening her mouth unless it's to give me a blow fam!" Cavell answered looking at her in disbelief. Babs approached Magique but she extended her leg ready to deliver a blow. "A bwoy, mind yourself yuh know, don't make me have to sic one of my byatches on you now!" Magique laughed leaning behind Monique. "You guys are acting dumb man, where do you think the chicken comes from that you get from Kentucky or that your moms cooks?" Wayne asked, surprised by their reactions. "Hold up blood, are you cussing my moms, trust me, you don't want to go there you know!" Marcus added, giving Wayne the dirtiest look he could muster. Wayne's heart raced, between trying to understand what they said, remember what he said, and think of something clever to say back, his face flushed crimson beneath his brown skin.

"What!?" he answered, a tad late, "Why would I be cussing your mum, I didn't curse your mother!" he continued standing to his feet. "Just cool Marcus man, he ain't cuss your mum! just leave him alone and stop trying to eggs up on the yout!" shouted a voice from some seats away. "Rare! Somebody like it countrified" Babs teased gesturing in the direction of the orator, a tall skinny girl with huge hoop earrings. "You homo donkey! you're such an idiot, no wonder you ain't got a girl, you wanna concentrate on getting one soon before Country here beats you to it, instead of running up those black and pink gums!" Laughter spread throughout the back of the bus as it turned on to Mare Street and headed in the direction of Clapton. As their ridicule continued, an older man, sitting a few rows in front turned to eye the raucous crowd. "A, don't watch that my yout! Dem a idiot if them can't look past your clothes!...strip off them clothes and what dem is...E!". The group silenced their jokes, pondering the man's words but as soon as his mouth closed, Marcus's mouth opened. "Oh shut up man, was anybody talking to you though...NO, just mind your business and keep your proverbs to yourself!" Wayne, grateful for the interruption, was horrified at Marcus's disrespect of the elder. He turned to the others for confirmation but instead, between kissing their teeth and agreeing with their friend, they too, turned their ridicule on the pensioner. Wayne thanked him for his efforts and continued to look out the window, only this time, he didn't care what they said.

By the time they got off the bus at Clapton Pond, he felt like a fish out of water; a poor relation, who could never quite amount to Cavell and his friends, though he wasn't quite sure that he even wanted to. As they turned into Springfield Avenue, his self-consciousness engulfed him even more acutely as he saw the crowds of youths liming in the street. "Nah bruv! What's that facie hole doing here, nah fam, that's not happening!" Marcus demanded eyeing up a crowd of boys in front of the house. "Shut up man, that's her cousin innit!" Sherrise whispered as they approached. Silence fell on both groups as the THM made their way past them to the front door. Marcus kissed his teeth audibly and animatedly brushed past the last one, "fucking idiot!" he spat, kissing his teeth. "What!...what!, did you say something bruv?, feel no-way you know, say what you gotta say!" A boy in a red hooded jacket, about seventeen or eighteen tried to push his way over to Marcus, but was stopped by another "llow that fam, dis is my cousin's barbecue yow, llow dat, there's plenty time for dat later!" The wearer of the red hood kissed his teeth but agreed and stepped back from the doorway and Marcus' retreating back.

Inside, the house heaved with bodies and a bassline Wayne smiled to himself that Semp would go crazy over. Cavell led the way, squeezing through the packed hallway to the garden, stopping every few feet to acknowledge a familiar face with loud animated gestures. With each stop, Wayne was once again openly eyed up and down, usually followed by a derogatory comment or giggle, and an introduction from Cavell as his 'junior'. With the back door in sight, Cavell was suddenly pulled off course by a screeching female, who proceeded to squeal with delight at his presence. As he waited what seemed to Wayne to be several very long minutes for the greeting to end, he stood awkwardly in the doorway, trying to look cool as his heart raced under the weight of eyes, real and imagined, on him.

The girl finally released her embrace and greeted the rest of the THM. "And this is my new boy, Wayne, fresh from yard!" Cavell explained. "Wayne, this is Ellie." The two exchanged hellos, as she half darted through the doorway, a smile spreading across her face as she went. "Oi, where you going, where's the drink den? Man is thirsty you know, and where's your sister?" Cavell kissed his teeth and continued on the way to the garden. "Yes cuz, what's gwarning my yout?" A tall muscular youth extended a clenched fist towards him as they made their way to the barrel full of ice and beverages. "Yes boss, tell me you got something good for me nuh!" Cavell asked. The taller youth laughed, "You done know my yout" he grinned ushering him to an oversized Yucca plant.

Marcus, Sherrise and Wayne followed the duo as they made their way to the corner of the garden. "Yeh that's the real deal my friend!" Cavell grinned before taking a couple more tokes and passing it to Marcus. "So what's good blood?" Cavell asked settling on top of an empty milk crate. "Trying to stay under the blue man's radar" his friend replied. "For real!" Marcus responded, passing the spliff to Wayne who discreetly refused. "Wha happen, you nah smoke?" the youth asked eyeing Wayne ominously. "No thank you." Wayne replied coughing from the cloud of smoke encircling him as the trio continued their conversation. "A, I got some fresh ting cuz, you man looking work?...we can twos?" the man continued, pulling out a knotted blue plastic bag containing clear button bags of weed. "Oh, so this is where you hiding, why didn't you come and say hi you pagan!" A voluptuous looking girl with long black hair approached the group, trailing the same girl Wayne had seen earlier behind her. Cavell stepped forward and embraced her. "Baby, I was looking for you, didn't titch tell you?" "No!" she replied kissing her teeth. "She was too busy eyeing up your friend!" "No I wasn't!" Ellie exclaimed, horrified that she would be exposed in front of Wayne, and made a mental note to get her sister back. "What, you like Wayne, Ellie? So you is that guy! Fam just land and he find woman already!"

Wayne and Ellie, both feeling increasingly awkward, were grateful for a sudden eruption emanating from the house, as the occupants of the garden descended on the back door to witness the cause of the commotion. In the middle of a packed room, Babs and two other girls battled each other for control of the tiny space as the increasing spectators egged them on. Tony Matterhon's Dutty Wine blasted through the speakers, sending girls shrieking with excitement. One girl in a polka dot mini skirt confidently attempted a dutty wine, only to land on her face, to the great amusement of the crowd, exposing her g-string in the process. "Oh no, my girl, don't try so hard, me will show you how it's done!" Babs screeched in between laughing and lifting the girl by her breast and her bum. Wayne was in awe of the scene as Babs proceeded to simulate penetration through her clothes as she leaned against the wall. Momentarily mesmerized, he finally looked away, wondering if the girl knew the back of her skirt had somehow become tucked into her waistband.

The evening progressed and Wayne found himself on his own. He was tired and not quite sure where to stand nor where to look, and longed for the solace of his bedroom. His belly rumbled as he sat on the top step surveying the thrashing crowd, wondering if he could make his way home on his own. "Did you get some barbecue?" a voice asked from behind him. "No, not yet" he replied, coughing to clear his throat. "Do you want me to bring some for you?" Ellie continued as she slid next to him on the step. "Yes please" he responded nervously. Within minutes, she returned with two plates, and the pair ate the jerk chicken and talked about Trinidad, school and their families, until Cavell finally found them after midnight. The barbecue continued until the early hours of the morning and by the time Wayne arrived home, his head spun with the events of the day. Sleep finally consumed him at 3am, as images of Ellie floated around his mind, and a smile settled itself on his face.

∞

The night before his first day of school, Wayne eagerly retrieved his uniform, pressed the few wrinkles out of his new shirt, and laid the outfit on his bed, complete with socks and freshly polished shoes. He covered the copy books his mother purchased, and with his best handwriting wrote his name on each one, neatly underlined with the subject. Finally, he sharpened his pencils and carefully placed everything in his brand new book bag. Despite his mother's warnings to get a full night's rest, Wayne hardly slept a wink, and soon enough, his alarm signalled 7.30am on Monday morning.

Ivy, already awake and busily preparing breakfast, sang quietly to herself and smiled as she heard the rumbling noise of the shower being turned on. Twenty minutes later, Wayne appeared in his uniform, clutching his grey book bag. Ivy took one look at him in his black blazer and red tie and a single tear fell freely down her cheek. He was so handsome, she thought to herself as her chest heaved with pride. For years, she yearned for the arrival of her son, for the opportunity to prepare breakfast for him, to wake him up for school, to straighten his tie or to fix is hair, and now the day had finally come. Today he would begin his great British education and the rest of his life. She silently hoped his father was watching over him as she wiped the tear from her cheek. Half an hour later, the pair, both immaculately dressed, awaited the number thirty-eight at the bus stop.

As they approached the school grounds, Ivy squeezed her son's hand in hers. "You ready babe?" Wayne laughed, "Oh gosh mums, yes I'm ready!" The pair smiled as they entered the playground which was already half filled with students, all eyeing the new boy as he made his way to the office with his mother. After a brief meeting with the Principal who praised Wayne's immaculate appearance and academic record, Ivy left with one last kiss goodbye and he was ushered to his line in the playground. By 9.05am he stood in front of his class, giving a short introduction of himself, and how he came to be there.

With thirty-two pairs of eyes watching him suspiciously, Wayne straightened his tie and began. "I have come to England to be with my mother who came here to make a better life for our family. I have come to England to increase my opportunities to have, do or be whatever I choose to have, do or be. I have come to this school to increase my knowledge because knowledge is power and as a young man, I believe it's my only line of defence!" Faces that seconds before, showed obvious disinterest and disdain, suddenly tuned in to the well-spoken, clearly unfashionable new boy. "Oh my motherfucking god!!" came a silenced but clearly audible voice. "Who says dat shit!" the voice continued. "Evidently not you Mehmet" Mr Ingrassia responded, as laughter peeled through the momentarily silenced room. A stunned Wayne returned to his seat as Mr Ingrassia thanked him for his comparatively enlightened words.

The first class was history, Tudors and the expansion of the British empire, a subject completely unrelated to the history he had been taught. "In fact it was during this time that your country, Trinidad, was discovered by a great explorer, Christopher Columbus" Mr Ingrassia added. Wayne was baffled by the attitude of his teacher's discussion. His history had taught him about the enslavement of the native Carib and Arawak populations and their eventual demise, a dark period, and certainly not the period of celebration that was being implied. "Actually, I see it differently. Before Columbus 'discovered', Wayne began, raising his arms to signify inverted commas, Trinidad, the Caribs and the Arawaks lived and prospered on the island which they had already named, Leri, Land of the Humming Bird." Two minutes later, "A! New boy!" came a stern whisper from the back of the room, "A...muppet! you best shut up you know!...I ain't got all day to be in dis shit hole!" The sniggering from the boys was audible, but to Wayne's surprise, his teacher, who Wayne was sure must have heard, completely ignored it as he continued to explain the Tudors and their impact on the rest of the world.

He left the classroom that day with a sense of unimportance and defensiveness, and for the first time Wayne wondered about his place in the world and what he could achieve. As the morning progressed, he settled into his routine, the differences between his education in Trinidad and this new school becoming more and more apparent. The few books and television programs he'd seen, painted a very different picture, and far from the heavy discipline, silent studious children and thick books he'd imagined, Upton Secondary didn't at first sight, seem able to offer him the education he travelled thousands of miles to receive. His form room, far from being an ornate brick or stone building, was a porto-cabin. The desks had clearly seen better days, the books were uncovered and dog eared, and the pupils, far from being impressed with Wayne's obvious intellect, scorned him as a 'boffin', kissing their teeth each time he raised his hand to answer a question, ridiculing his 'teacher's pet' antics.

At midday, the school bell signalled the approach of lunch time and Wayne made his way to the playground, along with the rest of his class. Although a typically cold autumn day, his adrenaline warmed his body as he sat in one corner of the playground with his back to the fence, waiting his class's turn in the dinner hall. He huddled against the breeze as he searched out Cavell amongst the throngs of boys on the playground, to no avail. Before long, a group of boys, some of whom Wayne recognised from his classroom, made their way over to him. "A, you're the new boy innit?" a smaller pale skinned boy asked. "You's a good boy innit!" another commented as the group laughed at the thought. "You got money for lunch or are you getting free dinners?" asked another boy with a heavy gold chain, neatly placed outside his jumper. "I don't know what that is but yes, I've got money." Wayne answered suddenly unsure of himself. "How much you got?" his inquisitor continued "Why?" Wayne answered holding tightly to the three pound coins in his pocket. "I'll give you four dinner tickets for two pounds" the boy answered signalling to another youth who produced a roll of dinner tickets from inside his jumper. Before Wayne could respond, the boy pushed the four tickets into his palm and extended his hand for the two pounds payment. Wayne looked at the orange tickets. He'd never seen them before and had no idea how to use them or that there was such a thing as a 'free dinner'. "Come on boss, what's the hold up, do you want it or not, I ain't got all fucking day to sell you fucking dinner tickets man, hurry up!" Wayne hastily retrieved two pounds and handed it over. "Cool blood! if you need anymore, just look out for me yeh!". The group left as promptly as they'd arrived and Wayne put the tickets in his pocket wondering how to use them.

Just then Cavell, Marcus and Babs rattled on the fence behind him. "Wha gwarn!" Cavell asked, touching his enclosed fist to Wayne's through the chain mail fence. "Just waiting for lunch, how come you guys got to go outside?" he asked enviously hoping to join them. "What, yuh no know say me ah de dan dada!" Marcus responded beating his chest. "In other words, fifth years can leave school for lunch!" Cavell translated. "I see you've already been hit up by the 'commerce man'?" Cavell continued eyeing the four tickets in Wayne's hand. "You best put three of them away before you go into the hall blood, you know say you're in possession of stolen goods and the walls have eyes yeh!" Cavell insisted. "How much did he charge you for them?" Marcus asked. "two pounds" Wayne answered "Two pounds! You got robbed bro!" Marcus shouted, laughing as hard as he could. "Don't watch dat, do your thing and we'll link later yeh". Cavell touched him and made his way to the shopping precinct on the other side of the high road. As the boys strolled away, Wayne made his way to the dinner hall, his heart racing at the prospect of the stolen dinner ticket in his hand. Friendless, he stood in the queue hoping his beating heart couldn't be heard by the boys on either side of him. By the time he collected his food and stood in front of the cashier, instead of producing the ticket, he dug deeper for his last pound coin and with a shaking hand, paid for it, not realising he was holding his breath until he seated himself on an empty table furthest away from the dinner ladies.

The hall hummed with the sound of students. Shouting, laughter and the clatter of tables and chairs, mingled with the sound of cutlery, teenaged digestion and the occasional vociferous declaration of disappointment with the food. Wayne sat quietly, observing his peers and wondered what his teacher in Tamana, Mr Ayoung would have made of the scene. He laughed to himself as he remembered 'the look' Mr Ayoung gave at the slightest disorderly noise and for a moment, he wondered again if he'd made the right move coming to London.

He tucked into his chips as the tables began to fill with bottoms and wondered if he would be eating alone. "Is anyone sitting here?" The voice interrupted his solace and he looked up. "I'm sitting here yeh", the tall dark skinned boy continued placing his dinner tray on the table. "You're new innit?" he continued. Wayne nodded his head between mouthfuls of burger. "I'm Ade, I'm in your class, what's your name again?" Wayne swallowed hastily and extended his arm. "Hi, Wayne Lopez" he continued awkwardly. "Cool". Two more boys dropped their trays on the table and sat with the duo, heckling Ade for some of his chips, and completely ignoring Wayne. Wayne looked straight past them to the window on the far wall, finished his pudding wondering why it was called 'spotted dick' and left the hall. Returning to his corner on the playground, he solemnly awaited the bell, jealously observing the boys on the playing field as the damp, cold wind, forced it's way into his body. The bell finally rang after what seemed like ages and he joined his class as they queued against the side of the dinner hall, awaiting entrance into their social studies lesson.

A few minutes later, he sat in front of a short stout grey haired man scribbling illegibly on the blackboard whilst demanding the class settle down. "Pay attention men. You only have forty-five minutes of my time and I suggest you use me wisely...are you with us Mr Jenkins?" he asked a late comer, casually making his way to a seat at the back of the room. "Mr Jenkins?" he continued sternly dropping a pile of papers on his desk as the boy stopped halfway to show his phone to another. "Yes boss, yes boss" the boy replied from the back of the classroom, slowly opening his notebook. "No need for 'boss', plain old 'sir' will suffice." "Yes boss!" the student replied eliciting a ripple of laughter from his peers. "Ok, last year we finished up discussing Enoch Powell and the effect he has had on the demographic and social profile of Britain. Who can remind me of what we concluded?" The class fell silent. Wayne had no idea who Enoch Powell was and after a prolonged silence, decided to ask. "Sorry sir, I was not here when this was being discussed, is it possible to give me a brief overview?" "Why certainly!" the teacher continued, happy to interact with an eager learner. Moans and curses could be heard from the entire class as the teacher began a biography of the infamous politician, stopping only to ensure the class took refresher notes in preparation for an impromptu piece of homework, clearly necessary as no-one had remembered.

The class was finally dismissed and the boys made their way to maths, the last lesson of the day. A couple of them pushed past Wayne, slapping the back of his head and giving dirty looks as they went out of the room, blaming him for the homework they were just given. "A, check out dis idiot!" an unfamiliar voice declared. He felt a sharpened pencil dig into his back as he made his way to the room on the top floor of the building; he looked around, realised he was encircled and continued walking.

"Oi, my yout! Don't ask so much fucking questions next time yeh! Man's got tings to do, places to go and people to see, I ain't got time to be no teachers fucking pet and I sure as hell don't give a shit about what happen to some grey man, much less write a fucking essay about it!...check yourself dude!...don't let me have to 'out' you on your first day!" The group burst into boisterous laughter, deliberately pushing past him so that he had to stop and hold on to the banister to prevent himself from falling. He squeezed a tear of frustration and anger from the corner of his eye, and sucked up the emotions threatening to escape his body should he dare to open his mouth. His anger simmered throughout the maths lesson as he viewed and reviewed mental images of the scene he had just encountered and what he should have done differently. The lesson passed without Wayne hearing a word of it, and as the bell signalled the end of the day, he couldn't wait to leave the building. He made his way to the bus stop amidst the throngs of uniformed boys, hoping to avoid bumping into any of the ones who cornered him on the stairwell, but mentally prepared for it, should in case he did.

As he waited for his bus, he felt something hit the top of his ear and brushed it off thinking it was an insect of some kind, but as he did so, he was hit again and again. This time, he brushed his face, picking up a piece of balled up paper. Still unsure, he turned behind him and was confronted with another group of boys, all solemnly glaring at him, daring him to say anything. He kissed his teeth and turned back around to await his bus. Laughter ensued behind him and Wayne cringed thinking about what to do if he was confronted again. The bus finally came with no incident, and he made his way to the back on the ground level. The boys all boarded the same bus, openly eyeing him, daring him to do something, but he did nothing, not because he was afraid, but because he didn't know what to do.

The bus finally arrived at his stop and he disembarked to a flurry of noise from the top deck. "A pussy! yuh better mind yourself you know!" "Fucking fool!" the boys hollered from the bus's slanted upper deck windows. Wayne tucked his hands in his pockets and went home, forcing the tears once again from his eyes. By the time he pushed his key into his front door, his enthusiasm for a British education and all the grandeur he imagined that it entailed, dissipated. He closed the door behind him and exhaled. Adrenaline flooded his body, causing his hands to shake as he removed his jacket and placed it on the hallway peg. His mind raced over the events of the day as his anger and irritation at the boys and himself, caused an uncomfortable dull ache to nestle in his belly. "How was your first day baby?" Ivy shouted downstairs as she heard the door close. Tears, about to be let free, were once again squeezed away as he cleared his throat and hastily walked into the kitchen. "Fine" he answered wearily lifting the lid of the dutch pot feigning interest in it's contents. He wasn't about to tell his mum about it, she would only worry and there's was no point to that; instead he took a deep breath, fixed his face and went upstairs in his usual jovial mood.

The week passed in much the same way as the first day. Wayne tried to settle in to his new school but as each day passed, he realised that although the schoolwork was a lot less and a lot easier, his ability outside of the classroom appeared non-existent. He'd always been popular in Tamana, but this wasn't Tamana and the rules, rewards and aspirations were completely different. He felt completely out of touch with his new environment, and worse still, no-one cared. It seemed to him as if everyone already had their position in a click, and he just didn't fit into any. Lunch hours were spent in the same corner of the school ground, trying to seem disinterested and happy to be by himself, all the while wishing Semp was with him, or he was in Tamana. He saw Cavell occasionally, parading through the school grounds, hailing almost everyone he passed by, but acknowledging Wayne only in passing. The school work was easy for him and what was new wasn't hard for him to grasp. His teachers found him eager, and willing, with discipline and manners, a joy to teach, a phrase they would repeat to the class, and one that ensured when the class was over, Wayne remained by himself.

By Friday, Wayne resigned himself to the corner of the playing field. He had no friends, nor any imminent prospect of finding any. He had no idea how to play the 'English' way, and as much as he tried to fit in, he stood out. His reverie was finally interrupted after lunch on the second week by what seemed to be a friendly voice shouting to him half way across the yard. His experiences the previous week taught him not to let his guard down too easily with his peers; so although he heard the voice, he kept his gaze steadfastly on the gap between his thumb and forefinger. "Fucking hell man! Are you hard of hearing or what?" the voice continued, in what seemed to Wayne to be an African accent. He looked up. "What up man!" The boy from the canteen continued, extending his clenched fist toward Wayne's folded arms. "You're from Trinidad innit, that's cool bruv, I'm from Ghana, I sit behind you in form room. Come on, I know say you're freezing sitting there, trying to act all cool and shit!" Wayne couldn't help the smile that flashed across his face. Ade noticed and held on to his arm to pull him up. Wayne stood, tucking his hands into his pockets. "Come on, let me put a little bit of that Trinidad sunshine back into your life man!" Ade continued as the pair began a trek of the circumference of the school grounds.

"How long have you been here?" Wayne enquired. "Two very long years my friend and since I am intending to become a doctor, that means at least one...two...three, four, five...six...seven...eight, at least ten years more!" Ade replied shaking his head in feigned disappointment. "My grandfather sent me to get the 'great British education', followed by a 'great British job', so I could send home some 'great British money'. I have a feeling the main purpose of my education is to look after him in his old age!" Wayne wasn't sure if Ade was being serious but laughed anyway. "How you finding it?" Ade continued. Wayne pondered the question. "How am I finding it?" he repeated as if unsure what the question meant. "Boy, all I could tell you is that it is very different and I feel like a fish out of water. It's just not what I thought it would be!" Ade kissed his teeth, "My brother, tell me about it, this shit is crazy dude!" The pair laughed as they surveyed the school grounds but by the time the bell rang, Wayne's perception of his situation was changing. His ready smile, hidden in the presence of his peers, shyly returned to his face. As he left school that Friday, he made plans to visit his new friend that weekend.

∞

Ade lived with his childless aunt in Homerton, a fifteen minute bus ride away. She sent for Ade three years ago when her brother, Ade's father passed away. He hadn't wanted to leave Ghana, his family or his friends, but he was now the man of the house. He knew his mother wanted him to go to make a name for himself and to return to help her raise his little brothers and sisters, so he went, he had responsibilities. Although his aunt loved him dearly, England was not the warm welcoming place he'd left behind and it took Ade weeks to learn to sleep without his brothers and months to understand the ways of his new peers. His aunt was approaching sixty, and had no tolerance for what she perceived to be spoilt, rude or stupid behaviours, and felt children, as a rule, should be seen and not heard and did not miss any opportunity to advise Ade as much.

As far as she was concerned, Ade's jobs were to excel at school and to do whatever she told him to do. Any deviation from this, meant too much exposure, too much free time, not enough discipline and not enough studying, which could all only mean one thing. You were somehow going to end up a criminal in jail, a scenario that would not befall Ade under her watch. Ade loved his aunt despite her inability to see anyone under the age of twenty-five as being responsible enough to be solely entrusted with their own lives. He knew she loved him too, despite her theories, but he missed his family and thought of them every single day. Unable at first to find any friends his aunt found satisfactory, he immersed himself into London life, filling his days with its' sites, sounds and tastes. By the end of his first year Ade had traversed the entire underground tube system, from Epping to Ealing and Barnet to Balham. His aunt, much like Ivy, usually worked long hours, leaving him to his own devices; and over the ensuing weeks and months, he became a frequent visitor to Wayne's home.

Neither had much pocket money, but between Wayne doing the cooking and assisting Andy on his painting jobs, and Ade helping out in his neighbour's garage, the pair explored as much of London as Ade knew, and which could be accessed by their bus passes and what little money they'd accumulated during the week.

"A!, come we go Southend tomorrow man" Ade announced linking Wayne at the school gates the following Friday. "Southend?" Wayne answered quizzically. "Yeah the beach man, the beach dread!" Ade continued. Images of Maracas beach cocooned at the bottom of St Joseph Valley flooded Wayne's mind. Coconut trees, bake and shark, clear waters and soft sands brought a smile to his face as he, for just a moment, submerged himself under a wave. "Yeh, let's go man!"

They arrived excitedly leaving Southend station the following Saturday morning. The promenade was quiet, and the stony beach gave an uninviting welcome to dirty debris filled water. Wayne thought of skipping pebbles across it's surface but the air was too cold to withdraw his hibernating hands from their pockets. After five minutes, the pair withdrew to the multitude of gaming and gambling machines. Within an hour, most of their money was gone and the boys decided to cut their losses, get a bag of chips and head back to the train station.

Standing on the platform huddled against the cold, Ade noticed two girls sitting on the only bench, and looking in their direction. The boys looked at each other and laughed, suddenly caring more about how they looked, than the cold wind threatening to penetrate their clothes. "Hold up, let me show you how it's done man!" Ade grinned as he made his way over to the bench. "Good afternoon ladies, isn't it a beautiful day?" he enquired throwing his legs over the back of the bench. The girls laughed and looked at each other, one smiled whilst the other kissed her teeth and pretended to frown. "Do we know you?" the serious one asked. Ade studied their faces, "No I don't think so...unless you have been to London or Africa or maybe America?" he continued. "No, sorry we haven't!" the pair answered, giggling as he dropped his bottom on to the seat. "Oh well then, I don't know you. My name is Ade, and you are...?" he continued confidently. "I'm bored and she's sleepy, what now?" replied the dark haired serious girl as her friend covered her mouth to hide her amusement. Ade laughed, "I see, you must be the joker in the pack, that's cool, hold on, let me introduce you to Mr Excitement!" Ade gestured for Wayne who unwillingly made his way to the bench. "Hey what up?" Wayne enquired in his coolest voice. Before they could respond, a group of boisterous boys jumped down the steps to the platform with two dogs straining against short leashes. They too made their way over to the bench.

"What you boys doing up ere den?" a short blond haired boy asked, sitting in the space between the dark haired girl and Ade. "Nothing" Ade answered with an unease that put Wayne on his guard. "On your bike den coon, can't you tell my dog's hungry?" the boy continued to the obvious enjoyment of his friends. Ade looked at the dog standing at his side. It was a white Pitbull that made his stomach flip as it growled at him. He breathed a silent sigh of relief at the muzzle securing it's jaws, then he looked at his friend and exhaled. Wayne knew something was up, he didn't know what, but he readied himself for whatever was coming. "Maybe you should take him back to your trailer park then." Ade replied coolly, sounding more English than he usually did. "What? What you fucking say?" the short boy responded exaggerating his walk as he stood in front of Ade's face. "Knock his fucking lights out Charlie!" his red haired friend shouted walking over to the inch and a half gap between Ade and his friend. Ade's heart was pounding in his chest, they were outnumbered two to one, plus dogs, and he was shit scared of dogs, especially Pitbulls. He kissed his teeth, holding the boy's glare, "I said, go fuck your sister, she's calling you!" The boy's face turned crimson, but before he could respond Ade leaned back and with as much force as he could muster, head butted him on the bridge of his nose. "Run Wayne!" he yelled as he steadied himself. The boys flew up the stairs and out of the station without looking back.

Taking the first corner they came to, they ran until they were out of breath and sure they hadn't been followed. Ade dropped down on to the kerb, holding his waist and struggling to catch his breath. "Shit man!" was all he could say before his heart finally started slowing down. "We gotta get out of here...now!" he added as Wayne, still visibly shaken though not out of breath, nodded his head in agreement. They both knew they couldn't go back to the train station. In unfamiliar territory they looked around for a clue on how to get out without getting jacked. With no other option and eager to put as much space between them and the white Pitbull, Ade and Wayne, staying off the main roads, began the walk out of Southend. "This country is different my friend, you can not apply the same rules you had back home and think everything will be set. Oh no, I'm afraid not! This shit is a different shit altogether brother!...the colour different, the texture different, the smell is different, the shape different, where it land ..." Wayne punched him on the shoulder, "Ok Ad, I get it...de shit different hyere!" The boys, moving in stealth mode, kept to back roads for almost an hour in the direction of London, until a bus finally passed them, stopping thirty meters ahead. The boys looked at each other and grinned, "Thank you Jesus!" Ade exhaled and they sprinted to the stop.

Over the ensuing months Ade and Wayne became inseparable. "Yes boss, wha' gwarn" Ade exclaimed as Wayne extended his fist at the front door, "I'm cool man, come through!" The boys excitedly made their way to Wayne's bedroom. "See it deh, see it deh!" Ade exclaimed throwing a game on to Wayne's bed followed by a handful of clearly pirated dvds. "Yes brethren! Where did you get these?" Wayne asked excitedly flicking through the cellophane wrappers. "Oh my days, you got American Gangster! That ain't even out yet!" he continued in amazement, ripping the cellophane packaging. "As my grandfather would say, it's not what you know, it's who you know, and I and I knows 'DVD Lyn'! five for ten pounds!" Ade sang animatedly. "Well I just give thanks that I know you cuz!" Wayne continued grinning as he eagerly placed the disc in the player.

The sound of agitated dog barking drew them to the window. In the half enclosed swing compound were a number of boys Wayne recognised from the bar-b-cue in Clapton. Two Staffordshire bull terriers pulled against their leashes as they tried to reach each other on opposite sides of the gathering. Girls sat on the wall, smoking cigarettes and drinking from cans, animatedly gesturing towards boys in the group and laughing unnecessarily loudly. "Oi dunduce! Is wha you ah look pon?" Babs shouted as he caught sight of the boys. All eyes followed his voice up to Wayne's window. "Dunduce? what you ah chat say, spell dat bomboclart!" Ade replied. "EH eh!" The group burst into laughter. "Dat younger is facety yow!" "I know, clearly he don't get enough licks!...Don't get bright, I don't want to have to come and knock the shit out of you again...come now and bring your phone, I need to make some calls!" Ade hesitated by the window. "You coming out or what?" Babs continued, "sounds like you need another lick down my friend!" Ade kissed his teeth as he withdrew from the window. "Let me go and see what this fool wants now,...you coming?" Wayne smiled and nodded in agreement and they made their way to the back door.

By the time he opened the gate, he was regretting his decision. In the crowd of fashionable teens, all of whom seemed to be adorned in Prada, Gucci and Nike, Ellie stared at him. His heart literally skipped a beat as he simultaneously became acutely aware of his attire, specifically the lack of sag in his slightly small, brand-less jogging bottoms. "Yeh what?!" Ade announced as he approached Babs. "What!!?" Babs exclaimed lunging at the unsuspecting Ade, pinning him in a headlock. "Beg for mercy nigga...pray to the Lord...ask for sustenance in this your hour of need!" he continued as Ade struggled to break free. The dogs barking increased in fervour and pitch, as the struggle continued to the entertainment of the jeering crowd.

"Look here, make your call." Wayne said after a few minutes, handing over Ade's phone. Babs took the phone and released Ade who sprung up immediately. "Next time mind who you talking to bro, your mother never tell you that?" he continued raising his arm and giving Ade a last slap across the back of his head. Ade straightened his clothes and kissed his teeth as one of the girls in the crowd asked if he was alright. "I'm cool man!" he responded trying to appear unaffected. "You're not you know!" she replied as she approached him turning his head sideways and withdrawing a bloody finger, holding it in front of his face. "Can you see this?" she asked comically. Ade looked at her finger and kissed his teeth. "Fucking dickhead!" he seethed between clenched teeth. Cupping his ear, he signalled to Wayne and headed back to the garden gate.

"Shit man!" Ade exclaimed as he saw the blood in the bathroom mirror. "That guy is such a cunt, what da fuck man!" Wayne sat him on the toilet seat and cleaned the blood from the side of his head. "The cut not deep, the blood stop already, you can calm down now" he exclaimed half laughing. Ade kissed his teeth, "he's lucky, that's all I can say, that cunt is lucky!" "You good?" Wayne enquired. Ade nodded his head. "Ok, I'm going for my phone, I soon come." Ade added getting up from the toilet seat. "I'm coming blood" Wayne replied surprised at Ade's bravery. Holding fresh tissue to his ear, Ade returned with Wayne, wishing he'd had the nerve and the opportunity to totally demolish Babs.

"Ahhh baby got a booboo!" Babs exclaimed comically as the pair approached. "Leave him man!" Ellie shouted, grabbing Babs by his collar as he tried to make his way to Ade. "You ok?" Ade kissed his teeth, "dont watch dat, I'm good!" he asserted, throwing the tissue on the ground. "The phone?" Wayne asked stretching out his hand. He'd already sized up Babs and was ready to take him on if necessary, there was no way he was going to make him look dumb in front of Ellie. Silence hung in the air for a few brief seconds. Wayne's heart raced before Babs finally stood up and handed him the phone. "Don't try to call your gyal tonight though...your credit's done!" he added nonchalantly. "That's fuckery!" Ellie shouted slapping Babs at the back of his head. "Cool" Wayne replied looking Babs in the eye for just a split second longer than was comfortable. "What you want some of what your wifey got?" Babs responded somewhat surprised at Wayne's possible disrespect. Wayne looked at Ade who kissed his teeth and shook his head. "Let's go my friend." "Yeh...later." Wayne replied nodding his head as he looked at Ellie, who returned his nod with a smile. The boys walked back to Wayne's, laughing audibly as they opened the gate. "And next time you come outside and want to hang around big people, learn to behave eh...because you will get fucked up again!" Babs shouted, thickening his Nigerian accent. The pair kissed their teeth in unison and shut the kitchen door. "Oh my days, did you see dat one in da red skinnys...she is F I T dread!" Ade joked, slapping Wayne on his back as they returned to the bedroom. "What?" Wayne asked still thinking about the smile Ellie had given him. Ade kissed his teeth, "that's a wifey dread!" "Yeh" Wayne agreed, "We've got to get some clothes blood" "hmp!...best believe dat!" Ade agreed.

Before they sat down and with the lights off this time, the boys peeped through the curtain. Just as they did so, Marcus peddled over to the crowd shouting "Black Ice! They're at the bottom of the estate! They're on the estate!" Within seconds the crowd dispersed in a flurry of expletives and threats heading towards Holly Street. Wayne and Ade watched them as they retreated out of sight. The boys looked at each other. "Come we go!"

Ade exclaimed. Wayne didn't need any convincing, and they excitedly ran out of the house in the direction of the barking dogs. They caught up with the Millitants just as they caught up with the 'intruders'. "Oioioi! What you people doing on my estate?" Diggy glowered, holding his dog as close to the usurpers as possible. Wayne recognised one of the boys from the Clapton barbecue and wondered if Marcus didn't. The intruder kissed his teeth and turned to his friend. "Check out this fool yow! Why, what you gonna do about it? What because you have your dog with you?" The boy reached to the ground and picked up two stones. "You wanna tango, come we go!" he continued, firing one of the stones at Diggy's dog Chaos. "You best drop them my friend..." But before Babs finished his sentence, Marcus pulled out a two by four from under his hoody and smacked it across the back of the bigger of the two youths. "Don't get fucking bright bitch!" he hissed spraying spittle on the intruder, kicking him in his throat as he lay on the ground. Before his companion could react, Babs swung a weighted sock towards his temple. The pair were temporarily immobilised. "Diggy...Chaos now!" Marcus shouted. The boy did as he was told, but before he could loosen the lead wrapped tightly around his hands and wrist, the pair struggled to their feet and started running as energetically as their dazed bodies would allow.

The THM laughed at the retreating infidels, valiantly conceding a head start as the chase began. The two boys ran swiftly towards the high road, stopping only to pick up some bottles and a piece of pipe. As they neared the lights of the high street they dared to lessen their pace, eager to catch their breaths. In the same moment, Chaos rounded the corner and made a grab for the bigger boy's leg. He screamed in pain as the dog's jaw closed around his calf. His companion kicked the dog with as much force as he could muster, but still Chaos held firm. Passers-by, offering no assistance, watched in amazement at the scene. The shorter boy, not wanting to be bitten himself, forced a piece of pipe between Chaos' jaws and his friend's leg. The dog whined as the metal was forced against his gums but sunk his teeth deeper into the boy's calf. Exhausted, the boy retrieved the pipe and instead, brought it down with as much force as he could inflict, at the side of the animal's head. Chaos howled in pain, finally releasing his grip.

Marcus, Babs and Wayne were the first to arrive as the taller boy hobbled against his friend only to be bitten again. Bile threatened the back of Wayne's throat as he took in the scene. Excitement and fear propelled him forward as the dog, now locked firmly onto the boy's arm, shook its' head violently back and forth, spraying blood as he seemingly attempted loosening it from it's socket. Marcus and Babs turned down their excitement as they noticed the stares of passers-by but did nothing to remove Chaos from his arm. His companion stood immobilised, eyes glued on the two by four Marcus swung back and forth as if warming up for a baseball game. Under the street light Wayne could see him clearly, he looked about his age, no more than fifteen or sixteen. His face was drained of any definitive colour as it dripped with sweat and glazed with globules of blood. He stood with one foot on the pavement and the other in the road staring at Marcus like a deer caught in his headlights. Marcus laughed comically as he slowly and indirectly made his way over to the boy, in the process, gesturing to Wayne to move behind him blocking any prospect of retreat. Wayne too seemed momentarily dazed. His heart pounded louder than he'd ever heard as he finally moved in the direction Marcus requested. To his disguised relief, their sudden movements seem to reanimate the boy. He exhaled audibly, shaking his head as if waking out of a daze before locking eyes with his friend. In the next moment, he lunged towards his free arm, jerking it as he tried to pull him away from the dog's grip.

A bus approached from the junction and he breathed a small sigh of relief in the knowledge they could make it out. His friend groaned in pain, now on his knees, and unable to make eye contact with him. He inhaled, and with as much force as he could muster, he yanked his friend upwards, determined to make it to the bus. The taller boy screamed in anguish as his arm popped from its socket. He heard the sound and felt the slackening of his grip. Bile rose till he could taste it on his tongue, but there was no choice, they had to make it to the bus. His plan was thwarted. Surrounded and blocked from view by the THM, Marcus swung his two by four, connecting with the side of the bitten boy's head, knocking him out cold on contact. The shorter boy finally released his grip and ran across the road jumping on the waiting bus. Breathless, he clambered to the top, looking for a view of what was happening to his friend, but all he could see was THM. All he could hear was laughter as tears ran silently and unnoticed down his wet face. "Oi Marcus, your dead meat!", he screamed repeatedly, eyeballing him as anger surged through his body. Marcus smiled, standing apart from the crowd, he bowed and blew a kiss as the bus pulled away from its stop and out of the Junction.

Wayne looked down at the intruder left behind, blood slipped from the corner of his mouth as he lay motionless on the ground. "Ok, let's go!" Marcus hissed staring at the window as the bus pulled away. "Black Ice bitch! That fucker is out! Spitting on the prone body, Diggy lifted Chaos and the group returned victoriously to the anonymity of the estate.

Adrenaline coursed through Wayne's body as he retreated with the crowd. Years of running through the undergrowth in Tamana had strengthened his leg muscles. He could easily have reached the intruder before the rest of the group, but he knew instinctively, he had to run with the crowd. He had no desire to draw blood nor to have his own drawn. The squad exuberantly returned to the corner of their swing park, cursing the audacity of the two intruders and commending Marcus on his militancy and aggression. Wayne stood quietly with his hands in his pockets trying to understand what had just happened until thankfully, he heard his mother calling his name. He said his goodbyes, touched Ade and walked home. He locked himself in the toilet and vomited until all that was left was bile.

"Baby, you ok?" Ivy enquired through the locked door. Wayne quickly flushed, wiped his face and opened the door. Ivy was startled by his appearance. "Babes, what's the matter?" his mother continued with obvious concern. "I'm ok mom, just feel a bit sick, I might be coming down with something", he lied, feeling worse at the prospect of telling his mum what had just happened. That night, fear kept him from looking out of his bedroom window. He was shook, and cried into his pillow for the first time, appeasing himself with the knowledge that the THM were his 'friends'.

He spent the weekend in his bedroom under the pretext of studying for Xmas tests. Ade knocked for him a few times, but instead of answering the door, he sat on the edge of the step waiting for the knocking to stop. Monday morning came around all too quickly, and he made his way to the bus stop hoping not to bump into anyone from Friday's crowd. As he neared the high road and the spot the intruder fell, he saw the same red brown stains on the concrete floor as was always beneath the post Mr Roxborough used to slaughter his pigs. He stopped in his tracks, momentarily mesmerised by the sight, automatically reliving the events of that night until he felt a stinging slap to the back of his head.

"Oi oi!" came a familiar voice as Wayne spun round, guilt and fear propelling him away from the stain. "What's gwarning my yout, I heard you was running with da pack on Friday!" Cavell laughed extending his fist. Wayne touched him weakly, grimacing at his comment as Marcus bounded up to the pair of them. He felt mucus at the back of his throat and coughed, easing himself away from the duo. "Yes boss!" Marcus interrupted and for the first time, extended his fist to Wayne as well as Cavell. "Fucking hell, dat idiot come clean over here to stain up my estate!" Marcus teased stamping on the stain as the trio walked past it to the bus stop. For a split second Wayne was stunned. Marcus's normal acknowledgement of him was either non-existent or a ridicule, and although this offer of a fist caught him off guard, it temporarily eased the uncomfortable feeling that nestled in his belly since Friday night. He extended his fist and for the first time, a feeling of acceptance and belonging enveloped him, as the three stood shoulder to shoulder at the bus stop.

As usual, the stop was crowded with students wearing the familiar black blazer and red tie. Any sense of uniformity however was somehow dampened with the array of styles in which the ensemble was worn. Long ties, short ties, fat ties, skinny ties, afros, some adorned with afro picks, cornrows, number one's, earrings, gold chains, baggy pants and tight trousers mingled in familial groups awaiting the number thirty-eight.

As they waited, the main topic of discussion was Friday night's usurper. The trio made their way to the back of the crowd, where normally Wayne in his unbranded and un-blinged attire, would not be permitted. Today though, instead of his usual position at the edge of the crowd, he found himself instead at it's heart, as Cavell leant on his shoulder listening to the varying descriptions of the night's events. By the time the bus came, Wayne had been included in more conversations than he had since the beginning of term, and the scene that had so shocked and disgusted him only a few days ago, was now embraced as his right of passage, his ticket to inclusion and without him realising it, his perception of himself changed.

∞

Christmas tests, scheduled to last the week began promptly at 9.30am with English. Class 4A nervously anticipated the test questions as Mr Ingrassia silenced his students, and asked for all textbooks to be closed as he passed out the papers. "If you don't know it now, you won't know it in the next five minutes!" he exclaimed as he walked the aisles. "but Sir!..." came a panicked voice from the back of the room. "Next term Mr Johnson, try paying attention to what I'm teaching you instead of whatever it is you and your buddies do at the back here, and I can guarantee you won't be in the position you're in now!" The boy kissed his teeth. "I tell you what, at least put your name on it and I'll promise not to give you a 'U'! Now, I can't say fairer than that can I?" Mr Ingrassia grinned at the cut eye the boy gave him and continued handing out papers.

"You may begin." Wayne scanned the paper and smiled to himself. An hour later and with twenty minutes to spare, he rechecked his work and raised his hand to submit his test and be excused from the class. Ade eyed him in dismay as barely audible snickering erupted from the back row. "What happened to you professor, not as clever as you thought A!" Mehmet of the 'back row boys' teased. Twenty minutes later, Ade caught up to him in the school yard. "What's gwarning boss, did you finish?" he asked concerned. "Course, that was a doddle!" Wayne exclaimed, surprised that they would even think that he hadn't, and wondered if it was possible that someone wouldn't.

The rest of the week passed easily for him. He'd already formed the habit of doing homework and revision almost every day, and so unlike some of his classmates, the tests were neither painful nor surprising, and he sailed through each examination. His status amongst the student populace too had changed. Instead of sitting by himself or joking with Ade during the lunch hour, he was now called upon to kick a ball, hear a joke, explain a problem and, coveted above all else, to hang with Cavell and the other 'too cool' fifth years.

Monday morning signalled the last week before the Xmas holidays and the return of the test papers. The school was subdued. The usual background noise was reduced to a silent hum as teachers in all classes returned the results; results that would make or break a great number of Xmas wishes. As usual Ade was late, and loudly entered the room as the register was being called. "Yo! Wha gwarn man!" he exclaimed, excitedly nudging Wayne to look in his ruc sac as he made his way to his desk. "Mr Odulajo!, is there something you wish to share with the rest of the class?" Mr Ingrassia enquired as Ade quickly closed his bag and made his way to his seat. "No Sir, sorry Sir" Ade answered feigning remorse and taking his seat as the test results were handed out.

"For fuck's sake!" came a frustrated voice from the back of the class. Wayne turned to see the orator as he was handed his test sheet and congratulated. Biggie, so nicknamed because of his stature, right hand man to Mehmet, sprang to his feet, knocking his chair over in the process. "I ain't having that man! Nineteen percent in history...nineteen fucking percent...he's having a laugh!" he glowered indignantly. "Calm down man, just calm down innit!" his friends urged as he gathered his belongings. "What, nah man, I ain't having that, this man is taking the piss!" Biggie continued, glaring at Mr Ingrassia. "Mr Browne, you can either sit and be silent, come forward and ask me a question, or make your way to your principal's office, choose one!"

Biggie locked eyes with the balding man standing in front of the classroom. He eyed him up and down as Mehmet urged him to take his seat. "Nah I ain't got nothing to say to you star!" he answered with as much venom as his words would carry. "Clearly there is something on your mind, spit it out, or do I have to pry it out of you like I would a dummy from a baby?" Mr Ingrassia continued from his seat behind his desk. The class remained silent as the pair engaged in their stand off. Mr Ingrassia finally exhaled. "OK, let me help you. I take it you're upset about your grade. Well, let's review it shall we. Your illegible handwriting, and inadequate punctuation is what makes your work incomprehensible, quite apart from your interpretation of the events, hence your grade. Perhaps if you chose to spend a portion of your free time addressing that issue, your grade would improve." The teacher stated succinctly. Biggie kissed his teeth. "Well if the work had anything to do with my history, I would take more time with it innit!, I don't want to know about no grey man's history, what is that going to do for me? what about my history? You people act like the rest of the world are nobody's and then you expect me to respect you and want to study you. How is not teaching me my history supposed to prepare me for my future. You're supposed to be preparing me for adulthood, but you're preparing me for a world where black people don't even get a mention!" he replied adamantly. "Yeah, why's that then Sir?" Mehmet interrupted, folding his arms and resting his chin on his open palm.

The remaining members of the class audibly agreed as Mehmet patted Biggie's back. Mr Ingrassia smiled and walked to Biggie's desk. "Listen my friend, why do you keep blaming everybody else for holding you back? Tell me, what's stopping you from going to a library, and borrowing a book about your history, and even more audaciously, why don't you sell one of those chains around your neck and buy a book?" Biggie kissed his teeth, "Fuck you man!" and slouched even lower in his chair. "Very well, I take it our banter has ended. In any event, I will not tolerate such disrespectful behaviour in my classroom, please make your way to the Principal's office immediately" Mr Ingrassia stated in a voice barely audible despite the unusual silence of the classroom. Biggie kissed his teeth as indignantly as he could. "Disrespect you? You've been dissing me since I came to this class, but it's cool dough, what goes around and all that...!" he continued as he gathered his belongings. "Yeh yeh, save it for the principal!" Mr Ingrassia interjected as the pair made their way to the office.

By lunch time, news of Biggie's fate circulated the yard. "Oi, did you hear about Biggie!? My yout got suspended fam... indefinitely! "Shit!" was all Ade could say as the pair silently made their way to the sheds. They gathered with the seniors in their usual spot, near the bin area at the back of the bike stand. Marcus and Babs were discussing their secret santas. "That fucking prick better get me something good yuh know!" Marcus menaced angrily. "Trust you to get picked by him!" Babs laughed teasingly. "I remember last year he got Heads a pack of handkerchiefs and my man was so proud of dem, about how 'they match your blazer' and all showing him all the different ways he could fold them!" "Yeh, well he better not try any of dat shit on me, cos he'll get tumped, best believe dat!" "So I heard you lot had some drama in your class today?" Babs enquired making his way through a pack of Fruitellas. "Yeh man, but Biggie's right though" Ade replied "we don't get taught shit about our history. Do you remember the trip to that art gallery?...was there any black people dough in any of the ten thousand and one paintings? We had to hear some nonce talk about Lord this and Queen dat, the only niggas was a mamie and a shoe shiner for fuck sake!" The group laughed. "For real dough, that's all there was!"

"So don't you guys know about the Caribs and the Arawaks, Frederick Douglas, Toussaint L'Ouverture, Marcus Garvey or Harriet Tubman!" Wayne enquired incredulously, for a moment understanding Biggie's outburst. Silence answered his question. Shit! That's real sad! I tell you what dough, props to Biggie, because if I'd said anything like that to my teacher in Trinidad, I would have got caned in front the class. And again at home." The boys burst into laughter as they made their way to the dinning-hall. "Rah!" "Fuckery!" "Innit dough!" "Pssttppss fuck that! They would have to catch me first fam!" "Blood, you had it rough!" Cavell teased. "I can't tell you the last time anybody tried to put their hands on me!"

Friday finally rolled around, and the school closed for the Xmas break. The pupils noisily left the compound filling the air with laughter and loud voices as they made their way to the bus stop discussing who expected what under their Xmas tree. "Blood, I just want a pair of dem Air Max's dread...the ones with da luminous..." Before Marcus could finish, Babs interjected kissing his teeth. "Oh for fuck sake! We dun know you ain't getting shit worth talking about Marcus, so best you stop da dreaming shit right now!" Marcus feigned offense. 'You don't even get a fucking Xmas tree in your house, what you talking about!" Babs continued as heat engulfed Marcus' face. The back of the bus burst into laughter as he lunged for the side of Bab's head. "Don't get defensive, everybody done know!! Xmas day is gonna come, you're mum's gonna be high, there's not gonna be any food, and you'll be lucky if you get a punch in the head from your step dad!" The laughter reached fever pitch as Babs ran to the front of the bus and down the stairs. "You cunt!, wait...watch...fucking African!" Marcus hissed as

Cavell pulled him back to his seat. "Don't watch dat my friend!" Cavell said, "...but it's true doh in it! The laughter continued as the bus pulled in to the stop in Dalston and they all alighted.

Wayne felt good as he opened his front door and was greeted with the sound of calypso coming from the front room, and his mum's singing coming from the kitchen. He usually came home to an empty house, retiring to his bedroom till Ade knocked for him, or Andy came home. He looked forward to the shifts that brought her home early, and not too tired to spend time with him. Today, the house smelt of cake and meat as Wayne opened the kitchen door. "Just in time my friend" Andy smiled as he walked in, quickly ushering him to the chopping board. Thyme, chive, onions, peppers and shadow benny, lay freshly washed on the board as Andy passed him a knife and reminded him that Santa Claus hadn't been yet. "Whatever" Wayne replied innocently as he chuckled to himself. Kissing his mother, he began preparation for the seasoning. The trio worked through the rest of the afternoon grating spices, mixing batters and marinating meat. Hours later, the lamb and chicken were cleaned, seasoned and stored away along with the pastelles, punch a creme and rum soaked fruit cakes. "Ok that's it, let's go grocery one time!" Ivy announced washing her hands. "Oh mum, I hate going grocery, please...I'm tired" Wayne grumbled looking to Andy for support. "I know how you feel," Andy responded laughing, "It's either now with the car or in the morning on foot!" Andy grinned as Wayne put on his coat and waited for them to get ready.

By the time they returned, night had fallen as they carried the bags into the house. "Boy, I tired, go back and see if my handbag in the car nuh!" Ivy asked her son as she packed away the shopping. Andy was still in the car with the last shopping bags, listening to music and smoking a cigarette. Wayne, deciding to prank him, stooped in stealth towards the car. Andy had already caught a glimpse of his shirt though and had already auto locked all the doors. Wayne heard the click, stepped on to the crumbled brick wall and threw himself across the car to the open sun roof. Andy ducked just in time to grab the packet of Maltesers out of his hanging hand, and was about to insert one in Wayne's nostril when four policemen surrounded them. The officers grabbed Wayne's legs and pulled him off the car. He was in shock, and instinctively tried to extend his arms to protect his face, but as he was pulled out of the sunroof, another officer grabbed hold of his arms. He screamed in agony as he was pulled down, hitting the pavement face first. Another two officers immediately knelt on his back, forcing his arms into a painfully unnatural position.

Ivy heard her son's screams through the open front door and dashed outside, just in time to see Andy being forcibly removed from the car. Panic swept through her like a tidal wave, followed instantaneously with unbridled anger. She ran the fifteen metres to the parked car, as police officers struggled to restrain her son, and he frantically struggled for his release. For a few moments Ivy couldn't move. She took in the scene trying to understand what was happening and then immediately sprang into action. She was screaming, but couldn't hear herself, her only thought was to relieve her son. Moments later, after trying to knock both officers off his back, she too was being restrained.

"Calm down ma'am!" one of the officers shouted, as she lunged towards her son whilst he attempted to remove her from the scene. "What the fuck!" Ivy screamed as the officer grabbed her arms and twisted them around her back. "What are you doing to my son!" she screamed at the top of her lungs. Between propelling her body forward and half dragging the policewoman restraining her, she made it over to Wayne lying face down on the pavement with a policeman's hand keeping his face pressed against the concrete floor. By now, a crowd gathered around the scene, and three more police cars with sirens blazing, drove on to the interrupted silence of the estate. The officer with his knee in the small of Wayne's back, reduced his pressure and asked his name. Wayne answered as calmly as he could, as adrenaline and fear coursed through his body. "Are you known to the police?" the officer continued. "No, no! He's not, can't you see he is just a child!" Ivy screamed "Why would he be known to the police!...Oh my god! Oh my god, Oh my god!" she repeated as information was passed to and from on the officer's radio. To Wayne it seemed a lot longer, but moments later, he heard his name and although not fully releasing him, the officers allowed him to stand as the car's license plates were checked. By now Ivy was hysterical, she'd never had contact with the police in Trinidad nor London, and couldn't understand nor process what was happening. "Why...why are you doing this?" she screamed alternating between shouts of outrage and moments of fear induced silence. By now a crowd of the estates residents lined the adjacent wall of the car park, intoxicated by the injustice of the familiar scene. "They do it all the time girl!" "Leave them alone!" "Ah so dem treat black people inna de ghetto!" As the scene progressed, the onlookers hurled abuse and protests at the officers to no avail.

"Why? why? what is this about, he hasn't done anything!?" Ivy continued. "He fits the description of someone we're looking for." The officer trying to disperse the crowd finally replied as if expecting his statement to quell the almost palpable aggression in the air. It was an unacceptable though familiar phrase, igniting the crowd into further abusive expletives and incredulous laughter at the audacity of the officer's reasoning. "Yeh we all know how that goes, all you grey man look da same to me too!" came an angry voice from the crowd. "What the fuck are you talking about! Why didn't you just stop and ask like a civilised human being? Why did you treat us like criminals before finding out if we were! For God sake!...unless you thought we were criminals....Do you think we are criminals?" No reply came and Ivy continued. "Why would you think we were criminals? Doesn't the law dictate innocence until proven guilt? why did you handle us like that, how dare you treat us in this manner?!" The crowd listened agitatedly to Ivy's cries, cursing the officers to release them. So there they were, on their estate, surrounded by two beast vans and four patrol cars in the week before Wayne's first British Xmas.

Minutes later, after a signal from an officer on his radio, Wayne and his family were finally given the all clear. "Ok thank you for your time, have a good evening." The officer stated as he released Ivy's cuffs. She said nothing but ran to her son. For a moment the family headed for an embrace, but just as she thought they were being let go, the officers began searching the entire vehicle, holding each IC3 as they were referred to, away from the other. Wayne's blood was boiling by now. Tears of anguish, anger and frustration fell silently down his cheeks as an officer kept hold of his arm, asking him questions about Andy. By now he'd learnt, the more he became indignant about the situation, the deeper the involvement became, and so he answered every question but with as little words as possible, looking past the officer as he did so. It hurt his sense of himself, to the very core of his being, but he wasn't about to show it, instead he kept silent and looked at his mother. She looked dishevelled and frantic. Her eyes were wide open and he could see she was afraid but finally she stood quietly, as close to him as she could, and smiled. Minutes later, the officers who moments before barred entry into the car park, now suddenly retreated to their vehicles. Ivy embraced her family, and thanked her neighbours. Andy hugged them both, and with his arms around them, walked back to the house. Christmas was spent in a sombre reflective mood in Wayne's household, insulated from the reality of just outside their front door.

∞

Wayne's aptitude for learning flourished as the months flew by, and his position as the brightest student in his year, was assured. His skill at art, his aptitude for numbers and his eagerness for words, amazed both his teachers and his mother. She herself was an ambitious woman, coming to London almost five years ago for just that reason. She wanted more from life for her son, and to give him those opportunities, she decided to go back to school. Becoming fully qualified would allow her the financial freedom to have the lifestyle she wanted for them both. It meant less time at home for a while, but she would have the financial independence to provide him with some of his wants and not just his needs. A theory she reminded herself of almost every day after coming home to a meal prepared for her by him.

Sometimes days would go by without so much as twenty words exchanged between them, and Ivy's heart ached with the guilt of her absence, but as she became more involved with her career, without realising it, she became less involved with Wayne. He didn't complain, he was sad sometimes but never spoke of it to her. Instead he would cook and clean so that by the time she came home, she could go straight to bed. Ivy was a proud parent and was soon lulled into a sense of security, which came from believing that his obvious natural talent, meant that he would be a doctor, lawyer or something else of skill and great rewards. By the end of the school year, Wayne was settled into his new London life and as the months flew by, he thought of Trinidad less and less. His confidence too re-emerged, as his friendships with Ade and the THM blossomed.

The impending summer though, brought thoughts of Africa for Ade, and thoughts of Ade's absence and solitude for Wayne. For Wayne, Ade was London, and his departure brought with it, his return to his bedroom and boredom as the holidays stretched endlessly in front of him. Ivy was either at work, school or with Andy, and by week two, his boredom threatened to replace his sanity. On day thirteen, he was awakened by the sound of dog barking streaming through his window as he rolled over and lazily stretched, yawning as he remembered yet again, there was nothing to do. Eyes still closed, he listened to the voices demanding silence from the dog and was startled as he heard his name shouted through the window. Trying to remove the smile that engulfed his face, Wayne eagerly made his way to the window, wiping the sleep from his eyes on the way. Cavell, Tasha and Ellie were seated smoking cigarettes on the remaining swings. Wayne's heart immediately increased it's rhythm as he gestured to Cavell with a nod of his head. "What's up my friend, you coming out? we're going up West!" Would it be ok with his mum? did he have anything to wear? and did he have any cash to spend? The questions simultaneously swam through his mind, but after a few seconds he nodded his head in agreement, and almost fell over his feet on his way to the bathroom.

By the time he emerged, they had been joined by Marcus, Babs and more THM and they made their way to Highbury Station. Heading for the first empty carriage on the Victoria Line, they animatedly pushed each other aside, jostling for the seat of their choice. Ellie sat next to Wayne, easily tapping his head as she sat down, whilst he himself could barely control his breathing.

His beaten up Converse stared out woefully amongst the row of gleaming Nikes, and he suddenly became conscious of his size nines. He squirmed in his seat as he tried to retract his feet, secretly surveying the attire of his companions. His initial excitement of being invited dwindled as he returned his attention to his too tight, too short jeans and silently prayed no-one noticed he didn't look like them. But it was too late. "Fucking hell Cs!....what da fuck..." exclaimed Babs pointing at Wayne with open arms. All eyes turned to Wayne. "What?" he responded inquisitively, feeling a distinct rise in the temperature of his face. Babs pointed from the top of Wayne's head, slowly making his way down to the scuffed tips of his Converse. Thinly disguised giggles and choked fits of laughter were met with open contempt as Marcus kissed his teeth. "You're fucking up da programme blood...you need to fix up! For real...you look like you should be in a black and white photo!" Babs continued to unveiled laughter. Wayne sat quietly, as his breaths became shorter in his chest. Unexpectedly, Ellie leaned forward and kissed his cheek, and his short breaths suddenly stopped altogether.

"Don't watch dat my yout!" Cavell smiled, "today you is getting hooked up!" Wayne's voice cracked as he opened his mouth and he quickly cleared his throat. "I cool you know, don't worry about me horse." he replied nonchalantly. "Yeh I know your cool...dats why you is getting hooked up! And you Miss Thing..." Cavell continued stretching his arm over Tasha to grab her sister's throat. "Behave yourself you, your breast ain't even full out yet and yuh playing de kissing game!" Tasha and Ellie looked at each other and to Wayne's relief, the attention moved from him to her and he could finally exhale. He spent the remainder of the journey praying she couldn't hear his heart pounding.

Oxford Street was bathed in sunlight as they emerged from the station. "Come on, let's go check Lenny, I'm hungry man!" Cavell announced putting his arm around Tasha and leading the Millitants down to the MacDonalds. "Is he working today though?" Babs asked. "That cunt is always working, let's go." Marcus answered. The foyer of the restaurant was packed as Cavell searched for the familiar face behind the counter. "There he is" Diggy pointed, "Ok grab a table people." Within a few minutes Cavell stood in front of the cashier. "Ten Big Mac meals please," he requested formally handing over a fifty pound note. The cashier rolled his eyes and retrieved the note returning with the order and forty-seven pounds and one pence change. "Nice." Cavell responded tipping his head before retrieving the trays of food.

Twenty minutes later, the meals were consumed and he announced cheerfully, rubbing his stomach. "Aite, belly full now! time to go to work...what, back at two?" Nods of agreement signalled a separation amongst the group as they gathered their belongings. Ellie opened her ruck sack and pulled out three shopping bags, each in immaculate condition. Stuffing her ruck sac into one and a t-shirt in the other two, she hooked her arm around Wayne's and they walked out arm in arm. Wayne had no idea where they were going, but it didn't really matter, Ellie had her arm in his and that was all he could think as they walked up the high street. They went into a few shops and he looked around feeling woefully inadequate. Ellie tried on a few things as Wayne waited for her, mesmerised outside the changing rooms.

By the time they reached the Nike store it was 1.30pm. "Ok, let's check this last one yeah, my bags are getting heavy!" Wayne immediately reached down to carry them, embarrassed that he hadn't offered sooner. "Aahh! ain't you sweet!" she teased, kissing him on his lips. "I need them," she replied looking into his eyes. "Thanks though." Wayne blushed, releasing his grip as they entered the store. Ellie survey the shop as if she was looking for the right section. Moments later she pointed to an area to the left of the entrance. "Alright, trainers this way!" The shop was full of Saturday morning shoppers and they had to wait to be served. They didn't mind, and browsed through the styles selecting their favourites. As an attendant became available, Ellie requested two pairs in their respective sizes and sat down, removing her trainers and placing them in one of her bags. Wayne sat with his back to hers and removed his shoes, tucking them under the seat out of embarrassment. The attendant returned with their selections and they tried them on, walking up and down confirming that they were indeed the correct pair, permitting their attendant to assist another customer. Returning to their seats, Ellie waited for the attendant to return, and feigning interest in two different pairs, requested their sizes whilst unlacing the shoes they had on. As the attendant withdrew her attention, Ellie gathered her bags and stood up. "Ok, these are the ones, let's splurt!"

Before Wayne could respond Ellie grabbed his hand and nonchalantly walked out of the store, stopping to admire a skirt on her way. By the time they reached the exit, his entire body felt like a throbbing vein. Though still battling the will of his feet, he soothed himself as he crossed the threshold of the store front, with no obvious pursuers on his tail. Without stopping or looking back, they made their way to the rendezvous point in MacDonalds, as he fought to return his breath to an even pace. "You ok babe?" Ellie asked, laughing at Wayne's flushed appearance as they fell into the booth "You haven't taken anything before have you?" she enquired earnestly using a tissue to wipe the sweat off his upper lip. "Yeh!" Wayne answered as if shocked at the question. "Yeh right!, you look like your about to have a heart attack, calm down!" Before he could reply, Marcus, Babs and two females, hands full of bags, sat in the booth opposite them. "So how you make out!" Babs enquired as Ellie pointed to Wayne's feet. "Wha!..a you dat blood!" he grinned at Wayne. "Ah yes man!" exclaimed Cavell as he dropped an over-sized ruc sac on to the table before heading to the toilets followed by Tasha. "You aite babe, how did u do?" she asked her sister on her way to the toilets. Ellie laughed, "ask him!" she replied laughing. Wayne felt naïve and embarrassed, and bowed his head. As he looked down at his feet though, exhilaration coursed through his body. They went shopping every day for the next three days and by Saturday, he had acquired three complete outfits that he tried on every night before he went bed.

∞

Wayne looked into the mirror and didn't recognise himself. From head to toe, he could have been any one of them. Smiling to himself, he slicked down his eyebrows and jumped the three flights of staircase to the bottom. Before leaving, he stopped in the kitchen, filling an empty flask with some of Ivy's Hennessy. Taking a sip for the road, he made sure to put it back in the same spot he found it. He eagerly reached the top of the estate, meeting up with Cavell and THM, as Babs rounded the corner screaming "Three 149s!...come on lets have yah!!" Ten fresh pairs of Nikes raced to the bus stop, jumping on the back as it pulled away from the curb. Before it arrived at Ridley Road market, it was already packed with Saturday afternoon shoppers as it made it's way up Kingsland Road to Stamford Hill. "I can't find my ticket!" Marcus bellowed, leaning into the ticket inspector's face. "Fuck off man!" he continued as the man insisted the ticket or pass be produced. "Do you speak English?...or you just playing dumb!, I've already told you, I can't fucking find it!" Marcus continued aggressively. "I must ask you to leave the bus then, or pay the correct fare" the inspector continued holding his ground despite the jeers coming from the surrounding seats. Marcus kissed his teeth ignoring the request as the man made his way to the lower deck.

Within seconds, the bus pulled over to the curb and came to a stop. Irritated passengers, unable to continue their journey cursed Marcus's attitude as they too made their way downstairs. Wayne sat uncomfortably in his seat. Marcus's eagerness to unnecessary ignorance was a weakness that irritated him. He kissed his teeth in the knowledge that he wasn't yet high enough in the ranks to challenge him but he imagined the moment he would be. It brought a smile to his face as he turned to gaze out the window.

Moments later the inspector returned, demanding Marcus get off the bus. Cavell kissed his teeth and tapped the back of Marcus' head. They were one bus stop away from their stop, as the remaining passengers audibly discussed the disrespectful behaviour vowing that teeth would have been knocked out, had Marcus been a child of theirs. "Come on you fucking maggot, now we're gonna have to fucking walk...you lucky it's a nice day!.. Ladies, let's go!" The squad loudly made their way off the bus, easily returning insults and dirty looks as they went.

At the gates of Finsbury Park, Ellie's heart skipped a beat as she observed Wayne approaching in the raucous crowd. "Oooohhh her sister nudged, "ain't that your boy?" Ellie feigned disinterest as the group looked in Wayne's direction. "But wha you a chat say... he scrub up good ee!" The girls laughed loudly, teasing her as the boys reached the gates. Wayne smiled when he saw her, and as he'd come to expect, his breathing shallowed. Reaching into his pocket he withdrew the flask, took a swig and passed it to her. Surprised, Ellie grinned and took a sip, coughing as the potent liquid burned it's way down her throat. The rest of the crew were already on the path to the fair but it didn't matter, they lagged behind, walking hand in hand. The fair was packed, music was blaring and the sun was high in the sky. Wayne felt the best he thought he ever had, and by the time he won a blue and white dolphin at the shooting gallery and handed it to Ellie, and she kissed him, he was the happiest person in the park.

Bumper cars, helter-skelter and bungee jumping later, the THM made their way to the gambling machines as Marcus received a text on his phone. He looked up and turned in the direction of a commotion at the park gates. "They're here!" he laughed to himself as he jumped off the platform, automatically reaching into his pocket for his trusted companion. "Boys, dem pussies trying to step up, come we got work to do!" Wayne's heart raced as the THM boys looked in the direction of Marcus' finger. He saw the commotion, his boys reaching for their weapons, and his legs jellied as he jumped to the grass, bringing up the rear as they converged in front the tarot booth. Wayne wasn't sure what was going to happen, or even what he was going to do, but he silently followed as adrenaline coursed through every cell of his body.

Within moments they were confronted by black bandanas. Black Ice boys. Wayne recognised some of them despite their attempt to cover their faces. Bucky the ranker, stood silently to the front. His reputation preceded him. He was also personally responsible for Marcus's mother getting dragged during her handbag snatch in Ridley Road Market, a retaliation Wayne heard for some outstanding violations on Marcus's part. Fear crept up the back of his neck as he hardened his face, and felt his feet follow his boys. Bucky was about to speak, but before any words were exchanged Marcus stepped forward, head butting him, leaving him dazed and off his guard. He grabbed on to the inside of his cheek dragging his face toward his expectant fists, firing endless punches as he dropped to his knees. Within moments Bucky stopped trying to defend himself and Marcus dropped his fist, releasing the boy's limp body to the cool grass.

Shock kept Wayne's mind and feet glued to the floor, but as he stared at the fallen body, his reverie was brutally interrupted by a blow to his jaw. The trajectory was off and it slid down his face, impacting with less than it's full intent. Still, the pain seared through his head and neck. He saw the youth approaching him again. He was heavy set and kept dancing around him. Wayne shook his head to clear the momentary fog. As his focus returned, anger instantaneously replaced fear and he sprang upwards head butting his violator with as much force as he could. It dazed him long enough for Wayne to punch him in his throat, but the connection was bad and the youth raised his arm swinging a sock, which this time hit Wayne's temple, sending him reeling to his knees. As he raised his hand to his face, another two blows followed to his jaw and the back of his head, each one ensuring he too was rendered useless to the THM. Wayne had never felt such deeply penetrating pain, his head felt ballooned to the point that he was sure it would explode as his body trembled into shock. He vaguely made out the shape of something round dangling from a swinging sock and heard Ellie's scream before everything went black.

The two sides engaged in a volley of fists and makeshift weapons until the sound of sirens forced a retreat. Wayne could feel himself being brought to his feet and half walked, half carried between two people before being pulled up stairs. He heard voices in the distance but couldn't quite make out the words. The excruciating pain had been replaced with a dull manageable ache but he wasn't yet ready to move any of his limbs. "You missed it blood! wake up, wake up man!" Something wet fell onto his face and he opened his eyes, sitting up with a jolt. The sudden movement sent shards of pain shooting through the back of his head as if arguing that it should not have been removed from the floor. He sat on the bed with his back against the wall, cradling his head in his hands unable to think or move. Ellie sat beside him, coaxing him to take the painkillers she held out to him before laying his head in her lap, gently massaging the obvious bruising with ice cubes wrapped in a bandana. "You ok my yout?" Cavell enquired stooping in front of Wayne to check out the damage to his face. "A little less pretty but you good!" he announced returning to his feet before retrieving the familiar shoe box from under his bed.

"Baddest! Yeh, I'm ready for de ital now dread!" Marcus declared jumping up and down, shaking his head and arms as if getting ready for a boxing match. Naz's 'Who killed it' blared from Cavell's stereo and the room full of voices sang in unison, "Look here , pretty mike shanked two-face al over some gal" drank Heinekens and smoked spliffs, retelling their accounts of their 'meeting' in Finsbury Park. Cavell reached across Wayne, passing a spliff to Diggy until he noticed Wayne extended his arm to intercept it. "Yeh I'll take a couple draws" he stated nonchalantly reaching for it. Babs eyed Cavell and the room hushed in surprise as Wayne inhaled the smoke. As was expected, he coughed and choked on the first pull and laughter erupted around him. Ellie herself had to contain her laughter as she offered him the bottle of water sitting between her legs. "Easy doggy easy...don't pull so hard fam!" Cavell advised as Wayne rested his head back against the wall. His head swooned and he felt queasy but he wasn't about to look even less ready in front of Ellie, especially since she had seen him take the beat down in the Park. So with eyes watering, he took a second drag, this time careful not to over extend his lungs. Momentarily holding the smoke in, Wayne felt every cell in his body relax and he became acutely aware of his body parts and more so, of Ellie sitting right next to him. The pain in his head seemed to fade into the distance, taking any discomfort or angst with it.

For the first time, he felt completely at ease with THM and reached out to pass the spliff to Diggy. His arm felt heavy but weightless at the same time, and he laughed to himself as he was forced to steady it to make contact with him. He handed it over but found he couldn't control his laughter. The more he tried to contain himself, the more he couldn't stop laughing. "Yes cuz, yuh ketch it dread!" Cavell teased. Wayne covered his face with his hands as he tried to control his laughter. His heart raced uncontrollably, he was sure he could hear it beating and was positive Ellie could. "How you feeling now babe?" she asked lightly rubbing the back of his head. "I..." he coughed and cleared his throat. "I cool" he answered with a smile. "Good" she replied leaning forward to kiss him on his lips. Her lips were soft against his mouth. He breathed in her scent and tried to act normal as she withdrew her caress. His face felt hot and flushed, his leg was uncomfortable and his arm lay awkwardly against hers. He could think of nothing to say and yet, the thought of moving from that spot was unthinkable. Ellie laid her head against his shoulder and Wayne felt the best he had in his fifteen years. He feigned interest in the conversations going around the room, and smoked and drank until 1am.

"Where you now coming from boy?!" Ivy asked opening the front door before he could turn the key. Wayne stumbled happily over the threshold, hugging his mother before trying to make his way to his bedroom. "What de mudder…!" his mother exclaimed catching the smell of alcohol and smoke as he approached her. "Wait…what yuh was smoking as well?" she continued pushing her son away from her. "Yuh stinking! Take off those clothes and get in de bath!" she demanded kissing her teeth and pushing him up the stairs. She struggled to help him undress but he pushed her away. In the light, Ivy saw the swollen mound distorting the side of his face. "Oh my lord Wayne!" she screamed holding his face to get a better look. He had forgotten about the beating and turned to look in the mirror. "Oh shit!" he exclaimed cupping the side of his face. It was the first time he got a look at himself and he grinned wondering how his face looked so terrible and yet hardly hurt at all. "What happened to you?" Ivy asked in earnest, shocked at his face, "Come let me wipe it down." Wayne flinched away from her as her hand pressed the lump steadily expanding at the back of his head. Seeing her distress at his face, he withdrew her hand from his head in an effort to avoid her knowing the full extent of his injuries. "Mummy, watch nah, bad man doh need he mummy to bade him yuh know!" he grinned cheekily, "and don't worry, I just fell off the wall at the back." Ivy was concerned, but he seemed ok and she allowed herself to be backed out of the bathroom. She had no idea he drank alcohol or smoked and was determined to find out, deciding first to put the kettle on for coffees. By the time she returned, coffee mugs in hand, Wayne lay sprawled diagonally across his bed. She wasn't about to accept his simple explanation though, it was 1am and he stank. Slapping his leg, she nudged him over to the side of his bed. Sitting on the edge, she handed him the hot drink.

"So where it is you coming from at this hour? You had me worried all night!" "Oh gosh sorry mum, I was just at Cavell's. I thought you were at work." Wayne replied sipping the hot liquid with the hope of settling his stomach. "So, since when you smoking and drinking papa?" she continued obviously annoyed. Wayne looked at his mother and smiled. "Actually mum can I get something to eat instead?" he asked, feeling a wave of nausea grip his body. Before she could answer Wayne felt the vomit making it's way to his throat. He darted to the bathroom just in time for the contents to hit the side of the toilet bowl. Ivy laughed uneasily and gently rubbed his back. "Hmph, you feeling like shit right?" Wayne nodded his head as he wiped his mouth. "Dat good, I hope you remember this next time you decide yuh big!" This time she laughed openly, pointing at his toothbrush to wash out his mouth. "Bake and cheese?" she asked wanting to soak up the alcohol in his system. Wayne nodded his head and returned to his bedroom. He felt high, queasy, ecstatic, hungry and guilty all at the same time. He could hear his mother muttering about the evils of alcohol but as he closed his eyes, Wayne didn't care. Today, he'd had his first proper kiss, everything was perfect. Ivy returned with his food within twenty minutes, but he was fast asleep. She smiled, covered his body and closed the door, hopeful that it was a lesson learned.

Wayne slept until 2pm the following afternoon. He awoke sluggishly and in urgent need of the toilet. Throwing his legs over the side of the bed, he sprang to his feet only to be forced to sit back down as waves of dizziness and pain enveloped him. His head ached and his mouth felt thick and tasted like vomit. He looked at his face in the mirror and startled himself. His left eyelid had completely closed and his cheek bone and temple were round with swelling. The back of his head had a knot the size of a golf ball, and as he reached the toilet, Wayne was sure he'd contracted a serious illness. He shouted for his mother but there was no reply, and for the first time in a long time, he missed her. Taking the water bottle from the fridge, he lay down across her bed, wondering what they discussed the night before. He tried to remember the events in Finsbury Park but it was too patchy and he pushed them to the back of his mind, favouring thoughts of Ellie instead. His face ached as a beaming smile attempted to spread across it. He felt sick but magnificent, and stretched his body, lazily smiling into his mother's pillow until he fell back asleep.

He finally awoke at eight the following morning. He knew his mother was home from the smell of frying fish wafting to the ceiling of the house, blowing gently across his nostrils. He got up and looked at his face in the mirror and kissed his teeth. One side was now purple and fully distorted. It looked worse than it felt, but how was he going to explain it to his mother. Opening the kitchen door with his usual greeting, he sat at the table with his head down. Andy sat drinking his coffee and reading the local gazette whilst Ivy finished frying the plaintain and began plating up. "Eh eh!, the dead wake up den ?" she teased. "You ready to eat?" she continued but before he could respond, she placed a cup of coffee, a piece of bake and a saucer of mackerel in front of him. "Oh geez-an-ages!" she wailed as she finally sat down to eat and saw her son's face in the unnaturally bright florescent light of the kitchen. Andy looked up from the newspaper, in the direction of Ivy's stare. "What de fuck happen to you boy?!" he exclaimed in shock. Wayne tried to grin nonchalantly as he came in for a closer look. "I fell off the wall at the back." "What...and mash up your face so!" Andy replied, sure that the wall hadn't caused the distress his face was in. "I'm alright man, Wayne continued, brushing Andy's hand from his face. "Stop worrying mum, I'm alright I just took a fall!" he continued trying to chew a piece of bake. "Unless you fall off a very high wall, land on your face, bounce, then drop on the back of your head...I don't see how you could end up looking like this!" Ivy concluded kissing her teeth and looking into her son's eyes as if she would see what really happened. Andy and Ivy looked at each other. Wayne knew they thought he was lying but stuck to his story.

Just then, the letterbox wrapped and he hurried to open it, relieved to be out of the hot seat. It was Ellie, Wayne closed in the door behind him. "Just came by to see how you doing babe...you look proper fucked!" she grinned. "Who's that Wayne, your food is getting cold!?" shouted Ivy from the kitchen. "It's just my friend, I'm coming" he shouted back. "That your mum?" Ellie asked smiling. Wayne nodded. "What she say about your face?" she asked genuinely concerned. "She's not happy best believe dat!" The kitchen door squeaked open. "I better go, you going ice skating tomorrow with dem lot?" Ellie asked aware that his mother could appear at any moment. "I should be, not sure yet dough, you going?" Wayne asked holding on to the door handle. "I think so..." Ellie replied kissing his cheek before hurriedly making her way to the gate, hoping she would get there before his mum opened the front door. As he watched her walk away, an uncontrollable grin settled on his mouth and he slowly but happily made his way back into the house.

"Oh yeh who's that then?" Andy asked, as Wayne sat down smiling, eager to fill his mouth with bake to avoid any such any questions. Ivy and Andy looked at each other and smiled as they awaited his response. "Who?" Wayne asked, not wanting to answer the question and stalling for time. Andy started to laugh but Ivy kicked his foot under the table. "Oh um, that's Ellie...she's just a friend of Cavell's" he finally answered with a mouthful of plantain. "Oh, she's just a friend of Cavell's...so why your face light up so!" Andy teased, burning his mouth on a piece of fish. "Oh ok" Ivy replied raising her eyebrows and looking straight into her son's face. "What?...what!" Wayne laughed, blushing under the weight of their stares. "Anyway, I have to get my arse to class, but as far as all this is concerned..." Ivy made a circle in front of his face with her open palm, "I don't believe you just fell off the back wall just so...I don't know what's going on with you, I know I haven't been around lately but you know you can come to me about anything right?" Wayne looked at his mother and smiled. He knew she loved him, but he also knew she would be unable to understand his life, and it couldn't be explained in black and white, which was the only language she spoke. "I good mum, for real it looks worse than it is...don't worry!" He embraced her and for a moment they both felt relief. "I love you, now you best get to class before you get a 'late'!" Ivy kissed her teeth and smiled, trying to believe his explanation as she made her way off the estate to the bus stop.

∞

The sound of Bob Marley's 'No Woman No Cry' hummed from the stereo as Wayne sat down the following morning to the breakfast his mother prepared for him after her night shift. His smiled as he lifted the tea towel covering the plate and happily made a cup of coffee before eagerly seating himself at the table. Folded neatly next to his plate was the local gazette with the headline 'Finsbury Park – Latest Battleground for Teen Thugs!' His stomach nose-dived as he picked up the newspaper, wondering if it was simple coincidence, that placed it so glaringly in his view. Panic engulfed him as he read the printed words. 'Saturday's family fun day was rudely interrupted by gangs of youths wielding an array of homemade weapons. Approximately twenty youths invaded the North London park, where a battle ensued just outside the perimeter of the fair ground. Onlookers report that the boys, aged fifteen to twenty clashed without any obvious incident. The Police arrived after just ten minutes but were unable to detain any of the perpetrators who fled into the crowd as the officers entered the park. Makeshift weapons including baseball bats, pool cues and gym socks containing snooker balls were found at the scene. The Police are appealing for any witnesses who have further information on the incident, to come forward.'

Wayne dropped the newspaper and slumped in his chair. His heart raced as he tried to remember the events and his involvement. Seconds later, he instinctively raised his hand to the mound at the side of his eye and his stomach dived again, this time at the thought of his mother or Andy putting two and two together. Feeling like an agouti caught in one of his grandfather's traps, he silently made his way back to his bedroom, avoiding any of the creaking steps so as not to alert his sleeping mother to his presence. In ten minutes he stood in front of Cavell's, newspaper in hand. "Bruv only now you see dat!!" Cavell teased shaking his head. His response did nothing to put Wayne's mind at ease and panic showed clearly on his face. Cavell laughed and lifted his hand on to Wayne's shoulder. "Come...come through...don't stress yourself...I have something for you. Wayne could already hear the music coming from his room. "Ellie's here!" Cavell announced shooting a grin just before they reached his bedroom door. He stopped and looked at Wayne for his reaction. "What?...just cool man" he replied smiling and feeling suddenly awkward. "Exactly!" the older boy responded, "just cool innit!" Cavell's room was full of smoke and the familiar faces of THM boys. Within minutes, Wayne's belly, moments earlier full of fear, was now full of excitement and pride that it was him and his crew that were reported about, and who sent Black Ice back to E9. He was a THM now, and it felt better than anything he'd experienced since getting off the plane.

The remaining days of the summer holidays, instead of dragging, now flew by, as Wayne's life revolved more and more around the True Hackney Millitants. Without realising it, his need to please his mother, was replaced by the need to please them. Ivy saw him less and less. He used to meet her after work sometimes, until, she assumed, he had gotten too busy with his friends, a fact she was glad about, remembering how lonely he'd been when he first arrived. She too was busy and anyway, he was looking happy and that was enough for her. As the summer progressed though, she began to feel less and less involved in his life. He didn't seem to be her little boy anymore, and despite her pleas to do something together, Wayne was always unavailable. In spite of the fact that it was Black Ice territory, which he couldn't explain to his mother, Wayne finally gave in and agreed to meet her after work. "Eh eh stranger, long time no see!" she teased, glad to see him sitting on the bench outside her building. As they walked along the dimly lit road, she huddled closer to him, commenting on the inches he seemed to have increased in height. He smiled. She knew he was pleased at the thought of his growing stature and deepening voice; a topic she often teased him about. As they cut through the back alleyway, Ivy felt his presence tense up and his eyes dart around, scouring the area for any unseen life. She hugged him closer to her "So how's your holidays going babe? Did you go to that careers fair I was telling you about?" she asked earnestly wondering how he filled his days. "Nah!" Wayne answered nonchalantly, as if a career was the furthest thing from his mind. "What do you mean, nah?" she enquired knitting her eyebrows. "No innit" he replied sarcastically. Ivy grimaced. "But why not, don't you want to know what prospects are out there, what some of your options are?" He kissed his teeth, "Nah that's Black Ice manor, I ain't going down there!" he continued kissing his teeth. "So what?...what do you mean that's Black Ice manor?" Ivy replied as anger threatened to bring forth curse words from her deepest being. "Look, we got beef with them so I ain't going down them sides mum!" he replied with undisguised irritation at her lack of awareness. "What do you mean beef?" Ivy asked, taken aback by his explanation. "Beef innit!...drama!" her son replied. Ivy's facial expression remained confused. Wayne kissed his teeth again. "War mum...there's a war on, true you don't even know!"

"What? What are you talking about, with who...and why are you kissing your teeth every minute, remember who you're talking to boy!?" Ivy returned, inflamed by the tone he chose to use with her. He kissed his teeth again, but this time caught himself midway and laughed. "The same mans that tried to rush me and Cavell the other day mum" he replied slowly, as if burdened to tell a boring story. "What do you mean rush you?, what happened...how come you didn't say anything to me?" she asked, conscious of the panic rising in her chest. Wayne kissed his teeth as silently as he could manage. His mother didn't have a clue. "I don't know, they always trying to jump us innit. Just forget about it mum...there's nothing you can do ok" "What do you mean...where?" she continued, alarmed that he hadn't told her when it happened. "E9 mum, but don't worry, I don't be about down there" he added, suddenly aware of how worried she looked and how much he'd missed her. "But this is E9!" Ivy exclaimed, looking around for the war her son had just described. "Exactly" Wayne answered, tightening his lips as if to emphasize his point. Ivy exhaled uneasily. She knew about the gangs but she didn't know her son was affected. She said nothing more, but the thought settled uncomfortably in her stomach as she allowed him to change the subject to chinese take away for dinner. Feeling calmer, Wayne hugged his mother. They hadn't embraced in a while and it felt good, but she couldn't help thinking something had changed.

The week before school began, Ade returned from Nigeria. Laden with strange foods, gifts and stories, he excitedly made his way to Wayne's house, eager to catch up on the events of the summer. Wayne opened the door expecting THM and was surprised to see Ade. He'd forgotten about his friend in Africa, and as they embraced, Ade could sense a formality that hadn't been there before, but said nothing. The pair retreated as usual to his bedroom where Ade told him of his adventures. "So what's been happening here cuz?" he enquired as he noticed the air maxs next to his bed. Wayne followed his gaze and smiled. "Yeah shit done changed up since you gone boy!" Wayne replied with ease. He got up and opened his window, closed his door and pulled out a box of Embassy cigarettes. Lighting one, he stood next to the window, extending the packet to Ade, who quickly declined with an undisguised look of shock on his face. "Since when you smoke!" Before Wayne could answer Ade kissed his teeth. "So you're one of them now? You walk different, you talk different, you look different, I guess I really missed out huh!" Ade exclaimed eyeing Wayne from head to toe. Wayne laughed. "Oh yeh, and me have woman now too...remember Ellie?" he asked, certain that Ade would. "Oh for real...?" Ade replied, openly shocked. Wayne nodded his head. "You jammy cunt!" was all Ade could say, extending his fist in congratulations. As if on cue, Wayne heard his name being called from the back. "Listen, I gotta go, what you doing?, come jam with us innit" Ade agreed and the pair made their way to the swing park at the back of the house.

"Oh, I see Mr Africa has returned" Babs teased in a heavy African accent as they approached. Fists were extended to greet Wayne whilst scornful looks were thrown in Ade's direction. "Yeh what's gwarning dude...you still making the play up West?" Wayne nodded "Oh cause we ain't got no room for passengers on this mission you know, drivers only!" Cavell continued looking in Ade's direction. Ade and Wayne looked at each other. Wayne felt bad but Ade made it easy for him. He kissed his teeth, extended his fist, exhaled and turned to leave. Diggy kissed his teeth, "I don't trust that brother you know, he love hitch up under the goody goody shit too much, he needs to remember he's a negro boy!" Ade stopped in his tracks. "What?...bless, what did you say?" he replied feeling conscious of the absence of his friend's support as Wayne stood next to Diggy watching him along with the rest of the THM. "Oh gosh, they done brainwash the yout, let me explain it in their terms, 'you's a nigger', act like it! Look at you..." Diggy motioned his arm from the top of Ade's head, down to his feet. "...you look square, grey, like you trying to kiss someone's bottom hole dread!...what, you think they gonna allow you in to their world because you got your belt resting up under your chin!" Laughter rose from the onlookers, but Ade stood firm. He looked at Wayne but his friend remained silent, avoiding his eye contact. Wayne felt bad for Ade, but he had to show his loyalty to THM. "You know what blood, I'm what I want to be, you are what they expect you to be, call it whatever you want boss! But give me the whole world any day, you can keep your little portion of it! Laters!" His fear and disappointment, firmly disguised until he left the estate, went unnoticed by Wayne.

∞

The new term began with less enthusiasm than Ivy was accustomed to. Lately Wayne's attitude was becoming more and more aggressive, but he was bruise free and smiling, and she was busy; so she put that down to his growth and increasing hormone levels. Ticking that box she refocused on her career, all was well in her world.

The first sign of trouble was a note from his teacher saying that Wayne disrupted the class during a test. 'It's just a temporary teacher mum...he didn't understand what I was trying to say, somebody threw something at me!" Wayne explained earnestly. "So why didn't you say that to your teacher?" Ivy continued, stunned that he would be sent home with a letter. Wayne laughed. "It's not like back in the day when you were at school you know mum!' he added trying to change the subject. Ivy exhaled shaking her head. She looked at her son for any signs of deception but found none. She was shocked, but thought she knew her son well enough to believe it was a mistake. "What, when do you think I went to school?" she finally responded. "Pre-computers mum, pre-computers, it's a whole other world out there now" She couldn't help but laugh. His sure smile easily erased any fear or doubt Ivy had in her mind.

Then came a second letter the following week, reporting his rude attitude from a different teacher. "Mum...mum calm down! You don't even know what happened. Wayne responded arrogantly. "What the fuck Wayne! What shit is this?" Ivy continued ready to get a belt. Wayne sensed her anger and lowered his voice. "Mum, the bus broke down and I ended up leaving my book on the bus ok. My teacher did not believe me and accused me of lying. I got a little vex and he said I was being rude!" Once again, though less readily, she accepted his explanation as she signed the letter.

'After all', she told herself, 'he was very bright and doing his homework would not have been a problem so the teacher must have been at fault.'

By the second Friday of the term, Ivy sat in the kitchen, this time reading a letter from the Principal with a note from a Sergeant Hobbit. Wayne had been involved in a fight. This time though, the letter also suggested a suspension. Wayne saw the look on his mother's face change as she read the letter. "Before you say anything, yes mum, I had to do it. I tried to walk away, but all I could hear was their disrespect...and whether you like it or not, whether you agree with it or not, I just can't let that slide out here mum!" Ivy's face changed, and Wayne's heartbeat increased. "What the fuck do you mean, you had to do it? Eh? Are you a jackass or something, don't tell me no shit. You've been acting fucked up for a while, but I thought it was a phase you were passing through, so I let it go!" Ivy screamed, standing in front of his face. "Mum, Cavell was in trouble, he needed help, what was I supposed to do, just leave him to get licks!" Wayne continued, slowly backing away from her. Ivy exhaled, lowered her voice and returned to her position in front his face. "So tell me something, if you're friend needed you to jump in front of a train, you telling me you would do it?" Wayne said nothing. "Fucking answer me boy! Is that what you're telling me!?" He still said nothing, silently kissing his teeth as he looked away. "I am almost positive that the answer isn't in your shoes Wayne, look at me when I'm talking to you!" He raised his head. "Is that it, how come we have a letter from the police? What do they want to see us about!" "I don't know mum, probably cause I took the postman's mail bag..." "What do you mean because you took the postman's mail bag, why did you take the fucking mail bag?" Wayne shrugged his shoulders attempting to describe the events to Andy. It had been a dare and he dragged it into the school compound whilst the postman delivered mail across the street. A new wave of tears streamed down her face, Andy whispered to her to calm down and reached for the Hennessy bottle tucked away in the corner of the counter.

"Mum, if I didn't help him, my life would have been over, you just don't understand!" "Your life would have been over? Oh so you rather listen to your friends than the person who gave birth and raised you, what, you don't think I can kill you too, just like that!" Ivy shouted suddenly noticing the low level of the golden brown liquid in the bottle. "Wait, what happen to this brandy?" she asked sipping on her drink and eyeballing the bottle. Andy, seeing the direction the discussion was going, admitted to spilling it, even though he didn't. Now wasn't a good time.

They sat in silence, uncomfortably looking at each other until she calmed down and spoke. "Wayne, life is about choices, you know this. You're choices tell me who you are, and right now...I don't even know you. I've always tried to show you that for every action there's a reaction, positive or negative." Without warning Ivy reached for his belt, hanging open through the loops of his pants, and stood up. "It's time for you to reap the consequences of yours." Wayne saw his mother reach for the belt still laced through his trouser loops. He smiled and nonchalantly tried to grab it. He should have tried harder. The belt, wrapped firmly around her closed fist came down with a permeating sting across his shoulders and back.

Shock momentarily immobilised him but as she rose the strap above her head, Wayne dove under the kitchen table, pleading for his mother to stop. She didn't. Instead she grabbed the foot sticking out, pulled of the sock and started beating his sole. The pain seared unhindered through his body. He kicked his legs to discourage her, but that just made her angrier. "Oh! So you want to fight me now! Ok mister man!" Ivy spat back, coiling the strap tighter around her fist. She ached inside as he tried to protect his body from the onslaught, but she couldn't stop. All she could think of was his life going down the drain, and she poured her broken heart into the blows. As she stopped to change hands, he darted out of the kitchen, almost flying up to his bedroom, pleading for mercy and begging her to remember that they'd agreed he was too big for licks. She ran after him, stopping on the landing before his room. She exhaled as the tears streamed down her cheeks. Finally exhausted, she dropped the belt. Her hands were shaking, and sweat glistened on her forehead as she caught her breath. Trembling, she pushed open his door. He lay on his belly facing the wall and holding a pillow to his face. "Now you know how it feels when you can't trust someone Wayne." she replied softly, and walked out of his room, closing the door behind her.

Ivy walked back downstairs still out of breath. She opened the back door and sat on its' threshold looking into their overgrown garden. She'd wanted to sort it out for months, but by the time she got home she was too tired, or it was too dark. Weeds, rubbish, over growth, lack of water, care and attention, had lain waste to her once well-kept garden. She sat, crying silently into the sleeves of her cardigan until Andy came in with a glass of brandy. She thanked him, received his hug and words of hope, then asked him to leave her alone.

She didn't know what to do, but she knew enough not to go back into his room in the state she was in. She suddenly felt very alone and the tears came down once more. Andy looked at her through the crack in the door and his heart ached. He wanted to hold her and tell her it was alright but instead, he silently climbed the stairs to Wayne's room. Wayne lay on his back staring at the ceiling. Andy could see the wet patch on his pillow and sat on the edge of his bed looking at the welts appearing on his body. "You ok?" he asked not sure what to say. "No not really" Wayne answered ignorantly, retaining his stare at the wall, forcibly ceasing the flow of his tears. "Look, you might not want to hear me but I'm going to talk anyway yeah. These boys, this THM that you're hanging around with, can't you see where they taking you? These boys are already lost and they don't even know it! They're boxing themselves in, limiting their potential, wanting something from nothing and when they don't get it, they beating up. The sad thing is, by the time they wake up, it will be too late. So what's left for them?" Andy paused to receive Wayne's answer, but he continued staring at the wall. "Crime my friend, that's all that's left. Deep down, they don't believe they can compete, so they don't live like they got a future, like they could be kings, it's not expected, and so won't be achieved. And where does that leave you...?" Wayne still said nothing and Andy stood up, tracing the line of a welt on his thigh as he walked to the door, "...an angry man in jail or a dead man in the ground."

A few days later on the last Friday of the Xmas term, sitting across from his form teacher, Ivy was beginning to realise just how deeply his new loyalties went. There were no more excuses to be made. The look on Mr Bertram's face, coupled with his tone told her, she should have taken more time, she shouldn't have been so willing to accept his sure excuses. Looking back at how stupid, busy, irritated, tired or just plain lazy she'd been, made tears come to her eyes, as all the missed warning signs now seemed so obvious.

It was taking him one and a half hours to get from Clapton to Dalston, twenty minutes away. As she thought about it, Ivy had to laugh, to hear Wayne tell it, his bus broke down almost every day, and she ate it up like butter on toast.

"You have been asked to attend today as Wayne has had a serious altercation with another youth. An altercation in which a knife was found in his possession." Mr Bertram looked at Ivy over the rim of his glasses and continued. "I'm afraid it's not just the altercation Mrs Lopez, Wayne's grades have plummeted and his attitude in class towards his peers and his teachers, has become detrimental to his, as well as the learning of other students." They both looked at Wayne with obvious disappointment. He kissed his teeth inaudibly and looked at the floor. "You guys just don't have a clue about what's going on do you! I told you mum, I had to do it. There's man in this school that are on my case, and I'm gonna juk them before they juk me, best believe that." Ivy's surprise soon turned to embarrassment and then rage as the information sank in. "Wayne is an exceptional student who has chosen to copy under achievers. It really is sad, but not unusual, I see it every day. Now, and feel free to correct me if I'm wrong Master Wayne, but as I see it, you're just coasting through your classes and one day, if you insist in finding fascination in class clowns instead of class teachers; you'll be in the middle of nothing, with nowhere to go except down.

As it is, and what I am about to say, I assure you, cannot be wriggled out of, I am suspending you for a period of four weeks as of today" Wayne stood and kissed his teeth, this time loud enough to be easily heard. "And you want me to succeed in life yeah?" he spat back at his principal, gesturing with his arms. "Suspended for four weeks?! Wait hold on, why are you excluding him for four weeks, he'll miss out on too much school work surely?!" Ivy exclaimed shocked at the Principal's decision. "Fine him! Let him come in early and clean the school! Let him stay late and help prepare for classes?" she insisted close to tears. "I am sorry Mrs Lopez. The decision has already been made and must now be implemented." Ivy was stunned. The look on the Principal's face told her not to bother pleading and she stood, collecting her belongings. There was nothing she could say. She thanked him and they left.

On the journey home, they said nothing. Ivy followed him into his bedroom and Wayne flinched at his door, making sure his belt was buckled and expecting a box or a slap, but that was not her intention. Again, they sat in silence until she felt she'd found the words needed to let him know what he was doing to his own life. "What's happening Wayne?" she asked after a while. He said nothing. His cupboard was open and she noticed the new clothes and shoes amongst his wardrobe. "Where did all this come from?" she asked, removing hangers bearing clothes she hadn't purchased. "Oh Cavell gave me them, they're too small for him." Wayne answered unflinchingly, without meeting his mother's eyes. Ivy looked at him and closed the cupboard.

"What's happening Wayne?" she asked earnestly looking into his face. "I feel like I'm losing you...like you're slipping away right in front my face!" Wayne felt the anguish in his mother's words and held on to her hand and exhaled heavily. "You're not losing me mum...you don't have to worry, I know I fucked up, but I just lost track for a minute but I'll get back on it mum, I promise you." Ivy looked at her son and smiled "Ok, but tell me something, do you think more of THM or of yourself babe? I ask because I'm scared you're losing yourself and what you stand for, before you even get started on your life.""

The question caught Wayne off guard and he laughed, surprised that he himself had to pause to check the answer. THM flashed across his mind and his stomach sank, not wanting to believe that he thought more of them than himself. He didn't answer. "Promise me something. I want you to represent yourself by how you act and what you do, not what friends you have or what clothes you wear ok? Don't just focus on your life right now, you have a future, and the ground work that you get through now, is what will prepare a future for you. I don't want you to be a failure Wayne. Hanging around with these boys, playing the arse in class, is not going to get you anywhere, is that what you want for yourself? What, do you think that being cool in school, or in your case now, OUT of school, is what will take you through life? Do you understand what I'm trying to tell you?" Wayne nodded his head in agreement but said nothing.

"I seriously don't want you hanging around with Cavell and these boys anymore, they are not helping you in any way! Wayne did you hear me?"

Ivy demanded feeling her anger rising and trying to hold on to her patience. "Yes mum" he replied wondering how that was going to be possible. Ivy inhaled deeply to try to calm herself, but even her breath was interrupted as she searched for words that her son would take heed of. "And understand this Wayne, your teachers already have their careers and their lives, and it doesn't matter whether you think they are nice or whether they like you or not, they will let you down just like your friends. It is for you to do the best you can with the time you have, so that you can make a great future for yourself. Do you understand, I need you to depend on yourself and compete with yourself, that way, you will always succeed regardless of the calibre of your teachers or the persuasiveness of your 'friends!' Tears finally freed themselves from their captivity behind Ivy's eyelids, and as Wayne put his arm around her, they flowed freely down both their faces.

∞

Ivy lay on her bed and looked up at the ceiling. She wondered if she should have beaten him. Moments later, she decided against it. They'd agreed that he was too big for licks now, and she'd learnt not to punish in anger, which was funny to her because it was only when she was angry that she would punish him. She self-consciously got up to pour herself a shot of Hennessy, feeling frantic and powerless at the sudden thought of her imagined future for him. Failing school, poor employment prospects, crime, getting arrested, going to prison, killing someone...getting killed by someone. Fear engulfed her, settling uncomfortably in the pit of her stomach. She tried to remove the thought from her mind but the more she fought against it, the more her mind brought it to the fore, stacking everything against her perfect dream.

As she sipped the clear brown liquid, Ivy closed her eyes and breathed, trying fervently to control her fears and quieten her mind. A few minutes later she opened them as a new thought came to her. 'The choices he makes, are impacted by, the presence and absence of things he experiences regularly'...what?" she said aloud, immediately sitting up to recall the words. It took a few moments for clarity to hit her, repeating them to herself until she understood. 'The choices he makes are greatly impacted by the presence and absence of things he experiences regularly' Standing still, she mentally reviewed her son's days. 'What does he experience regularly?' she asked herself, eagerly grasping at the potential solution. For the first time, she looked at the London behind the double decker buses, Oxford and Cambridge, Buckingham Palace and the Peter and Jane stories of her childhood. As she did so, she remembered the look on his principal's face as he passed his judgement, as if Wayne was just another product of his environment, to be tolerated whilst being processed. Not nurtured and groomed, challenged or awakened. The physical pain in Ivy's heart winded her.

Waves of helplessness coursed through her as tears ran down the side of her face, pooling in her ear. 'How had the THM become so fucking important?' she screamed in her mind. As she searched for an answer, another thought occurred to her. 'Have you been a good parent?' The question popped into her head, taking her breath away and immediately stopping the monsoon of thoughts that consumed her. She exhaled and mentally reviewed the last six months of their lives. Of her life. 'Work, school, Andy...Wayne had always been busy...happy and busy. We'd both been happy and busy...too busy to really connect, but surely he could have come to me if there was something troubling him...my door was always open...but was I always there?" She answered herself out loud, feeling the full weight of her new discovery. Ivy sat up and wiped her eyes. "Was it my fault?!" she asked herself tentatively hoping the answer would be no, but wondering if she could really be blameless. It was ok for him to be out, or about to go out, she never queried it, maybe because it made it easier for her to fully embrace her busy life, minus the guilt of her absence. Rushing in the morning to get him to school and her to work, too busy for small talk, TV dinners, hanging about on road doing what the fuck she didn't know. Day in, day out. "Oh my god...it's my fault!"

The realisation dawned on her that she was not there on most days for most of the day. She checked in physically for a couple of hours, to tidy up and cook, then she usually was so tired and frustrated, she didn't have time for any quality interaction. She threw herself onto her bed and bawled silently into the pillowcase. She was not there, nor was anyone else. No mother, no father, no grandparents, no uncles, no aunts, no cousins, no guidance, no positive input to dilute the madness of his experiences. In that instant, Ivy became acutely aware of the value of her family, the value of their companionship, support, guidance, assistance and the importance of being amongst them. His grandmother had always told her that it took a village to raise a child and the truth in her words suddenly and acutely dawned on her. "I thought I could do it by myself...but I can't can I?" Tears flowed incessantly down her face until she was forced to turn over the pillow to it's dry side. Ivy wondered if indeed, she had made a mistake. Isobel hadn't wanted her to take him to London. They'd argued about it, and the older woman insisted he remained in the security of his father's home, that he was not yet ready for a big city, and how would she manage on her own, Ivy remembered how she felt. She could comprehend nothing but that he was coming back to London with her, and what her mother-in-law said through her tears, went completely over her head, after all, the best place for a child was with it's mother. She felt caged, 'was it possible to grow a strong healthy seedling in such a malevolent garden?' Angry fearful thoughts filled her mind as she finally drifted off to a dream filled broken sleep. She woke with a start. Drenched in sweat she looked at the clock on her nightstand, it was 10.59pm.

Wayne lay awake in his room too, thinking about his mother's words and how he could possibly obey them. She hadn't tried to beat him and he loved her even more for that, but she still didn't have a clue. She was trying to fit a round peg into a triangular hole. Wayne smiled to himself and exhaled. What was he supposed to do, just blank them? 'I just can't do that' he answered himself angrily. It wasn't that he disagreed with her, but they were his peeps, his mentors, his bodyguards, his brothers, his family. Because of them, he no longer looked like he just stepped off the banana boat, because of them he now got respect on his estate, because of them he could walk about on road, because of them he got Ellie. Wayne kissed his teeth. 'I ain't leaving them, how could I!' But how could he explain that to his mother. She wouldn't understand him, she didn't know what it was like on the streets. She couldn't see it, because it didn't affect her. There was no-one marking her as she walked down the road, no-one sending threats to her. He was in too deep, he needed them now, there was no way he could stay away from the Millitants. They were his protection from everything else.

He yearned for a pull on a spliff and looked out the window to see if Cavell's bedroom light was still on. It was. He dressed himself and looked in the mirror, wondering what his grandmother would say. Two hooded track suit tops, scarf, oversized baseball cap, black gloves, and, hanging carelessly off his bottom, his grey track suit, unzipped over his trainers. No coat. If he was honest with himself, he looked like someone he would cross over the road to avoid on a dark night. Instead he smiled, he wore the standard attire of any inner city youth, the thugged out, 'don't fuck cause you'll be fucked. If he didn't look like that, he'd be an outsider, an easy target, after all he didn't live in the Sesame Street world his mum seemed to, so how could he look or behave in a Sesame Street way?'

Wayne kissed his teeth and looked at the time. Ivy would be asleep by now so he gently opened his door and looked over the bannister. Her light was off and he gingerly made his way down the stairs walking carefully on their edges to avoid too many discernible creaks. Thunder clapped as he eased his front door closed. He scanned the estate. No-one was about and he pushed his hands deeply into his pockets and ran to Cavell's house, ducking his head against the icy rain drops. "What's up blood?" Cavell answered surprised to see his younger at the door at that time of the night. "What your mum not home?" he teased as they made their way to his bedroom. "Yeh, but I'm stressed man, you got anything?" Wayne replied smiling to himself as he smelt the weed in the air upon entering the room. "What's up my yout...come, tell your daddy?" Cavell continued taking a pull on the spliff and handing it to Wayne. "It's my mums man, Mr Bertram suspended me innit, and now she don't want me hanging with you lot!" "Fuck me!" Cavell replied, "Give me my shit back den!" he continued extending his arm for the spliff. "Yeh right" Wayne replied, ignoring him and inhaling his deepest drag.

Cavell grinned. "I hear you're mum yuh know blood, but she got it twisted. School ain't all that it's cracked up to be yuh know. What do you think just cause you're a good little boy and you go to school every day, you're gonna have a good life?" Cavell paused to kiss his teeth. "Listen man you're a black yout in a white man land, you dig me, and they don't want you here, best believe dat! What, do you think you're gonna get a big job when you finish school or something? Yeh right, more like a shit hole job where they treat you like a cunt and pay you one-fifty for the week, I get more than dat standing on the street corner for one afternoon cuz! Do you really think any big company is going to hire you? Fam it's a fucked up world out dere bruv!" Cavell paused to grunt and retrieve his spliff. He exhaled the smoke. 'When you live around here yeh, your options are limited. The schools are shit, waste of a man's time! Them teachers ain't interested in you my friend, and best believe they don't think you have a 'bright future'! The popo is the same, well you should dun know dat, they ain't here to protect you, they is here to contain you, to mentally strangulate you!" Cavell grinned at his rhyme "I know you feeling me. So what's left for you, the streets, the ghetto, and when you're here, it's all about respect my friend...your rep and your cred! That's something you have to cultivate, do the right things, say the right things, look a certain way, it don't happen just so!" Wayne smiled, he knew that from first-hand experience. It wasn't until he linked Cavell that he felt safe, respected or qualified to get a female like Ellie. "I hear you blood" he answered blowing the remaining smoke out his lungs. "And you're not going to get it from listening to your mums, cause these niggers out here can smell dat shit, and they'll go straight for your jugular, and you won't even see it coming fam! You gotta make sure your shit is on point!...twenty-four-seven-three-sixty-five...and the biggest part of that, is having your mans dem to back you." Cavell paused and eyeballed Wayne. "That's why we march together my friend. Divide and conquer, unite and prosper!...ain't that what the man said" he continued animatedly. "You gotta protect yourself my yout, it's kill or be killed out here so make your choice. Stick with us and you know everything done cook and curry, or, be the momma's boy your mum wants you to be, but you better have one eye on the back of your head my friend."

Rain poured incessantly, consuming the city in an aroma of wet concrete. Wayne hugged his hoodie close to him as he ran the metres from Cavell's to his front door. In Homerton, the frenzied scene at the bus stop, drew attention from passers-by who looked, but silently refused any sense of responsibility to act and drove, or walked on. Even the other would be passengers at the stop recoiled at the scene but simply turned away. Hearing her girlfriends come to her rescue, Micha regained her composure and began, aimlessly at first because of the position of her head, throwing punches until she connected with what felt to her to be Tasha's crotch, whilst her girls focused their assaults on Tasha's head until she loosened her grip. Ellie tried in vain to save her sister from the attack. She scrambled on to the backs of two of the assailants grabbing extensions and weave as she tried to remove them with her weight and sheer force. She succeeded, but it was a temporary victory, as she too was kicked to the ground and pummelled by the others.

As she fell, Micha shouted to her friends to catch the scene on a mobile phone. In a chorus of agreement, four mobiles were produced, recording the beating with a back drop of laughter and delight. As if acknowledging their potential break into the 'big time', the beating increased in viciousness and audacity. The sisters tried to protect themselves from the onslaught, but as kicks and punches rained down on their bodies, at some point, Tasha lost consciousness. Micha saw her body relax, arms which had only a few seconds before, been protecting her face, slumped to her side. She signalled her girls to stop and surveyed the damage they inflicted. Satisfied with the result, she bent over Tasha's still body. 'Don't fucking come back round here cause we'll be waiting for your muppet arses...Biiyatch!!' she spat into her ear. Stamping on her leg as she got up, Micha eyed her whimpering companion and laughed, daring her to try anything, anything at all. Ellie held her stare, but she knew there was nothing she could do, and silently watched them flee the scene in adrenaline soaked victory and in panic.

She tried to sit up, and as she did so, pain coursed its way down the left side of her arm and she screamed in anguish as she looked at the pink flesh and white bone protruding at the side of her watch. She looked around but there was no one to call, she screamed at her sister to get up but Tasha didn't respond. She slid closer to her, trying to pull her sister closer, but Tasha still wouldn't move. It was then that she noticed her sister's face and the blood pouring from the gash on her scalp. Before the scream of horror could escape her lips, Ellie too fell unconscious.

Micha and her girls ran towards the estate in fits of laughter, pausing only to ensure they were not being followed. Once there, they scrambled to the first darkened stairwell to catch their breaths, remaining there, until they were certain they had not been followed. They proudly reviewed each other's actions in the 'battle', mocking the feeble attempts of the two transgressors in defending themselves. They applauded the most ferocious amongst them, recounting her bravery and physical superiority over the two who dared to step up in their manor. As their adrenaline rush subsided though, and quiet fell amongst the girls, they each retreated into their own thoughts, surveying themselves and each other, noticing as if for the first time their bloodied hands and shoes.

A plump girl finally spoke. "She looked in a bad way man, do you think we should call an ambulance?" she asked sheepishly, perhaps through guilt or just fear as she attempted to wipe the blood off her top with a used tissue. Silence hung over the girls as they reflected on the comment, and on what they had just done. Before guilt could consume, Micha warned against it, reassuring the group that a passer-by had probably called an ambulance already and anyway, they were THM bitches. The plump girl agreed, and continued wiping her top, cursing the blood of the enemy, for making it difficult for her to go home unnoticed. As if by magic, any guilt at their actions subsided.

They remained huddled together in the stairwell for a while, but as time passed, one by one, they dispersed in the direction of their homes, all ensuring that their individual journeys did not take them past the bus stop, and the scene of their violence. Micha was the last to leave. Her mother was out for the night and so wouldn't notice her empty bed, but even if she wasn't, her home was the last place Micha wanted to be, and would happily risk a beating for not being there. Curfews suddenly seemed unimportant, and, as the last of her friends left for home, she preferred instead to call Bucky, for only he would understand what she had just done. And only he would be able to offer her the understanding she now so desperately needed.

∞

The next day, Wayne slept until the afternoon and was only woken by the sound of stones hitting his window pane. He rubbed the sleep out of his eyes and looked through the window. It was Cavell gesturing for him to come downstairs. The look on his face told him something was up, and Wayne held his breath as he quietly made his way to the back door. He peeked in his mother's bedroom and noticed the time on the clock. She'd already left for work so he jumped down the remaining flights and threw open the door to the back garden. "It's Tash. She's in the hospital man, they got jumped down E9!" Wayne's heart somersaulted in his chest. "E9...with who? ... why...?" Cavell stopped him before he could finish. "I don't fucking know blood, just put on your shit let's go find out innit!" Wayne left, returning ready in less than two minutes.

Visiting hours were over by the time they got to the hospital, but the boys snuck in and searched the beds for the familiar faces. In a room at the end of the corridor, they finally caught a glimpse of what looked like Tasha before a nurse noticed them and asked them to leave. "Oh my God!!...Oh my God!!" was all Cavell kept repeating as he took in his girlfriend's distorted bandaged face. "Oh Shit" Wayne gasped as he too looked through the sliver of window on the room door. "I'm afraid you two gentlemen will have to leave!" announced the nurse, opening her arms to usher them back down the hallway and through the double doors. Cavell kissed his teeth and looked through the window. Her eyes were closed. Swollen shut. He put his hands on his head and squeezing back tears, he left the ward. "Where's Ellie?" Wayne asked. The nurse looked at him like he was wasting her time. "Did you not here me...I said GET OUT! Do you want me to call security cause I can do that you know!" Wayne exhaled and started to the door. "Look please mom, I just want to know if her sister is ok?" The nurse opened the door for him to leave and as he stepped over the threshold, she spoke. "Are you referring to the girl who came in with her?" Wayne nodded eagerly. She has some cuts and bruises and a broken arm, but she will live." She closed the door and Wayne exhaled, running to catch up with Cavell at the lifts.

The boys left the hospital in silence, each absorbed in their own thoughts. Marcus and Babs, just back from Tasha's house, were outside. For Cavell, only scenes of Tasha's distorted, discoloured face circled around his mind. He couldn't understand how it happened, why it happened and most of all, who did it. Wayne was in shock, but relieved that Ellie was going to be ok. He couldn't believe it either, shit was going too far. Shock turned to anger as Marcus and Babs told them the whole story of what happened at the bus stop. His imagined image of it sickened him. Bile rose to the back of his throat and tears stung his eyelids, but he refused to let them roll freely. Tears were a blatant sign of weakness and he wasn't in the mood for Marcus's heckles. A dizzying sensation of restriction and panic engulfed him as rage flooded his being.

"Give me a fag" Wayne asked Cavell, brushing past Marcus and accidently stepping on his heel. "What's up with dis cunt?" Marcus asked gesturing to Babs "What, you can't feel dat you treading on man's foot?" Wayne kissed his teeth. "Whatever man" he replied as he lit the cigarette. "You best check yourself my friend, cause I don't tolerate no junior trying to step up, you understand...wait is you crying darg?!" Marcus continued smiling, glad to have been the reason for his tears. Wayne kissed his teeth and stopped in his tracks. "And what!...What's your fucking problem my friend?...From day one you've been on my case, running up your ashy fucking gums! What! You ready?" He continued, taking two long strides positioning himself in front of Marcus. Marcus laughed and looked past him to Cavell. "You best tell your dog to back off fam. I don't wanna have to cripple the cunt!" he replied laughing as if he'd just heard the best joke. Before Cavell could respond and to Wayne's own astonishment, he swung for Marcus, connecting with his temple. The four boys looked at each other in stunned silence as Marcus stumbled backward. Wayne shook his fist loose as fear momentarily encroached on his thoughts, but adrenaline quickly pushed it away.

"Fucking behave!!" Babs shouted jumping in front of Marcus and wagging his finger with a sly smile at Wayne. "Check yourself, come, let's get out this shit hole manor!" The rain began to fall and with it, tears Wayne tried to contain, were fully released. His heart ached for Ellie. He felt stifled, cornered and boxed in. 'Was this adulthood, is this what growing up and seeing the world was about?' He inhaled deeply as if trying to breathe in strength from the air, instead he breathed in the smell of wet concrete and exhaust fumes. Looking up at the sky and as the rain disguised the tears rolling off his face, he exhaled until there was no breath left in his body. ,

Cavell kissed his teeth. "What are we doing about this boys?" he asked through an almost closed mouth. "Cause it's on!" "Best believe dat it's fuckin ON!" Marcus continued, "I'm ready!" Wayne added as Babs nodded in agreement. "For sure for sure!" "Bless...come we go then, there's shit to be done." Cavell dug his hands into his pockets and the unit moved on. "Don't think I'm letting that one slide yeh" Marcus whispered as he picked up his hat that had fallen next to Wayne "I don't expect you to" Wayne replied. They passed the bus stop and walked the mile uneasily back to their turf. They didn't know what yet, but they knew this would not go unchecked, and agreed to hit it the following evening, tooled up for whatever Black Ice had to offer.

Wayne was unwilling to return home when he saw the light on in his mother's room. He couldn't be bothered to make up a lie about where he'd been, or listen to a lecture about why he shouldn't have been there. He crashed at Cavell's, to the boy's great surprise. "Eh eh...somebody untie the apron strings or what!" Babs teased. "Whatever". Wayne replied, pushing thoughts of his mother to the back of his mind.

The following day as agreed, the THM gathered at Cavell's. Marcus was agitated, he walked into the room as if he was about to break into a sprint and paced up and down until Cavell told him to sit down. "We ain't got time for this shit. Look what's happening around us!! It's all hands on deck right now dread. Ain't no time for no jackassisms!" Marcus seethed animatedly. "We need to think this shit through cause we ain't got time for no mistakes. What's wrong with you blood? Sit down just fucking calm your ass down yeh, we need to think!" replied Cavell, irritated at Marcus's tone. "Ain't no time to come up with no long plan yo! What da fuck blood...we need to take action now! We need to handle our business! We need to let mans know they can't approach like that!" Wayne could see Cavell's irritation rising. "Ok so what do you suggest big man? What do you wanna do!?" Cavell asked standing in front his face. Marcus lifted his t-shirt and revealed a 9mm tucked into his knock off Calvin Klein shorts.

The boys gasped audibly. Already beating hearts quickened their pace as Marcus brandished the dull piece of metal in the air. Wayne's mouth fell open as Cavell reached over for the weapon. "What da fuck!...Where did you get that!" "Don't worry about it, I told you, we need to handle our business fam!" Marcus replied. "Well I guess that's it then..." Cavell announced with a grin. "Looks like we've got a date!" The room exploded into a chorus of cheers, whistles and howls, as the gun was passed amongst the boys. "Nobody can step to us now dread!" Marcus continued brandishing it like a trophy. "Yeh man!, these muppets gonna learn the hard way!" "Man's can't think they can step up without consequences!" DMX's 'Bring ya whole crew' blared out of Cavell's music system. The volume was too loud and it sounded distorted but they didn't care. They were the righteous, and they were empowered to take revenge. Keisha banged on the door but they didn't answer. The noise was more than usual, and darker, almost threatening. She wished her mom was home, and sat on her bed with the pillow over her head, hoping instead that the electric in the meter would run out. By the time they left that evening, each boy was tooled up and ready to inflict as much damage on their enemy as they could physically dish out. And it was right that they should, or so they thought.

It was dark by the time they got to the estate in E9. Caps were lowered, hoodies pulled up, and scarves wound securely around their faces, shielding them and their identities from the cold night air. Ducking into the bins in front of the park, they had a clear view of the alleyway running alongside the estate. Going by the graffiti on every surface, it was obvious Black Ice territory, and the preferred route on, in and off the estate. It would only be a matter of time before they showed up, so they each settled in, six per bin to await the arrival of any or all members of Black Ice. Wayne felt claustrophobic after half an hour and cracked the lid of the bin. The estate was almost silent under the night sky and he eagerly breathed in the fresh air. It was a good position, the overhanging estate ensured any approaching footsteps could be heard well before the owners' arrival.

Wayne's urge to stretch became unbearable and he rose to breathe in a gulp of fresh air. "A, close the fucking lid, I can hear that cunt Bucky man!" Wayne ducked back down and listened to the approaching sound. Within seconds Marcus tapped on the walls to alert his boys in the second and third bins. The voices and footsteps were upon them. Wayne's heart beat so fast and loud he was sure the others could hear it. His weapon of choice was the baseball bat Andy gave him, and he held it tightly as the steps passed the bin. Moments elapsed as adrenaline and fear stormed their bodies simultaneously and Cavell gave the signal to out. Tights stolen from mothers, sisters and girlfriends covered each boys face as they silently climbed from their hiding spaces, taking cover behind any object that would provide the shelter. "A pussy I got something for your girl!" Cavell shouted lighting a cigarette. He inhaled deeply waiting for a response. Bucky turned to see where the voice came from and saw a lone figure about fifteen metres behind them. "You what?" he replied laughing with his companions, certain he couldn't have heard what he thought he heard. Not on his estate. "I said, your loose pussy bitch, you know, the one with the one hang low and the droopy lips, you know, your best gyal, favourite ting!?"

Bucky couldn't believe his eyes nor his ears, and for a split second wondered about the green he'd just smoked. "What da fuck!" he looked at his five companions and around the estate. They were alone. "This guy has to be some kind of cunt, to try creep up on me, on my estate, and by himself. Come we go handle this real quick, man is hungry blood!" he added wondering what the fuck was in the boy's head. "Done know cuz!" The four boys walked back up the alley-way and as they drew closer Bucky made out Cavell's face under his fish net tights. "Oh my days!" he exclaimed throwing his arms in the air. "You slippin bitch, is you crazy?" The boys were incredulous. "You know where you dere pon?" one of them asked menacingly eyeing Cavell. "Well you must be either stupid or crazy because you're not going back home to your girl tonight....but you know dat right!" Cavell grinned and discarded his cigarette. "I don't think dis bitch heard me yuh know, A! yard yout, tell your friend...I got...something for him wifey!" Before Bucky could reply, the youth punched Cavell in his mouth. "Pussyhole watch your mouth, yuh forgetting which part you is or what!" Cavell's head flew sideways at the unexpected blow and he grabbed tightly on to the handle in his pocket as he tasted the blood at the corner of his mouth. He laughed briefly as if joining the jovialty of Bucky and his boys. "I just remembered, I got something for you too chieftan." Cavell slowly removed his hands from his hoody, and in one movement, passed the blade across his assailants face. The youth screamed, stunning his companions and sending the THM into action.

They encircled the Black Ice boys, releasing their anger in a volley of blows, all the while waiting for the sound of Marcus's gunshot. They had the upper hand and within seconds, two of the Black Ice boys were out cold. Marcus laughed at Bucky and his remaining standing companion. "Boy your soldiers can't take the heat, what kind of cunt holes you got there badman?" Before he could reply, Marcus opened Bucky's mouth with the barrel of his gun. He said nothing but his companion held on to Marcus's leg and begged for mercy. Cavell laughed, stamped on his arm and kicked him in the face until he passed out. "Do your ting" he gestured to Marcus "time to splurt innit." Marcus slowly squeezed the trigger but the pin wouldn't release. He tried two more times. "Fuck sake! It's not letting off man!" Bucky used the moment to move his mouth off the gun but Marcus swung the butt to his temple as hard as he could and he dropped to the floor. "What? what kind of pound shop shit is that!?" Cavell exclaimed in disgust at the gun's failure to go off. "Fucking finish him off!" he continued, wiping his knife off on Bucky's shirt. Blows were inflicted without restraint as Marcus drained his anger into the now still bodies on the estate's pathway.

Before they could finish, a shot rang out from the tower block behind them. Momentarily unsure it was a gun shot, the THM froze, but as a second followed by a third shot hit concrete, they each ran for protection behind the limited cover offered by the bins. Seconds that seemed like minutes, passed as the boys huddled for cover. Shook and rooted to the spot, they were helpless as the bullets hit the bins and the red brick wall behind them. "Shit...we gotta make a run for it boys..." Cavell whispered finally, but their faces told him that wasn't going to happen. "We got no choice...that's all there is to it." Raised on their haunches, they readied themselves for the dash. The shots suddenly paused and Cavell slowly stood up. He looked in the direction of the gun fire but saw nothing "Ok, wall to wall, let's go!" The boys darted out from behind the bins and the shots resumed. Within seconds they made it out the alleyway, but they didn't stop until they reached the cemetery dividing the two wards. Out of breath they fell on the tombstones and overgrown grass, lungs and limbs burning with exhaustion. It was then that Wayne noticed the warm liquid running the length of his jeans. All at once a burning sensation and a pain unlike anything he had experienced in his lifetime seared through the top of his thigh. "I think I been shot..." The last thing he saw was the look of shock on Cavell's face.

∞

Ivy was at home cooking when her phone rang. "Hello" For a few seconds, all she could hear was screaming and crying on the other end, and hysteria began to wage turmoil in her stomach. She could just about make out the sound of Angela's voice. She was screaming and incoherent. "Angela, ANGELA! Where are you? What's wrong?" Ivy shouted, as panic coursed through her being. Worst scenario images of her son immediately gripped her thoughts. "V, V!...come, come pleeeaasseee" Her voice sounded horrific and caused Ivy's panic to send bile to the back of her throat "Where are you Angela?" "I'm at Homerton Hospital...Ivy, Wayne's been in a shooting." Her friend's words winded her. "I'm on my way!" In one minute, she was standing at the bus stop, it wasn't until she sat in a seat that she tried to regulate her breathing.

On the journey to the hospital, Ivy's heart alternated between coming to a full halt, and racing at a pace conducive with the Grand National. Feelings and thoughts flooded her now fully awakened mind and kept her in a state of numb shock. Her main thought was deliberation as to whether he had been the shooter or whether he had been shot, both thoughts equally sickened her and bile finally eased its' way from the back of her throat, falling easily to the floor in the space between the seats.

It was a busy night for the front desk. Ivy entered the hospital and went straight to the counter. The tired looking nurse finished dealing with a patient, took Wayne's name and asked her to wait. She could barely breathe as she waited, agitatedly tapping the counter while the nurse got the information. Two women sat consoling a third, who seemed in such anguish as to bring about her own death. A tall male companion spat passionate words to her and anyone else who listened. "No exposure, inadequate education, misaligned priorities. By the time they grow out of childhood, and realise what being a part of the world really means, they are secluded. They have to remain amongst their own for there just is no room for them elsewhere. Perhaps that's why it has become even more important to respect what the streets are all about. Perhaps that is why the gang culture flourishes so easily, regardless of the lives it takes. That becomes the main place for them to shine. They don't have the guidance to shine anywhere else. Sad. I don't blame them, at least not entirely. The streets are their teachers..." The Emergency Room patrons grew silent, encouraging the orator as they tuned in to his words. Enthused, the man eagerly continued. "My father once told me that as a black man, you have to fight ten times as hard to succeed. I remember how he would regale and remind us of what it was like for him. The first generation of blacks to migrate to England after the Second World War. The influx of West Indians looking for a better life. I wonder if they ever thought one day that their son's sons would get this lost?" The woman wailed even louder as the nurse returned with a colleague who took Ivy's information and directed her to his ward.

Angela stood outside the double doors but Ivy didn't see her and walked straight past. She entered the ward not sure what to expect, holding on to her chest as if she were afraid her heart would fall out. Wayne had been placed in a side room with an officer guarding the entrance. And there he was, lying perfectly still. His left leg had been immobilised and extended upwards. His face was slightly swollen, a drip and monitor attached to his arm. Ivy exhaled audibly, despite his injuries she was ecstatic that her son was alive. She gingerly approached the bed, unsure if he was conscious, but to her surprise and relief, he cracked open his eye lid and gave her a quarter smile. "Lord Jesus thank you God! Thank you Jesus, thank you God!" Ivy's knees gave way and she almost slumped to the floor.

The shooting was reported on the news over the ensuing days, but there was no mention of the altercation between Black Ice and THM. Both manors were relatively quiet to the untrained eye, but behind closed doors, a great war was being strategized, by both sides. Wayne was in agony but glad to be alive, relishing the attention he hadn't realised he'd missed from his mother. The bullet went through his thigh, literally missing his femoral artery by a tenth of a centimetre. A fact the surgeon made a point of letting him know, could have cost him his life. It was excruciating to stand, but they both knew he could so easily have been taken, and because of that, Wayne embraced the pain. Ivy was at his bedside every day, nursing him back to health and promising to spend more time with him. When she asked about the incident he knew he couldn't tell her the truth and so, like the police officers to come, he told her he was totally unaware of why or who shot him. That's what she'd assumed, and so it was an easy pill for her to swallow. The police interviewed him a few times, but he didn't have much to say and with no leads, and time passing, it seemed futile to expect any arrests.

He didn't see the Millitants in the first few days. His nerves, which he had to mask from his mother, were permanently on edge as he waited for their arrival and news. But as time passed without a visit, his gratitude for his life was soon replaced with the reality of his situation. Thoughts of abandonment festered in the absence of his boys until finally, he didn't care if they had his back or not, Wayne wasn't about to let his shooting go unpunished. He couldn't, even if he wanted to. Finally, at the end of the week, and after visiting hours, Marcus, Babs, Diggy and Cavell, turned up at his bedside. "What's up my yout?" Cavell announced looking for signs of damage to his leg. "Yes boss what up, what up!" announced his companions. Wayne remained silent and looked at Cavell. "I dunno, you tell me...I been stuck here in this bed fam, you're the one that's out innit!" he finally replied. Babs started laughing. "Oh oh, I think he's on his period...no wait...my girl does that same shit!" Babs walked to the bedside and began stroking Wayne's head. "You missed us innit!" Wayne cut his eye at him and faced the window. In his thickest African accent, Babs continued "the baby boy has missed his fathers...do you feel abandoned son? Don't be afraid my child, we will never aaaabandon you!!" Wayne couldn't help but smile and he kissed his teeth. "Whatever innit!" he replied trying to still the smile spreading across his lips. "We're here fam, we got your back but we had to lie low innit. We couldn't just come up in the place and don't know what's gwarning!" Cavell added. "For real though, stop being a pussy. So you ain't said nothing to no-one have you?" continued Babs. Wayne shook his head. "Good!, cause tonight, we're going back for them bitches" Wayne exhaled and tried to sit up. "That's what I'm talking about, we can't let that go!" "Let that go?" Cavell kissed his teeth. "Never that my friend...never that!" "So what you going to do?" Wayne asked eager for the insight. Marcus kissed his teeth. "Why you feel you need to know that, what you planning on getting up and coming with?!" Wayne said nothing. "Yeah , that's what I thought, so just quieten your arse down innit, cause right now, you don't need to know!" Cavell looked at the clock on the wall and gestured to his companions. He knocked his chest with the side of his closed fist. "We out, and remember you're one of us, we got you fam."

The following week, news of another attempted murder filled the headlines. Ivy cringed as she read an article on her way to the hospital, Wayne was being discharged and as she read, she half hoped he wouldn't be. His eagerness to be with his friends caused her stomach to churn, but she was determined to keep him out of harm's way. She breathed a sigh of relief as the hours passed and he showed no sign of wanting to leave the house. By 8pm he was already in bed and Ivy left for work, confident that he was safe and secure. By 8.15pm Wayne was standing in front of Cavell's house. He knew his mother wanted him to stay in, and couldn't be bothered to argue with her. He also knew she had to work so he just waited till she left. Cavell greeted him at the door, patting him on his back. "They let you out blood!", he asked surprised. "Can't keep a good man down cuz!" Wayne replied grinning and limping towards the stairs.

"Come, you reach just in time, shit's about to go down!" His room was filled to standing room only with THM boys. They cheered and bumped fists as he entered, teasing him jovially about his limp. "Don't study dat my friend, it will fix back, and we took two of them for that! Best believe bro!" The room exploded in a chorus of whistles, cheers and stamps. "Alright! Alright!" Cavell continued, raising his arms to quieten his boys. "Listen, we not done yet! and we won't done till we finish that fool Bucky!" Marcus added. The room erupted once again, only this time Keisha banged on the door with news that her mother said it was time for them all to leave. The boys spilled into the cold night air, replacing gloves and pulling stringed hoodies against the wind that whipped through the estate. After making their plans for the following night, the Millitants dispersed into the shadows of the estate. Wayne returned home, consumed with images of the following night's revenge.

"A, I got the night off and I thought we could watch a movie together." Ivy announced jovially the following day as she entered his room. He answered "great!", but thought 'fucking hell!' and groaned to himself before pulling the quilt off his face. "Actually I can't mum, not tonight." He added nonchalantly, trying to think of what it was he could say he was doing. "Why?" Ivy asked, not wanting to hear anything about THM. "I have to do something." Wayne continued smiling as he made his way past her to the toilet. Ivy knitted her eyebrows. "But you can't even walk properly, where do you have to go...what you have to do?" his mother continued from outside the toilet door. Wayne kissed his teeth softly, "I just have to do something innit!" he replied, wishing he'd thought of an excuse last night whilst he couldn't sleep. "With who?" Ivy demanded, fear growing in the pit of her belly. "Cavell and dem lot mum alright!" Wayne returned with a snap. "What de arse you telling me boy!, I told you, I don't want you hanging out with those boys!" Wayne kissed his teeth again, this time loud enough for her to hear. "Boy you want me to fucking cuff out your teeth...kiss dem again...go on fucking kiss dem again!" his mother dared from outside the toilet. Instead he exhaled and sat on the toilet bowl, waiting for her to leave.

Ten minutes later she was still outside the door as Wayne quietly turned the handle hoping she'd gone. "You're not leaving this house tonight eh!" Ivy stated adamantly, standing in front the door frame forcing him to squeeze past her. "Whatever!" Wayne replied signalling that she move so that he could pass. "Oh yeah?!" Ivy's open palm engaged the side of his face, forcing him to retreat back into the bathroom. "You must feel yuh big! You carry on Mr man, like I said, your arse better be in your room all fucking night!" The slap took them both by surprise and Ivy retreated to her bedroom so he wouldn't see the tears in her eyes. As she walked away, Wayne, still in shock, held on to his face, cursing her under his breath. He eventually got up to return to his bedroom. "I fucking going out tonight, watch!" he stated ignorantly, loudly, though not too loud for her to hear.

The day passed and evening slowly turned into night. Wayne cracked his door to hear if his mother was still awake. Hearing nothing, he peeped over the bannister checking for light coming from her television, and there it was. It was 9.30pm and he was due to meet the boys at the end of the estate at ten o'clock. He silently dressed without creaking any of the floor boards before attempting the climb down the stairs. He cursed under his breath as each step creaked beneath his foot until, half way down, he decided to go back up and try a different route. Unbeknownst to him, Ivy and Andy lay awake in bed listening to the boards give away his position. Wayne returned to his room and looked out the window. It was at least a ten metre drop; unless he could lower himself and shimmy sideways to the fence.

Despite his painfully injured leg, he was determined to represent with his boys and exact his revenge. He climbed out the window, lowering his body and extending his bad leg to reach the top of the fence. It didn't work. His leg couldn't take the weight, but already out the window, he had no choice but to skim it, or to fall. His foot slipped off the thin wooden slate and he fell, bad leg first, to the ground. Wayne screamed in agony as his stitches burst, ripping apart the partially healed wound upon impact. He lay on the ground, trying to tolerate the pain as he clutched his leg. Ivy and Andy heard his scream, jumped out of bed and ran to his room. Her heart skipped a beat when she saw his empty bed, but before panic set in, Andy called her to the window and she looked out. Relief, worry and anger competed for air time in her mind in the seconds it took for them to reach the back yard. "What happened Wayne?" Ivy asked, kneeling at her son's side. "I fell mum" he answered weakly though still ignorantly. Andy knelt to scoop him up and the trio returned to his bedroom

He lay back on his bed, groaning in pain as Ivy checked his stitches. He winced as she replaced the bandages but she felt no empathy, only frustration and anger. "It serves you right, those who can't hear does feel!" Wayne kissed his teeth aloud this time. "Mum, if I don't deal with this, this way, I might as well go and jump under a bus! You don't live in the London I live in mum! Seriously, you don't have a clue! It's not all about work hard and everything will be alright like some fucking promised-land shit! That may apply to some but it does not apply to all mum, it's just not that fucking easy!" Wayne was conscious that he swore, but he wasn't going to apologise or take it back. He felt too experienced and too old to be told what he could and couldn't do. "You wouldn't survive one day in my shoes mum, so there's no point in me trying to explain, or you trying to advise me is there?...just know that unlike the goldfish in your pond, there's sharks in the water that I swim in ok!" Ivy felt irritated. "You're right, I don't understand why you've been kicked out of school! I don't understand why you have a bullet hole in your leg! And no, I definitely don't understand what's so great about your THM that you will jump out the fucking window!

Listen, I might not live in the London that you boys have created for yourself but I live here too, it's just that I know that when I make a bed, I have to lie in it, and so the bed I CHOOSE to make, doesn't have the fuckery that is so clearly in yours!" She suddenly admitted to herself that what was lost, by far outweighed what was gained in bringing her son to London. Isobel had been right all along. Maybe it was time to throw in the towel, maybe it was time to go back home. "Alright, you clearly need to get off this fucking merry go round you're on, and if you can't do that for yourself, I'll do it for you. You need a time out, I'm booking a flight to Trinidad!" Wayne kissed his teeth and tried to turn up his stereo as Ivy walked out of his room. His torn stitches throbbed angrily as DMX's 'Slipping fallin can't get up' came through the speakers in front his pillow. The next morning, Ivy visited the travel agent and Angela visited the morgue.

∞

Cold Showers

Rage, rage against the dying of the light...do not go gentle into that goodnight. Dylan Thomas

The Captain signalled the aircraft's descent, as Wayne returned from the toilet and buckled his seat. Clear blue skies dotted with the occasional puff ball clouds filled the small window. Waves crashed gently against the tiny island, as if cocooning it from the rest of the world. For a moment, thick dense foliage seemed to consume it, until the interruption of winding roads and galvanized rooftops broke it's monotony, a far cry from the view Wayne remembered as the plane landed at Heathrow almost two years before. He smiled to himself as he pictured his grandparents and he relaxed for a moment, it was good to be home.

His grandparents, Isobel and Papee, helped to raise Wayne after their son, his father, passed away. They moved to the home his father was born and raised in, when Tamana was still untouched virginal bush, offering no roads, electricity, cultivated land or running water. The pioneering pair made it their new home. Isobel at sixty-nine, was a force to be reckoned with. Though she often appeared domineering and abrupt, her husband, children and grandchildren were the focus of her life. She stood five feet seven inches off the ground, and possessed a full rounded figure. Make-up-less, Isobel wore her thick hair pulled back into single plait, always covered with a scarf. She was still beautiful even at this age, a natural beauty emanating from her very being, and which spared no time for the frivolity of vanity. Knarled hands and chipped finger nails, testified to her life with her husband, raising ten children and turning their twenty acres of dense bush into the plantation her family could live on, as well as off of. An expert marksman, Isobel's no-nonsense approach to life enabled her to raise her family, through good and bad times, instilling pride, love, respect and ambition, as true markers of a Lopez.

At seventy, her husband was the gentler of the two. Preferring to leave the disciplining of their children to his wife, his approach centred around the learning of a lesson in any situation. Whilst collecting dasheen bush in a small ravine, he was bitten by a mapapi snake which, in the end, left him with no calf muscle on his left leg. Since that day, he could no longer do the fourteen hour days on his land. A fact which left a heavier burden for his wife to bear and brought tears to his eyes when she left their bed early to ensure the coffee had been ground and brewed before he woke up. At five feet nine and inspite of his bad leg, Papee's quiet presence and manner, revealed a strength in his aging body and rose his stature beyond his physical measurements. He saw every opportunity as a moment to learn and enthusiastically taught his children about the world around them. A hunter matched in marksmanship only by his wife, Papee, a born flirt, was always ready with a compliment for a female specimen regardless of her age, size or physical appearance. His charm captivated the women of Tamana, and did not go unnoticed by Isobel, especially when accompanied by his favourite, Old Oak White Rum, a fact which caused many a 'lick down' threat from Isobel. Wayne adored them.

He sat back in his seat and closed his eyes, but the smile suddenly slipped from his lips as Marcus's parting words to him as he dropped off the gun, replayed for the thousandth time. "Cs is gone now cause of you. You got some catching up to do. Do what you gotta do innit...don't make me come for you!" The tension in his stomach, a constant companion throughout the flight, swiftly increased it's fervour and made its way to his head. Almost instantly, anger bubbled without his conscious awareness at the back of his throat, as he churned over the thoughts and events that brought him here. Anger that soon found an outlet, in the shape of a white couple with too much baggage, holding up the queue of passengers attempting to disembark. Wayne resented their presence. It seemed unfair that he should visit their country and feel so unwanted, yet their visit to his land, was being welcomed with smiling faces and helping hands. His irritation peaked as he saw the long local nationals' queue he was greeted with at customs, compared with the empty foreign nationals' line they stood in, with their matching suitcases and tourist hats.

By the time he saw his uncle in the crowd of people waiting to welcome their loved ones, Wayne hoped the couple would be robbed or at least catch dengue. He fought to control the irritation that engulfed him as he made his way over to the familiar face. Seconds later he was almost swept off his feet in a bear hug that instantly returned him to age ten as his uncle greeted him. Unexpected tears flowed freely down his face as he returned the embrace. Thoughts of the white couple vanished from his mind and his body relaxed for the first time in a long time. He was home. He placed his suitcase in the back of the pickup and they left the airport. "I stopping for a drink...you want one?" his uncle Terrence asked, pulling over in front of Cognac Shack just off the highway. "Yeh I'll take a beer." Wayne answered nonchalantly. Terrence smiled at his nephew and made his way into the bar.

Minutes later he returned with a beer and a shandy. "Yuh big, but you're not that big yet!" he announced, handing Wayne the shandy. Wayne kissed his teeth, he would have liked a rum and coke, but wasn't about to battle with his uncle even though he felt much older than his physical age, and a lot more experienced than his uncle. Familiar irritation threatened the back of his neck once more as they continued their journey to Tamana. He thought for a moment about the Wayne that left Trinidad. It seemed like a lifetime away, as far removed from the Wayne knocking back a sorrel shandy, as a dog was from a cat. He inhaled deeply as they continued their journey under the descending night sky. Shops became fewer, and houses further and further apart as the smoothly tarmacked highway gave way to dense undergrowth and narrower potholed roads. The familiar earthy aroma of trees, rain and fruit penetrated Wayne's senses and he inhaled even deeper. "So how it was, and how is your mother?" Terrence asked breaking the unusual silence. Wayne mulled over the questions in his mind. "Well, it's different from here that's for sure" he finally answered, wondering what his uncle knew of his life. "Well obviously, but different how...what did you experience up there that you couldn't down here, what did you get from it?" Wayne closed his eyes, the past two years flashed through his mind as he scanned for something his uncle wanted to hear. Nothing came that was worthy of regaling, and an uncomfortable silence pervaded the truck.

He ached silently as images of Cavell's lifeless body filled his mind's eye. Before he could stop it, vomit surged forth from his stomach. Terrence veered off to the side of the road as he saw his nephew heaving, and helped him out of the truck. "Oh god, what they do to you up there boy!?" he asked, as he gently rubbed his nephew's back and held him steady. Tears breached the rim of Wayne's eyes but he forced them back down. A few minutes later, his body heaved once more, releasing the last of the bitter yellow liquid, and he sat down, trying to steady his spinning mind. "Ok I good Uncle, let's go" he stated finally, getting up unsteadily. "Take your time, we ain't in no rush, just relax yourself. I have a bottle water in the truck, hold on, I'll get it and you can rinse your mouth." He returned with the bottle and a few minutes later, the journey resumed.

After a few moments, Terrence squeezed his nephew's shoulder, "Wow! So it was dat good eh!" Wayne smiled and looked out of the window. His stomach was empty but he still felt sick. Cavell was dead and he was on his way to his grandparents' house. 'Cavell's dead.' The words swam round and around, stirring a quandary of emotions that caused him to squirm uncomfortably in his body. Sleep at last brought him some relief, as the last of the day light turned itself over to the black night sky, blanketing the thick foliage around them.

He slept uneasily until his uncle turned off the ignition and shook him awake. "We home boy. Here, drink some water, throw some on your face." Getting out of the truck he removed the suitcase and waited for his nephew. Wayne emerged moments later and gave a sheepish grin. "You ready?" Terence asked, "As ever," Wayne replied, feeling far from it. "Well you know your grandmother. She's been cooking all day and tell everybody to come for food because she grandchild coming home!" Wayne grinned, he wasn't in the mood to be passed amongst his uncles and aunts but he knew better than to fight it.

They heard the sound of laughter and the pounding of his grandmother's mortar coming from the back. "Here we go!" Terrence teased as Wayne took a deep breath, before making his way to the thatched roof covering the hammocks at the back of the house, and to a barrage of screams, welcomes and hugs. He was passed around and inspected like a dog at a dog show. Wayne felt uncomfortable, unsure of what they knew of his London life and the choices he'd made, and although it annoyed him, he pretended all was well. But he wasn't the same little boy that left so happily, bright eyed and bushy tailed.

"So tell us all about London!" exclaimed one of his uncles, squeezing in next to him on the hammock. "Oh my days! I'll get up shall I?" Wayne winced, trying to ease himself up out of the canvas swing. "Did you see the Queen, how you doing in school, how your mother doing, did you get a girlfriend yet?" Wayne blushed and grinned and in an instant he was back to ten years old again, but it irritated him and intensified his sombre mood. "Nah uncle, do you?" The laughter in the gathering died down at his response. "Listen I'm tired, going to hit the sack. Good night" Wayne got up to make his way to the house. "What you say?" his uncle asked, stopping him with a shovel handle. Wayne kissed his teeth. "Nothing uncle" he replied trying to barge past the solid guava wood. Isobel sensed the rising friction and interrupted. "Leave de boy nah, he had a long day, Wayne you go ahead, we'll see you in the morning." She embraced her grandson and silently ached at the tension that stiffened his body. He walked up the backstairs before realising he had to pee. The toilet was in the back and he had no intention of returning to his family, so he walked straight through the house to the orange mangrove and relieved himself under the night sky. He heard the silence amongst his usually loud family and kissed his teeth. Exhaling loudly but not too loudly Wayne went back inside talking to himself as he went. "You guys must think I'm that little boy who left here... but trust, you're in for a shock!" he said loud enough for them to hear.

Kissing his teeth, he fell on to his bed. Within moments, several mosquitoes found their way to his bare skin. He raised his hand to slap them but missed. His irritation inflamed, he chased them with a rolled up pillowcase until he swotted each one. Satisfied, he lit the cockset on the night stand and waited for sleep. It eluded him with thoughts of the last few weeks, and by the time he did fall asleep, he couldn't wait to get back on the airplane.

∞

Wayne opened his eyes at 10am the following morning, and for a few brief moments smiled as he inhaled the familiar scent of his grandparent's house. The sounds of traffic, intermittent police sirens, and music left on from the night before, sounds which greeted him every morning and which were his constant companions through sleep, were suddenly noticeable in their absence. He lay on the mattress staring up at a cobweb in the corner of his room, inhaled and stretched his body, inspecting his room for any changes. There were none, though it seemed at lot smaller than he'd remembered. He smiled to himself as he noticed his feet reaching the end of the bed, proud and surprised that he had grown that much. A few seconds later, he remembered why he was there, and the heaviness to which he had become accustomed, returned. As did his anger. 'Why Cavell? What the fuck!' Banging his clenched fist against his temple, Wayne exhaled a roar that brought his grandfather to his bedroom door.

"Hey boy, what's up, you having a bad dream or what?" Papee asked. "You want some coffee?...come outside and eat something, Isobel left your breakfast on the stove." "Where's granny?" Wayne asked rubbing his eyes as he made his way to the back. "She in de garden as usual." Papee answered, pouring a cup of coffee for them both before sitting down. Wayne ate his breakfast whilst his grandfather sharpened the blade on his cutlass. "So what's been happening gramps, how you guys been....did you miss me?" His grandfather laughed out loud. "Boy miss is not de word nah, your grandmother take it real bad." Papee exhaled, "but we just glad to see you now." "Me too." Wayne replied, acutely aware that his plan for London had irretrievably capsized. "Look, finish sharpening this ting for me eh, I need to empty a load boy!" his grandfather exclaimed heading for the small wooden structure housing the toilet

Wayne grinned and reached over for the smoothly worn stone. He looked around the compound noticing how little things had changed since he was a little boy. Dried corn cobs still hung from the rafters of the backhouse. The weather beaten coconut branches of the thatched roof were home to an array of jars containing an assortment of seeds sitting quietly next to garden tools, old ice cream containers, biscuit tins and crocus sacks, all neatly held in it's eaves. The mortar and pestle stood where they always did, near the scorched earth of Isobel's coal pot. The 2 fourteen feet benches enclosing the area, still bore the carvings he'd left behind. Wayne stretched lazily, looking around the neatly cut perimeter of his grandparents' home. He smiled to himself as he sprinkled the stone with water, and sharpened the long blade of the cutlass as his grandfather returned, exclaiming relief as he did so.

"How come you guys haven't put in a inside toilet?" he asked realising just how used to England he'd become. Papee laughed out loud. "That is crazy talk now man! You could be in a house lying down comfortable-comfortable, and then your grandmother go and use the toilet, you know what kind of problems you go have right dey!" Wayne grinned. "When I go inside dey. I good you know. I doing my thing nice and easy and relaxed. I don't have too squeeze my bottom for it not to make too much noise when it land in case somebody here meh, or try and light a match to take way de scent. A, I shitting like a king dey dread!" Papee exclaimed unnecessarily proudly Wayne thought, grinning at the old man. "Oh gosh man, yuh mouth so big, you have nothing better to tell de boy on his first morning home?" Isobel joked, making her way from the side of the house, dragging a crocus bag behind her.

Wayne admired his grandmother. As she drew closer in her black rubber garden boots, thick black belt with a selection of knives and small tools in her waist, head covered with a wide brimmed straw hat and scarf that had clearly seen better days, she seemed not to have aged a day since his departure. She looked rugged and beautiful at the same time. Wayne ran to carry the bag for her, even though he knew she didn't need the help. "What assness your grandfather telling you?" she asked teasingly, releasing the strap from her shoulder to his arm. "You want a cold drink?" Wayne asked suddenly wanting to release her of every burden she'd ever carried. Isobel sat heavily on the wooden bench. "Oh gosh boy yes, that would be nice, thanks!" He retrieved a plastic tumbler and filled it with ice before adding homemade lime juice. He handed it to his grandmother and took a seat at her side. She took a long drink and rested the cup in her lap. "So you reach home boy!" she exclaimed slapping his thigh. "It's so good to see you." Wayne beamed from ear to ear feeling once again like the child he'd left behind.

"I missed you guys too granny, believe me, life over there is completely different from what I was expecting!" Isobel nodded her head and drank the last drops of the sweet and sour liquid before crunching down on a piece of ice. "Yeah, so what was it like, I want to hear all about it...but hold on, let me take a quick shower and then you can tell me. Shell these peas for me in the meantime." Isobel passed a colander of freshly picked pigeon pea pods to Wayne and headed for the three walled open air structure erected in the middle of a pepper tree patch, about ten meters from the toilet. "Ole man, come and scrub my back for me nuh?" she shouted to her husband on her way. Papee reluctantly threw a leg over the side of the hammock in an attempt to get up. "She still don't even let a dog rest around here!" he muttered under his breath, winking at his grandson. Wayne sighed and smiled to himself. 'Yes, it was good to be home.' In that moment his heart felt as light as it had been for a long time. He inhaled deeply, tasting the air as he breathed it in. A wide uncontrollable grin covered his mouth as he retrieved a pea pod, pressed it and cracked it open, releasing nine fresh pigeon peas inside.

Then he wondered what they knew of his time in London and his familiar unease returned. He yearned for a cigarette and hurriedly shelled the remaining peas. "I going shop and come back right, anybody want anything?" he asked eager to feel the smoke in his lungs. "No thanks, you have money?" Isobel yelled from the shower. "Yeah I'm good, see you in a minute." Wayne put on his shades and began the fifteen minute walk under the hot morning sun. Things hadn't changed at all it seemed. The seasonal trees were in full bloom. Red cashews hung heavily on the tree at the end of the driveway and he clambered up the incline, picking a fat fruit. He twisted off the cashew nut hanging from the bottom and bit into the sweet tart yellow flesh. Juice ran down the sides of his mouth and he wiped it off with the back of his hand.

The road was still a compilation of stones, grass, dirt and pitch, forming a pathway of potholes and crevices that were the cause of many a suspension failure. In the light of day, the overgrowth of trees and plants on either side of the road invited him in with its cool shady coverage, moss covered stones and ripened fruits. He passed them unnoticed, focused only on his desire for a cigarette, and walked at a 'London pace', to the shop. It was almost empty apart from two elderly customers, who each turned to look him up and down before finishing their conversation. Wayne recognised them from the village and patiently waited his turn at the counter. After what seemed like ten minutes but was in fact two, of what seemed to him to be unnecessary repetition of her granddaughter's husband's appreciation of alcohol, he kissed his teeth. The trio stopped and looked at him again. This time the attendant kissed her teeth. "Do you want something?" she asked wondering why he had his shades on in the shop. By now Wayne was biting back irritation. "Duh, what do you think I'm doing here!" He kissed his teeth before she could answer. "Look just give me a pack of Benson", he continued pushing a twenty dollar bill over the counter. "We don't have Benson!" she announced almost happily. "For fuck sake...!" Wayne muttered under his breath, rolling his eyes in exasperation. "Look, what cigarettes you got?" She pointed to the row of DuMaurier and Broadway on a shelf above his head. "Just give me a pack of DuMaurier." She put the pack on the counter and he grabbed it, and walked out the shop. "Your change!" she shouted after him. Wayne stopped in the doorway, lit a cigarette and walked off. "But what de ass is dis!" the clerk announced looking at her remaining customers. The three looked out the doorway in amazement wondering what kind of parent would have raised such a child.

His sense of irritation was in full swing, made all the worse by his failure to purchase a cold drink, but he wasn't going back, the cashier was lucky she didn't get a thump in her face. Wayne inhaled deeply, savouring the rush of chemicals appeasing his brain. A spliff and some Henny would have been better, but he was grateful for the cigarette. His surroundings went unnoticed once more on his return journey, as he walked the quiet country road deep in thought, wondering what was happening back in London. 'Was Cavell dead because of me? What am I gonna do about it?' The couple at the airport returned to his mind and as if like a magnet, brought with them every disappointment and disrespect of the past months; from his suspension, to Ellie's attack, his gunshot and finally Cavell's murder. By the time he arrived at the red dirt track signalling the entrance to his grandparent's home, Wayne was seething uncontrollably. He stubbed his toe in a pothole and cried out, less in pain, as in anger, disappointment and grief.

He paused with his hands clasped firmly on his head and looked up the driveway to the back of the house. He could see his grandmother peeling cassava and knew she awaited him. As he looked, he thought of the things he would tell her and it sickened him. Tears fell unnoticed down his face as he stared at her, trying to formulate the correct words to make her understand. No explanation came, and moments later, he veered left. Leaving the bright light of the baking sun, he dropped down into the seclusion of the cocoa garden on the other side of the road. The cool forest floor, covered in fallen leaves and moss covered stones, swallowed him up, and he took off as fast as his legs, the uneven ground and thick foliage, would permit.

Startled forest dwellers flapped their wings and screeched in disapproval at Wayne's sudden intrusion into their world. Their cacophony covered the sound of his feet crushing the undergrowth beneath, and was soon joined by the sound of a dull roar, rising in crescendo with his breath. It continued until he tripped on an exposed root and fell into a shallow crevice. There he lay for a while, and just cried, and as he did so, the forest was silenced. "Cavell's dead because of me. What the fuck am I gonna do? What the fuuuuuck!" he screamed at the forest, as if expecting some kind of response. There was nothing. The solace and renewed vigour he usually felt in the bush eluded him. His mind did quieten it's barrage of chatter, but the scars his thoughts left behind maintained the familiar pit in his gut. He knew Marcus awaited his return to put things right, and he had to be ready....with a plan. "C's, I promise you man, Bucky's mouth is gonna be biting the kerb! Believe me man, I promise you that!" he shouted earnestly. Cried out and drained, he finally sank back on some leaves to catch his breath and his bearings.

After a while, a manicou scrambled through the undergrowth, jolting him out of his thoughts as it made its' way across the forest floor. The animal slowed down just a few meters from Wayne and it irritated him, passing so carelessly in front of his anger. Didn't it know how easily it could be killed? He picked up a stone to throw at the animal, lying still as it approached. In that moment he pictured his grandfather's many lectures about the value of all life and his face when he'd caught him pouring salt on a toad's back. It was in striking distance but Wayne dropped the stone and watched it pass. He lit another cigarette and inhaled, but the smoke was rough on his dry mouth and throat. Exhaling, he looked around for something to quench his thirst. A fat burgundy cocoa pod beckoned to him and he eagerly twisted it off its' tree branch, cracked it open and scooped out a mouthful of fleshy seeds. Wayne had no idea of the time, but the sun was no longer over his head. Grey clouds covered the previously blue sky when he arrived back at the road. His anger had quietened, but left a debilitating feeling behind.

∞

"Oh gosh boy, I say you get lost?" Isobel greeted as Wayne walked over to her. "One sec granny, I'm just getting some juice, I was down in the garden for a while." She immediately noticed the difference in his demeanour and looked at her husband. It saddened her. Ivy told her about his suspension and shooting, they were shocked and heart-broken by the news and couldn't wait for his return. He himself though, had never alerted them to anything not going to plan. "So come, take this plate and sit down, tell us all about London." Wayne smiled weakly as Papee passed him the plate over filled with callalloo, macaroni pie, fried plaintain, pelau and stewed chicken. His taste buds salivated as he positioned himself in the hammock. His belly rumbled as the fork approached his mouth.

The trio ate their first mouthfuls in silence before Wayne worked out what to say. "To be honest, I didn't even really want to come back here." Isobel and Papee kept their eyes on their plates. "I don't know what mums told you, but what she thinks sending me back here will do, I don't know, but all it's doing, is frustrating me and delaying the inevitable." Silence hung thickly in the air as forks scrapped across plates and food was swallowed and digested. "Since I left you, I've had to grow up and grow up fast granny! You don't have a clue what I've been through, and yeh I know it's changed me, but all it's done, is open my eyes to the reality of life...and it's a fucking bitch for real!" Isobel flinched at the ease of his choice of words, but didn't stop him. It was clear as day that he had changed, he seemed to be carrying a weight on his shoulders under which his normal perspective had become stifled and broken. Whatever he was holding on to inside, had to come out, she could see it was poisoning him, and her heart swelled with angst as to what he might say next. He needed help, something had derailed him from his dream of a good education, a good job and a good life, from his reason for going. Her heart ached, but she alleviated her fear with the knowledge that he wasn't going to leave her, he wasn't going to return, not until she'd put it right.

"Every day I wake up, I'm in a place that, well the best way I can explain it, is that it's a different vibe from here," Wayne continued swallowing a mouthful of pie and callaloo. "How yuh mean different?" Papee asked. Wayne exhaled and looked across to the thick foliage at the edge of the compound. "Well, first to begin with, imagine a place where you're always trying to be more, to have more or, to be seen as more....and at the same time, there's no real more to have. I don't meet people that are routing for me and sending me good vibes on my way! More likely than not, they want to diminish or extinguish me. That's just how it is. Do you follow what I mean gramps, can you imagine what that would be like? And you're just in it every day feeling more and more anxiety?" Papee looked puzzled at his grandson's words but nodded his head. "Yeh I think I can" he answered unconvincingly. "Ok, imagine a game of snakes and ladders yeah, only, when it's your turn to roll, there's suddenly a hundred snakes and only two or three ladders." Papee looked at his wife as she winced with her grandson's words.

"For a long time I spent most of my time alone. When I wake up, mum's not home, and if she is, she's too tired or busy and I don't want to disturb her, not that she would understand anyway. She lives in a different London to mine." Wayne continued. "What you saying, what your mother is not there for you?" Isobel interrupted alarmed. "Nah granny, I'm saying she can't be. I'm not taking anything away from her, I love my mum, and I know she's just doing her best to make a better life for us, but in the meantime I'm growing up, and I'm doing it alone. There's no family, no community to watch over me. Sometimes I think there's no God." Isobel and Papee looked at each other again. They had never partaken of religion, but God? that was a different matter altogether. But still, they said nothing and Wayne continued. "There's absolutely nothing to do unless you got money, and even then, you have to have people or you're just alone. No one to say let's go camping, let's go river, let's do a barbecue, let's just go and talk shit under the stars. Nah, none of that, it's not that kind of place.

Anyway, I met some fellas though, they kinda saved me, and suddenly, I didn't feel like I was on the outside looking in anymore, I was part of it too. If it wasn't for them I'd be up shit creek without a paddle as Papee would say." Wayne smiled, giving Isobel a thumbs up as he bit into the chicken leg. "Anyway basically, London is divided between the people that have and the people that don't yeah, and for the people that don't have, life has different rules. And there's a separate set of rules for boys like me. I have to defend my shit...at all times, against whatever comes at me...and believe me when I say there's always some shit coming at me. So I end up damaging someone, or getting damaged by someone. So back to my boys, the True Hackney Millitants, THM for short." Wayne continued proudly. "Mum don't want me hanging around with them, but to be honest, the more eyes I have, the safer I am!" Papee and his wife looked at him quizzically, not really sure where he was going but he was so emotional, they remained silent, paying close attention to his pain more so than his words.

Wayne paused to catch his breath. He could feel his eyes glazing over but refused to release any tears. He lay back on the hammock, rocking himself with his hand on the dirt floor, allowing anger to consume him instead. "You want a drink or what?" Papee asked, sensing his grandchild's pain. Before he could answer and to Wayne's great surprise, he got up and went into the house returning within moments with three glasses and a bottle of White Oak rum. Wayne's anger ebbed as he handed him a small glass, quarter filled with rum and two ices cubes. He looked at his grandfather with a smile that turned into a giggle then a laugh. Papee looked him in the eyes and returned his smile. "This is one of those once in a lifetime things eh, don't let me see you with a bottle eh because as big as you is, you're not too big for licks!" "I know gramps!" Wayne assured him, wondering if they knew how familiar with alcohol he had already become.

"So what about school?" Isobel asked licking sauce from her fingers. "School...wow...you know I've been suspended I take it?" Wayne replied stirring the ice cubes with his finger. "Yes" she replied in a tone that told Wayne she expected a good explanation. "Well, again, it doesn't really have the same vibe as Tamana Sec, its' not really about learning there, no-one shines too brightly, and the teachers don't expect or even particularly want you to. Maybe they're just tired I don't know, but I'm never inspired at school." "What? what nonsense you talking boy? What you mean it's not about learning?" Isobel demanded knitting her eyebrows. "Nah it ain't granny, it's about what your sneakers are saying, and how facety you can be. You can't just be, you have to be one of them and it's about survival of the fittest. No-one wants to hear about what grade you got, or talk about what you learned. And the teachers ain't got time for you, just don't disrupt there forty minutes and fuck off when it's over! You can't question what they say and they don't want to hear your version of events or what's going on in your life...they don't get any respect, at all gran, nah for real...but that's because they don't give any either."

Wayne knocked back some of his drink. The sound of the forest dwellers suddenly seemed loud in the quiet of the evening. It was hot and muggy, but a cool breeze blew, gently cooling the tiny sweat beads on his forehead. "I got suspended for defending myself and protecting my rep. My reputation, the respect I get from the streets is the only thing I have worth a flying fuck, and I ain't about to let no chieftain step up and disrespect!" "What?" Papee interjected. "One boy from Black Ice tried to step to me and

I put him in his place. And before you say it, no! I couldn't go and tell my teacher. They wouldn't have done anything, and, it would have made me look like a cunt, and after that, I would have been shit under everyone's shoe!"

Silence hung in the air as his grandparents visualized the memory of his time in London. "Where's Black Ice?" Isobel asked eager to understand the full picture. "It's not a where, it's a who granny. Remember I told you about the 'have nots' fighting over the little they have?" His grandmother nodded. "Well, Black Ice are just one lot, but they're our main enemies. They could fuck us up on sight and we do the same. That's just how it is." Wayne turned to his side and pulled at his shorts revealing the wound at the top of his thigh. "It was one of them that gave me this." He continued matter-of-factly. "Lord father eh, it sound like you're living in a war zone, not England! Papee almost whispered, refilling his glass as Isobel traced her finger along the line of the scar. "So what about the police?!" she eagerly interjected, determined that his story have a happy ending or at least a way out. Wayne laughed until he almost fell out of the hammock. "Well now you really got it twisted! No-one goes to the five-o granny! Again, I'd be a sitting duck if I did that, you don't snitch gran, you handle yours. And anyway, do you think they care what happens to us. I am a target for them just as much as I am for Black Ice. These people stop me at the drop of a hat, hold me up at the side of the road, empty out whatever I'm carrying, turn my pockets inside out, lean up on my chest, kneel down on my back!....all this, while people are just going by, watching me like I'm some kinda criminal! Why?, cause that's just how they see me gran, that's just how they see us, and how they deal with us reflects that! Do you know what that does to your mind after a while...to your spirit?"

Wayne downed the remainder of his rum and looked toward the bottle. Papee looked at Isobel and grinned. "Go ahead mister" she replied turning her head as he refilled Wayne's glass with more alcohol than was necessary. Wayne gladly took it, hardly noticing the look that passed between his grandparents. "Do you mind if I smoke?" he added grinning slyly. "Hmph...knock yourself out!" Isobel replied, wanting to slap the cigarette out his hand and stamp it into the dirt. "Ahh yes!" Wayne exhaled, quickly retrieving the pack from his shorts pocket, he awkwardly lit one and inhaled.

"Anyway, my boys handled me when I got shot innit, they took care of it whilst I was laid up. Now it's my turn to defend it, Cavell's dead and where am I...? In fucking Trinidad...no disrespect! I ain't gonna see him on the estate, we're not gonna hang out, he's just gone and he ain't fucking coming back, and it's all because of me"

By now Wayne had a good head, he was glad of the opportunity to talk without being berated. He wondered momentarily how it was that he was drinking, smoking and cursing in front of his grandparents, but the thought was fleeting. After all he'd been through, they must see that he had grown. He felt like an adult, refilled his glass and sank back into the hammock, swinging it nonchalantly. Isobel and Papee's concerns churned like butter in their bellies, but they showed no fear and encouraged Wayne to tell his truths. They allowed him to drink and smoke with abandon. Papee squeezed his wife's leg as he refilled their glasses. "You good chic?" he asked as he handed her the glass, "Yeh, I just listening to my grandson, but hold on a minute let me heat up the stove so I can reheat this food, we need to finish eat and soak up this fire water" she replied retreating to the kitchen. "Aye ya yi!... that's why I married you yuh know, cause you does read meh mind!" he replied, kissing his wife as she made her way to warm up the food on the stove. "You alright granny?" Wayne asked squeezing her free hand as she walked by. "Boy yuh home, there's nothing else for me to be but great!" She returned the squeeze and gave him the chore of carrying the plates to the stove.

"Granny, you know it would be so much easier if you had a microwave right" "Nah nah nah!" Papee intervened, "Mi-cro-wave!...no thanks! Yuh ain't see how strong and healthy I is? That's fresh food cook on a open fire...with love. Microwave does do that?" Papee grinned rubbing his belly. "Gramps, just cause something using new technology, it don't mean it's bad yuh know!" Wayne replied laughing. "Yeah and it don't mean it good either, not so?" Isobel returned and shut them up. "As far as I see it, I know what in the fire, what's in the oven, what's on the stove, what it is I make and what it will do for me. What is a microwave, what is it doing to the food to cook it so fast, I have no idea, but it don't sound good! I will stick with my old stove!" his grandmother continued cheerily. "I don't know, but I know it would save you a lot of time." Wayne countered. "Time!, time to do what?...for me to cuss your grandfather!" Isobel countered. "Oh Lawd no!, doh encourage she with dat nuh, I does get more than enough of that already!" Papee urged, cleaning his toenail with a knife. "Yuh see?! Dat is de shit right dere why I does have to cuss your arse as soon as your eye open in the morning!" his wife countered pointing at the knife cleaving his toenail. The trio burst into laughter. Papee began his rendition of Gregory Isaacs 'Night Nurse', grabbing Isobel's hand to draw her for a dance. She smiled and gave him a quick two step before returning to the stove. They ate, talked and drank well into the early hours of the morning. Wayne told them all his fears, his anxieties and his disappointments, and in return they enveloped him with love. He was their Wayne after all, he had just picked up a little 'dirt' on his journey but they had plenty of soap and water. The coup rooster crowed before they went to bed.

Isobel couldn't sleep. She would have been getting up in an hour or two anyway so after seeing her men to bed, she sat on the veranda in her rocker and meditated. As the light of day replaced the quiet disguise of night, she watched the sun come up and wondered about the London her grandson lived in. She knew it wasn't perfect, no big city could be, but it hadn't crossed her mind that it was as he'd described. The bright happy enthusiastic child that left no more than two years ago, had returned a bitter and angry young man. His mind, trapped like a caged animal by his experiences and changed expectations. His thoughts were eating away the old carefree Wayne, changing his perception until what remained seemed a bundle of ignorance, intolerance, angst and fear. He was lost, and without the right guidance, he was following the blind.

The early morning quiet was broken by the sound of moaning coming from Wayne's bedroom. Isobel ran inside and found Papee standing in his doorway. I can't wake him!" Papee whispered. Wayne was still asleep. He tossed and turned mumbling something inaudible to his grandparents. The fan was on and focused on him but beads of sweat covered his face and back, making his earlier crisp sheets, now damp. Isobel shouted his name as she approached his bed. He bolted upright then lay back down. He was still asleep, but this time his face was relaxed and he lay still. They observed him for a few moments then quietly left his room leaving the door wide open. For the first time in a long time Papee felt helpless. He usually vanquished his children's 'boogy man', only this time, the 'boogy man' seemed bigger and more powerful than he was. He embraced his wife. "Girl what are we going to do for this chile?" he asked eager for guidance. Isobel exhaled, I don't know boy, I just doh know...I know we have to fix it though, because if we don't, who will?"

They looked at each other, trying to find the answers to a game they knew nothing about. Wayne's dreams continued throughout his sleep, interrupted only when Isobel brought him out of his reverie with cool compresses and soft strokes, only to return when complete sleep consumed him again. It was the same for the following two nights. He awoke dishevelled and unrested, spending the days in a cloud of anxiety and irritation, unwilling to take part in anything that required his mental attention. By the third day, Isobel had had enough.

∞

Wayne woke at 10am, five hours after his grandparents. He felt weak and unsteady. Relieving himself in the outhouse, ensuring he checked for insects under the seat before he sat down, he cursed the idea of having to shit under such conditions. It irritated him that his grandparents did not want an inside toilet, and that he had to keep an eye on a spider in the corner to make sure it didn't drop on him. As he left, he picked up a stick and killed it, feeling a slight improvement in his mood as he watched it's legs contract in death. He looked under the tea towel in the kitchen and found a plate of smoke herring and eggs with two hops bread. Pouring himself a cup of lime juice, he cursed the absence of a microwave to heat it up his meal and sat in the hammock, wondering what he was going to do with himself until his stay was over. Nothing he envisaged interested him and he kissed his teeth. There was still ten more days of his stay, but all he could think of was London, and what awaited his return as he rocked himself back and forth.

He dozed off again until he was woken by the sound of a familiar voice approaching the house. "Morning!...Morning!". Wayne sat up, rubbing sleep from the corner of his eyes just in time to catch an orange his closest friend since childhood, Semp, threw at him. Semp grinned from ear to ear, stepping forward to embrace him. "A horse, what's de scene!" "Rah boy, you get big dread!" Wayne replied, surprised at his friend's stature as he scoped him from head to toe. He remembered Semp the way he'd left him, not as this 'man' that stood in front of him. "Fuck me, what you been eating dread?" Semp laughed, flexing his muscles and easily pushing Wayne off the hammock. Wayne kissed his teeth, picking himself up off the floor. "So yuh back for good or what?" Wayne kissed his teeth again. "No!" he replied indignantly feeling irritation creep back into his being. Semp felt awkward, he'd heard about Wayne's visit to the village shop, but didn't expect the attitude to be applied to him.

"A check this out!" he continued eagerly showing Wayne what looked like a worn out old amp. Wayne kissed his teeth again "make that yourself did you?" he asked, lacing his words with scorn. The look on Semp's face caused the laughter in his throat to choke him as he heard the words come out his mouth. "Not from scratch no." Semp replied, turning on his heels to leave. "Anyway, tell your grandmother I pass through..." Wayne stood up, "look sorry man, I just got a lot on my mind right now...sit down nuh." Semp grinned easily and sat on a bench. "Well offer a man a cold drink nuh, wha happen, yuh left your manners up de road or what?" he teased as they sat in momentary silence. Wayne got the drink and gave it to his friend. "So?...what's de scene, fill me in cause I just hadda know what have you acting like a cunt so!" Wayne chuckled and exhaled. A part of him was glad to excite Semp with his London adventures, and he retold the tale of his woes with Black Ice, THM, and the London of his experience. Semp listened incredulously, shook by the picture his friend painted.

"You have to take a life?!!" Semp asked in disbelief as Wayne finished his tale. "You ready to take somebody's life horse?...or you ready for your mother to bury you?" he continued sombrely. "You can't tell me you're ready! I don't care what you been through, or how fast you had to grow up, no man ready for that! take it from this backward country arsehole!" Semp announced vehemently. "No, but I gotta do what I gotta do though! And my mom won't be burying no-one!" Wayne returned adamantly. "So you're going to allow a group of 'not so bright' boy dem, to steer your life? is that what your telling me?" Semp continued. Wayne was incensed. "What the fuck do you mean? You stay there and feel you know... trust, you don't know shit!...dickhead! All I can say is when I get back, somebody's going to feel it, trust me!" Semp kissed his teeth. "You had to be a cunt!...I rather stand up and take my chances on my own, Jah know!, I rowing my own boat mister, cause nobody know me better than me, and nobody love me more than me, so I and I is not going to war for nobody!" Semp insisted, shocked at his friend's acceptance of his apparent fate.

Wayne was unimpressed by his response. "Whatever man, you do you innit. Let me know how that goes for you." The pair sat in uncomfortable silence. "You got any cigarettes?" he spoke after a few moments. Semp smirked, "nah dread, I doh smoke" "Why doesn't that surprise me." Wayne replied scornfully under his breath. Semp laughed out loud. "Boy you best leave that tantrum shit for somebody it will impress yuh know!". Before Wayne could respond, his grandparents returned dishevelled with sweat and dirt. Bags of pommeracs, silk figs and sapodillas hung between them on a guava stick pole, balancing on both their right shoulders. The boys both got up to relieve them of their burden. "Oh gosh boys thanks!" Isobel exclaimed releasing her load and kicking off her heavy garden boots before dropping down on to the cool concrete steps of the house. Papee went straight to the full barrel of rainwater, scooping out a calabash bowl first for Isobel and then himself. They washed their hands, faces and necks whilst Wayne brought them each a cold glass of lime juice. The silence between the boys lay thick in the air. "What you did today Wayne?" Isobel asked massaging her shoulder. "Nothing" he replied lazily. She was woken by his groans again the night before. They didn't seem to be getting any less intense and she was unsure what to do about them. All that came to mind was to keep him busy and so that's what she decided to do, and Semp's arrival couldn't have been more timely.

"Why you boys don't go and check the spring at the back of the fig trees, I think some branches need trimming?" Wayne exhaled audibly, "nah, I ain't really feeling that you know granny." Semp kissed his teeth. "Boy, your grandmother asking you to do something for she!" Wayne's anger returned in full glory. "A, fuck you nah boy!" he spat at Semp. "Granny you want me to fix something for you?" Isobel, still taken aback by her grandson's reaction, extended her arm, and, reducing her voice to a whisper, she held her grandson's hand. "Wayne, since you reach back here, you acting like somebody here do you something, you cursing in front of me, you drinking hard hard hard and you smoking right in front my face. I leave you to it cause I say is something you going through and you will work it out, but now!...now I not so sure. You need to take a time out. Get off that merry-go-round. Think some different thoughts, or you will make yourself sick, depressed, mad or you'll end up somewhere you don't want to be!"

"Breeze out your mind!" Semp added sincerely. "A, I say fuck you nah boy!...and Granny you have no idea what you're talking about, how you going to help me?, no for real, what do you think you're going to do? It's not about getting up early and doing a hard day's work, fresh coffee and bathing in the rain anymore granny. Just leave me alone...and no!, you can't fix it by sending me up on the land with Semp for fuck sake!" Wayne heard his words but he couldn't stop them. Stunned silence hung over the group for a few moments. "I'm going shop." he announced finally, running inside for his wallet. Before they could respond, he was on his way down the road, eager to get a cigarette, a drink, and away from them.

Papee and Isobel watched him go. "Isobel, I don't think there is anything we can say to him that he will hear right now. But just how we want him to see shit from our perspective, we have to look at things from his. All we can do is let the dam burst, and be there to minimise the damage." The three sat for a while until Isobel got up returning from the kitchen with three bowls. She passed the cassava and the salt-fish to the men. "Here, you cut up this and you clean that...food still had to cook. And yes I hear you ole man, but I don't think he can handle it, we have to step in...I can't see him go through this no more, it crippling him!" Tears slipped easily down Papee's face as he looked at his wife. "I know baby, I know...I just not sure how. This is a new generation in a different place..." They sat in silence once more, trying to figure out the best way to help the boy they each loved.

"Salty soup." Isobel spoke after a few moments, standing motionless as the idea formed in her mind. Papee and Semp looked at each other. "How do you fix salty soup?" Before they could reply, Isobel answered her own question. "Dilute it with water and add some provisions" she spoke smiling "and its' the same way we can change his mind!" Papee wasn't sure where his wife was going, but he knew her well enough to feel confident she would know exactly what to do. "Right now his mind is so messed up with the pain of his experiences, that there's no way out of it, it's like he's on a merry-go-round and he's creating more and more shit every time it goes round'. The only way he's going to hear us, is if we dilute it, stop it or at least slow it down. We have to stop the chain of thoughts going around and around in his mind. It's the only way we can make room for new thoughts, new thoughts carrying better feelings. They digested the information for a few seconds. Semp tried to keep up, not really understanding the older woman's train of thought. "How are we going to do that though?" he added. "One thought at a time, one idea at a time, one degree at a time. We have to shift his perspective and his perception will change itself." Isobel answered, now sure of her new plan. "Do you think it will work?" Semp continued, unsure that anything would be able to get through his once best friend's new hardened skin. "It has to work, if it doesn't, I can't let him go back, it's as simple as that. He is my grandson and I won't lose him to...something that's not worthy of him." Tears flowed silently down Isobel's cheek. It was the first time Semp had ever seen her cry.

The afternoon cooled as grey clouds covered the sky. Wayne walked briskly, relishing the feel of the breeze as it brushed past his face. His heart, already beating quickly before he hit the dirt road, tightened in his chest until he was forced to sit at the side of the road to catch his breath. He sat with his knees up and his head resting on his arms. His breath came in short gasps, whilst his mind swam incessantly with thoughts of anger and violation. He felt out of control, and it added to his building rage. He exhaled energetically, trying to calm his mind and control the frequency of his thoughts until he rose, steadying himself and resumed his journey. Within minutes, he stood in front of the closed weather beaten shop doors. "For fuck sake!" he shouted clasping his hands at the back of his head. He felt like screaming but sucked it up as he noticed an old man seated on his porch across the road, eyeing him as an unfamiliar. "Take a fucking picture, it will last longer...cunt!" Wayne shouted as he walked past the house. The man said nothing and Wayne continued home, consumed with anger, frustration and helplessness.

Thunder clapped overhead but he didn't care, the soft pitter-patter of rain gave way to the drumbeat of heavier drops on galvanized roofs and tree leaves. He embraced the rain, allowing it to flow unhampered through his entire being as he walked the short journey home. By the time Papee saw him in the road at the end of the driveway Wayne was sitting in the dirt, bawling uncontrollably, and this time he didn't care nor was he aware, of who saw. "Isobel!...Isobel!" Papee shouted as he ran to his grandson. Semp and Isobel looked to Papee and darted after him. She held her chest as she saw the crumpled figure in the road and ran to him. "Wayne, Wayne? Wayne!" she screamed with no response. She fell to her knees and embraced his body into her chest, rocking back and forth. "It's ok. It's o.k. It's o.k. Come, everything o.k. I know, I know, go ahead baby, go ahead and cry, let it out, let it all out. They sat for some time as she rocked him back and forth, earnestly trying to soothe his anguish.

"Granny what am I going to do?!!" he whispered finally, repeating the question. "We'll figure it out baby, we'll figure it out." Papee sent Semp for the umbrella and tried to gather up his wife and grandchild, ushering them inside from the rain. Wayne's tears racked his body and he held on to Isobel longing for a release from his consuming thoughts and the debilitating feeling they brought. Isobel hugged him tighter, and sang Amazing Grace over and over, until finally his sobs eased and his body lay still and silent in her arms. She wiped his rain sodden face and kissed him. "I love you, let's go get out of these wet things ok." Wayne exhaled and nodded his head in agreement. Papee and Semp, standing over them with an umbrella and a piece of siding, eagerly helped them up.

Wayne closed the door to his room and stripped off his wet clothes. His mind felt numb, but he realised the thoughts that terrorised him on his return from the shop, were no longer swirling through his head, and he breathed a sigh of relief. A sense of calming serenity settled on him that seemed to cocoon him. It came with no solution but it gave him a reprieve from his mental torture, a feeling Wayne welcomed and missed. He could breathe. Isobel knocked on his door, pushing it open at the same time with a mug of fresh brewed chocolate. Wayne smiled. "Sorry about that granny" he said, taking the mug of steaming liquid. "Sorry for what?" she replied sheepishly, holding his face in her hands. "What because you was crying? Boy bawl if you want to eh, how you mean, how else you going to move that ball of badness you had stick up inside you." Wayne laughed out loud. "I never understand dis ting about man doh cry or man shouldn't cry or crying is a sign a weakness! It takes a real man to cry eh, and when he does, his tears bring a healing that can't come from medicine or anything else. Tears release the negative and make room for the positive. Always remember that eh, that's one of the tools God gave you, use it!" Papee stuck his head around the door, clearing his throat to draw Wayne's attention. "Yuh give meh a fright dere boy, how you feeling?" he asked jovially. "I good gramps...sorry about that eh." "Boy hush your mouth eh...sometimes you have to go through the darkness to get to de light!"

∞

By the time they emerged from the house, Semp had already set the cassava to boil and was frying the saltfish. "Oh gosh boy, your mother trained you good!" Isobel joked as she sat down. Wayne felt embarrassed to see his friend, but he sucked it up and apologized. Semp kissed his teeth. "I not studying dat dread, yuh forget is me you dealing wit or what!" Wayne smiled and nodded his head and the two boys embraced. "Alright, enough of that gay shit!" Semp announced passing the strainer to Wayne. "I have to go organise some music for de dance tomorrow. I passing for yuh bout ten." Before Wayne could respond, Semp darted off, hoping to reach his destination before the rain began again.

It was late as they sat down to eat, Wayne wasn't hungry but he knew better than to say it. They ate silently, each wrapped in their own thoughts of how to move forward. "Do you ever reconnect with God child?" Isobel asked interrupting their silence. Wayne half laughed, "what...how do you mean, pray?" he asked consciously noting that God had never been a real part of his life, and also that he didn't feel like talking about it. "You know, plug in, recharge, realign yourself with your inner being, with God...reconnect with your source, seek guidance, seek counsel?" she clarified swallowing a mouthful of watercress . Wayne sniggered. "No...God don't come round Hackney too often granny!" he chuckled shaking his head. Papee and Isobel looked at each other and grinned. "But what de ass is this! Child, God is always everywhere, and in everything including in you, and she's always trying to communicate with everybody including you." Isobel continued sure in her conviction. "What...'she'?" he asked quizzically raising his eyebrows. "And anyway, since when you in to church granny?" he continued poking her, remembering her distaste of the 'Sunday Morning' Christians passing her scornfully as she tended to her crops. She kissed her teeth and smiled, " First to begin with yes, she's a she, when she's not a he, or a it, so yes deal with it, God is a woman too!" The pair laughed as Isobel eye-balled them, but easily conceded their agreement.

"Seriously now, no I'm not talking about religion, or church or even the bible!" Isobel added adamantly. "No she mean God, the big cahuna! The beginner and the ender!" Papee answered listening intently to the discussion. Isobel continued, "Religion has distorted God, it's turned her into this far away, jealous, vengeful thing, contained in an old time book, and who only speaks to a chosen few, who must be sinless! When something happens, they claim 'oh, it's God's will', as if it just happened to them, like they had no part in it; and when it's something bad, it's, why God do this to me or worst yet, there is no God!

Its' your attention to something that brings it into your life, whether through worry and fear or through appreciation and hope, it's your attention to something, good or bad, that brings it into your life. It's you exercising your 'free will', not God's will.

Then they want to say for you to love God, you must wear this, or say that, or be like this or do that...and if you don't, then what...what she don't love you or you not good enough? Then these same church goers want to scorn you! Do you really feel God, this magnificent energy that cannot be created or destroyed, cares whether you having sex before marriage, or that you gay or that you did not go to church on Sunday?" She paused to kiss her teeth and Papee continued. "Religions breed separation and hierarchy. And that is where it is wrong from the very beginning, because God say, we are all one and we are all equal! So if you're making a church, based upon such a fundamental mistake, how I go follow you again after that! So no, we not into religion, but we are into God, very much so. Very much so! We just see her differently because we approach her directly. I don't look to interpret a passage in a bible, or go to church and ask a priest! I speak to her directly and I get a first-hand response, relevant specifically to me, now.

The bible on the other hand, has been written and rewritten so many times it contradicts itself and it's separating people from God, and from each other." Papee lamented vigorously before returning to the pot. "It's true, so now people don't really take God seriously or at least, not enough to have the faith to believe she answers every prayer every time." Wayne kissed his teeth ignorantly. "Yeah right!...No he...she...don't!, that's not true granny, come on." Isobel could hear the pain of shredded hope and disillusionment in his voice. "He don't talk to me, and he don't answer my prayers, I can tell you that...straight up!" he exclaimed vociferously, as if cheated out of a birth-right. Isobel put down her plate, and moving a stool, she sat beside the hammock, resting her hand on Wayne's knee. "Wayne she talks to everyone all the time!" Isobel looked into his eyes to make sure he understood her conviction. "She speaks, but the problem is you don't know how to ask for what you want, and you don't know how to hear her give you the answer darling."

Wayne exhaled and kissed his teeth, Isobel smiled. "Tell me, how exactly do you pray...do you pray?" she continued fervently. "Like everybody else..." he countered, eager to disprove her theory. "When I want something, I beg him for it, try to offer something in exchange, promise to be good, then I wait for it to come. Incidentally, it hardly ever does." Isobel laughed knowingly and reached for his free hand. "You see, that's why I don't like religion, it's unplugged your connections to your creator, turned her into a pappi show! Listen eh, you trust me right?" she asked seriously. Wayne nodded his head and Isobel continued "God is my best friend, she's bigger, broader, wider, deeper and funnier than any 'god' in any bible or in any religion! I will seek counsel with her before anybody on this planet...including your grandfather, and he knows dat and vice versa!" "Ok, I go take dat one." Papee responded agreeing with his wife. "Wayne, look at me child, we are not separate from God! God is an immensely inconceivable energy, not a puny egotistical physical human. We are a minute portion of his energy in a physical body. There is God in all of us, and through that spirit, that energy, we all have the power to create whatever we want. It is our choice, not his will.

We communicate and manifest our prayers through the energy we are vibrating, how we are feeling, and not as people believe, through our words. So when you pray, be clear on what it is you want, but instead of begging for it, feeling the absence of it, worrying and crying about it, just ask once and spend the rest of your prayer on why you want it, and on appreciation of what you already have. If you spend your prayer and your time begging and worrying about something, since all prayers are answered, you will receive what you are energising, what you are vibrating, what you are feeling, which is more of the same, more to worry and cry about, and then you say shit like God don't answer my prayers!

Instead, spend your prayer in appreciation. Give thanks for anything that you feel real appreciation for. It could be one thing or many things, it could be the sunny day, a part of your body, something you have achieved or received, anything, so long as you can feel the emotion of appreciation about it. Then wallow in it, feel it and your energy will vibrate it! Then you must receive what you've energised, more of the same, more to appreciate. Trust me baby, life doesn't just happen to us, we guide it with our thoughts and our emotions."

A tear escaped his eyelashes and rolled down his cheek. Wayne looked at his grandmother as he took in the impact and energy of her words. He believed in her, but if what she was saying was true, how was it that he had not heard it before? Why then was life the way it was? If there was such a way out, why didn't everyone know it? Surely hope and empowerment would be in the air he breathed, not the powerlessness and contraction he inhaled daily. Isobel saw the doubt on her grandson's face and smiled to herself, at least he was listening. "Yeah I know, hard to believe it's that easy right, but it is, it's as simple as that. Sometimes though, I know you can get so caught up in shit that you can't feel appreciation for anything! In those times, you're fully disconnected from your source, your spirit and there's only one thing for it. Meditation, the silencing of your thoughts baby. Only when you quiet your mind, will you become connected to who you really are. And when you practice your connection, trust me child, you will receive the inspiration to do anything you want in your life You will feel different too, calmer, empowered, able, in control!

Wayne exhaled audibly and placed his head on his knees. "I dunno granny man, you make it sound so simple, but it's not." Isobel stroked her grandson's head. "It is darling! It just depends on your perception of yourself in relation to everything else. Test it, you've got nothing to lose right? Test it then. Start a daily routine and see what happens. Every morning I wake, before I even open my eyes too good, I appreciate. I appreciate your grandfather, the smell of the morning air, the coffee I'm going to drink and my toilet! Whilst I'm still in my bed I think about them and smile until I ready to get up. After my coffee, I go sit on the veranda and I just quiet my mind and breathe for fifteen minutes. This keeps the channels between me and my spirit open, and readies me for receiving. I do this every day and my life has been blessed...Not so?" she asked looking at both Papee and Wayne. Papee smiled and nodded in agreement. "Begin it Wayne, begin this process, make this routine a part of your life, begin it and I promise you, your perception will change and your life will just open up, like a completely new bud."

Isobel paused and looked at her grandson. Wayne chewed over his grandmother's words. "Do it!" his grandfather concurred enthusiastically nodding his head. "Your grandmother definitely more in tune than me, but I can vouch for what she saying. Over the years I've had and done my fair share of shite!" Papee grinned at his wife and Wayne smiled in acknowledgement. "So I know what she talking about, first hand! Sometimes you find yourself in so much shit, and the more you try to figure it out, is the more you drowning...in shit!" The trio laughed as Papee animated his words. "Them times there, your mother can't help you, your father can't help you and your friend can't help you, but you know damn well you need help eh. So what you going to do? You're so disconnected that you can't think of anything to appreciate, and even the thought of meditation will make you want to cuss your mother! But believe it or not, that's when you need it the most, because that's when you're disconnected the most. Them times there, don't think just breathe, just breathe, consciously breathe and start breathing every day. Soon enough the brakes come on and as your grandmother say, the roller coaster will stop!"

It felt good to Wayne to hear his grandparents' words. They sounded plausible and he wanted them to be possible, but his life wasn't as easy as that, and he was no saint. It may work for them, but he doubted it would work for him. Isobel looked at her grandson and his expression revealed his thoughts. "Just try it baby, when you think you're losing your mind, just talk to her, and I promise you, if you take time to be quiet, you will hear her and you will receive. Just like when you're hungry, you need good food to full you up and keep you well, you need appreciation and meditation to keep you centred, empowered and inspired. Without this process I would be lost, your grandfather would have sent me basodee crazy by now! yuh think is joke, he not easy yuh know!" Isobel added pointing from her husband's head to his feet. Wayne laughed. "Alright granny, I'll try it." he replied, knowing full well he wasn't going to. Papee laughed, manoeuvring a missed bone to the tip of his tongue to spit out. "Well, what I go tell yuh boy, experience is the best teacher!" he added, holding out his plate and gesturing to Isobel for a refill. Isobel looked at Wayne, "This mudder arse want me to forget you here this evening yuh know!" she complained annoyed but jovially.

Wayne wanted a cigarette, though his craving was a lot more manageable than he expected. He felt calmer than he had in days. His shit was still there, but had somehow been removed from his mind's centre stage. He lay back on the hammock and wondered why he wanted a cigarette until he fell asleep. Isobel stared at his face, serene in it's peacefulness. She covered him with a sheet and kissed his forehead before lighting a cockset under his hammock. He slept straight through the night without any disturbance for the first time since Cavell passed away.

∞

He woke refreshed at 7am the next morning, to the sound of his grandmother berating his grandfather. "I could dig dasheen whole day, and still have to come home and cook food and straighten up de house...what you think I just like to do that?!...you just use any excuse to go and lime!" Papee sniggered and tried singing a tune to appease her. "Oh God doodoo, let meh take a ole talk nuh" he teased. She hit him at the back of his hand with her wooden pot spoon. "No!, not when there is shit to do. It's already seven o'clock, you kill any duck yet?" Isobel demanded, annoyed at his inability to grasp the term 'hurry up'. "Woman I am going to deal with it, John just ask me to check de pen before..." Isobel didn't bother to let him finish. "Check de pen!...check de pen, check de old talk and de rum!... not today!" she shouted, returning to her seasoning. Papee walked out of the house. "Eh eh, yuh wake up! was your grandmother mouth ent?" he chuckled heading for the fowl coup. "What happen?" Wayne asked rubbing sleep from his eyes. "Miss Gloria and Madam Betsy looking to bad talk somebody again, dey coming up de road and she find she don't have enough duck!" he moaned loudly. "Ohhh" Wayne groaned, turning over in the hammock. He remembered the area's news carriers only too well.

"Can I come with you by John?" he asked, hoping not to have to deal with an inquisition as to his whereabouts over the past few years. "I hearing yuh eh!" Isobel announced coming down the kitchen steps before he could answer. "Morning darling, don't mind your grandfather, he just want to go and lime, and come back and see food and everything miraculously appear!" Wayne laughed getting up to go to the toilet. He wasn't up to an interrogation and he knew that's exactly what was going to happen. "Yes I have things for you to do too, so don't get any of your grandfather backside ideas. Organise yourself and let's get this show on de road, and by the way, the duck is for Terrence and dem, they coming to kill the pig later and Miss

Gloria and Madam Betsy are coming to help me clean the sorrel...thank you very much!"

"Granny I'm helping, but I don't really want to see Uncle and dem right now you know...for real" he replied hoping for an easy out. "But is now more than ever you need to be around your family boy!" Wayne kissed his teeth and exhaled loudly "Oooooh granny!" he yawned throwing himself back into the hammock. "I just not in the mood to see them right now, I can't be bothered to talk about shit..." He winced as he heard the word. He was conscious of the language he had been using, but the thought of cursing in front them now, seemed sacrilegious and he tried to catch it before it came out his mouth. "I mean 'stuff'" he continued grinning. "Hmph!" Isobel sighed, returning his grin. "Yeh that's cause of the things you're holding in your mind, the thoughts your keeping...take a break nah, what yuh think your problems will eat you cause you turn your back on them? Worrying about a problem when you don't have a solution just makes it bigger and attracts more problems to you. Boy laugh and joke, be happy for a while. Put down the load, rest your mind, it will make room for a new perspective, a solution, or God forbid, the problems just might solve themselves altogether!" Wayne sighed lazily, comforted by the wisdom of her words. He knew he'd have to face them sooner or later and resigned himself it would sooner. "Ok Granny, but Lord knows I ain't got no time for Miss Glory neither Miss Betsy!"

The morning passed in a bustle of activity. Wayne didn't have a moment to think about what awaited him in London. He helped his grandfather catch hold of three ducks before twisting their necks, submerging them in boiling water and plucking their feathers. He swept the compound with the cocoyea broom and washed down the dog house before sitting with his grandparents to chop up the 3 buckets of seasoning needed to prepare the Xmas meats. The smell of finely chopped thyme, spring onion, chive, shadow beni, garlic and pimentos inflamed their taste buds, encouraging them to break at 11am for an early lunch. After a plate of curry duck and dumplings prepared by Papee, Isobel conceded to their request. "Ok, allyuh could go on, but remember they coming about four o'clock for the pig eh!" "Lord Father!, how come yuh send meh such a wonderful woman ?" Papee asked, one arm extended to the sky whilst the other tugged at her dress.

"Man move from here eh, Wayne, take your grandfather before I change my mind or before Madam Bet..." "Good afternoon,' came the voice from the front of the house. Isobel grinned at her husband. "Go on." She said softly. Wayne donned his grandmother's boots and the pair headed through the bush, shortcutting the journey to John's house, and avoiding the Inquisition into his escapade to London. Isobel had every intention of letting them go. She wanted to keep Wayne busy, keep his mind in the present, too busy to worry about what lay in wait for him, or what he'd been through, long enough for him to change his perception of his life. She smiled as she watched them head past the advocado trees. Everything was going to be ok, he was home and she would take care of him just as she'd done his father. This time she knew she had one week left and unlike her son, she knew the form his devil would take. She closed her eyes and squeezed out the thought, focusing on her breathing until it disappeared. It was enough time. It would have to be.

"Boy how you looking so miserable so!..what you leave your woman in England or what?" A heavy set man wearing a torn t-shirt and well-worn loose boxer shorts greeted them warmly. Wayne couldn't help but smile. "No...I just have a lot on my mind right now Uncle" he replied shyly. "What, woman problems?" John continued deftly peeling an orange before passing it to him. Papee laughed, "Man, not everything stem from a woman yuh know, oh gosh!" John kissed his teeth. "Man, every single problem I had in my life, I sure I could trace it back to a woman!" he announced assuredly. Papee laughed even louder. "I take it Carina not home then?" he replied. John grinned at Wayne. "So tell me all about London, the bright lights and the big city man!" Wayne exhaled audibly. "What, it was dat bad?" John asked raising his one eyebrow. Wayne sat in silence, not sure how to answer.

'Was London that bad?' he turned the question over and over in his mind until he could find an answer. "No, but the people real different Uncle." Papee could see him struggling and answered for him. "He just got tie up with the wrong crowd." "Orhor" John continued as if he fully understood, eager to berate a naughty child. Wayne felt inflamed at the simplicity of Papee's answer and John's response. "No!, that's what I mean gramps, you guys just don't get it. You still got this idea of everything being perfect in

London, like some kind of fairy tale or something! That is so far from the reality it's not even funny!" "Go on..." John encouraged, intrigued by Wayne's outburst. "Right now, there's a war on, or at least that's how it feels to me! My life's in real danger, and that's just normal, that's just how it is. When I get back there, I have to watch my back and I have to be ready to slaughter somebody for not giving me proper respect. Right now, my boy is dead because of me, and man and mans just waiting for me to get back to deal with that liberty...and I'm going to!" The adults looked across Wayne at each other. "Whey boy, dats a real heavy burden yuh carrying dey boy!" John returned softly. Papee grunted, "Yuh telling me! Man Isobel don't even want him to go back!"

Papee was glad his friend broached the topic. Eager to hear his view, he sat quietly whilst the two spoke. "And how you planning on dealing with it?" John continued. Wayne kissed his teeth, as a tear of frustration rolled down his cheek. "I don't know Uncle...but it's a life for a life innit." "But what de arse is dis! You serious boy?" Wayne nodded his head. "So how is it your fault that your friend died?" John asked, amazed at the words coming out of such a young mouth. "He was avenging me Uncle. I got shot innit, and whilst I was laid up, he went to deal with them and got shot himself." Wayne replied. "Jesus Christ!" John exclaimed, horrified at Wayne's predicament. "Uncle, everybody have their own turf and every turf wants to feel like they're the boss, you understand?" John nodded his head. "So you ready to take a life? do you know what that feels like, cause I can tell you it's not nice, and you going to carry that with you for the rest of your life?" "I don't have a choice Uncle, whether I'm ready or not, it's going to happen, that's just how we're living." John shook his head. "That's not true, you always have a choice boy, in everything, every day. But to be able to make that choice, you must know who you are, you must be confident in yourself and where you want to go. If not, you will choose based on what people are doing around you. Anything this one or that one says or does or expects, is the bandwagon you will jump on, because you don't have your own rules to follow. And how can that choice be right for you? they are not you, so it will always be a wrong choice for you, that's why you must always keep at the back of your mind, who you are and where you are going, that way you could never be misled or misguided."

Papee smiled at Wayne, "Yuh understand him?" he asked passing him another orange. "Yeh, I hear what he saying" his grandson answered. "Good." John slapped him on the back. "Just think about it, because to me, and I is just a old fart country farmer eh, something is missing or a link is broken or damaged or something, cause it sounds like all yuh feeling powerless or hopeless or both, but instead of addressing that, all yuh trying to feel good or empowered by making each other feel small. But that is not respect, that's just fear and that can only be maintained by causing more and more fear. If respect is what you're looking for, and not a hole in the ground or a hole in a jail, you need to take a long hard look at yourself...a long hard look." John paused checking Wayne's face as if to determine whether he was understood. "Not so Papee?" he continued, hoping Wayne would marinate on his words. His grandfather agreed, vigorously nodding his head, trying to quickly swallow a mouthful of orange pulp. "Wayne is a young boy, he's a good boy, and sometimes in life you forget where you're going because of everything going on around you. It might cause you to get on de wrong bus, but, it is what it is. What to do from there now, is de crucial point, de game changer, shall we say; will you continue on the wrong bus or do you have the nerve to get off and get on the right one that's going where you need to be?" Wayne heard the words of his elders and tried to make sense of them. They rang true and simple, but he knew that was because he was away from it all, he wasn't so sure how they would sound back on the estate.

Before long, John heard Carina return home, shouting about the fence repair before she even reached the front door. "Oh shit!" The three laughed quietly as he rushed them over to the damaged fencing, posing as if they'd been working on it all day. "Three hard back man and all yuh in the same spot I left you in since this morning! Don't try dem tricks on me old man!" Carina quarrelled playfully. John attempted to explain but she cut him off with a look. "just fix it!" "Yes darling" he answered robustly, muttering to Papee and Wayne under his breath, "yuh see what I mean when I say woman is the cause!" The trio laughed until Wayne's sides hurt.

∞

"Granny I can't believe you still juking clothes on a juking board!" Wayne announced, earnestly concerned that she should still be washing clothes like that at her age. Isobel smiled, wiping the sweat from her forehead. "Boy I'm used to this, don't worry about me." He hung a pile of wrung clothes on the line for her, and sat on the steps watching her finish the wash. "How you doing baby?" she asked, "how you feeling about things?" Wayne stared at the soapy bubbles cascading down the juking board. "I alright granny." he answered finally. Isobel smiled. "You is a soldier like your father, but I know you're carrying a heavy load. I can't help you carry it, but let's see if we could make it a bit more manageable nuh?" Wayne looked up, "how you mean?" he asked curiously. "It's all about perspective, you either looking from the perspective of the problem or you're looking from the perspective of the solution. Just a guess, but I would say you've been looking at the problem, not a solution." she grinned, raising an eyebrow as Wayne reviewed his mind set before acknowledging his agreement. "There's no solution to this granny, not as far as I can see anyway, taking out Bucky is the only thing I can do!" "That's because you're looking at the problem, and incidentally, taking out Bucky won't solve anything, won't revenge still be on the menu, or is it all going to be friendly after you do the deed?...I doubt it!" Wayne said nothing and exhaled.

"You do know you can choose how you want to feel right?" Wayne looked at his grandmother and raised an eyebrow. Isobel smiled. "It's true. And do you know that you vibrate the energy of what you feel? That vibration, is the language God speaks. God gets your vibration and returns to your life things that match that vibration. So how you consistently feel, is like a magnet that attracts more of how you consistently feel into your life. Remember every request or prayer is answered every time, but you have to speak the language, words are not heard, vibrations are felt. So when you're feeling doom and gloom, what do you think you will get in your life...more shit to feel doom and gloom about, problems! Scientific fact my dear! But when you're feeling good, feeling happy, what can you expect to see in your life....more shit to feel good and happy about, solutions!" Wayne exhaled again and almost kissed his teeth. "Granny, how can I possibly feel good with this hanging over me, my life is fucked! Excuse my language. What is there for me to feel good about? seriously, I can't think of anything but Cs and Bucky, and trust there's nothing good there!" "I hear you child, but you CAN feel good, you just have to choose to, and decide that you're going to feel good. And when you do, you'll realise just how much there is for you to feel good about. And the more you practice feeling good, the more you open up to seeing a solution popping up in your mind just so just so! And I say practice, because I know shit does fly every day eh." Wayne laughed as his grandmother paused to point at his grandfather. "But so long as when you take stock at the end of the day, the biggest part of the day, you spent feeling good, feeling happy, then you going in the right direction, you're sending the right vibes as you young people will say. No matter how dark it gets, I want you to always remember, God matches vibrations...emotions, and sends you experiences to sustain that vibration, that's how prayers are answered. Shit will still happen, but when it does, don't focus on it, just choose to feel good and you will experience more to feel good about, and less and less to bring you down!

Wayne couldn't remember the last time he was happy, he was either ok, or not ok. "To tell you the truth granny, I don't really see happy that much...not in me or the people around me...and I can't just get happy just so!" Wayne replied cynically, though intrigued by the conversation. "Of course you can!" Isobel responded adamantly. "Happiness is a choice, just like anger or sadness eh! Always remember that, don't wait for something good to happen to get happy...choose to be happy and something good will come...be stressed and something stressful will come! That's how life works...every time!" His grandmother's earnestness made him giggle. "I serious boy" Isobel continued. "Come help me wring these jeans." Wayne jumped up and took the bucket of rinsed clothes. "I'll do it granny" he answered eagerly retrieving the pile of trousers. She smiled as he kissed her on the cheek on his way to the clothes-line. "Wring dem good eh, I don't want to have to wait till in the morning for them to dry!" Isobel teased. She watched him as he wrung the pants, shouting at him to shake out the creases before hanging them. "Yes ok granny!" he replied, exaggerating the shake.

"Do you know the phrase, 'I'll believe it when I see it?" she continued as he returned to the step and sat at her side. "Yeh" Wayne answered. "Well you know what I've discovered boy?" Wayne had no idea and shook his head. "Well, what I've discovered, and I'm talking through experience eh..." Isobel paused, raising an eyebrow to emphasise her point. "I didn't pick up all these wrinkles and grey hair for nothing you know!" Wayne grinned in acknowledgement. "Anyway, what I've discovered, is that the real truth is 'I'll see it when I believe it.'" Isobel waited for Wayne to digest her words, wondering if he would accept the contradiction. "You understand where I coming from?" Wayne slowly nodded his head trying to visualize her statement. 'I choose to be happy, in spite of what's going on around me, so when shit does fly, like when Miss Mary start talking her shit or blight take the pigeon peas or your grandfather working my last nerve, I don't dwell on it, I give it five minutes, some good curse words and I move on. Remember, it's how you feel that speaks to God and how you feel is what is sent to you. If I dwell on it, I will stay vex, and if I stay vex, I can guarantee that they, somebody or something else, will do something again to get me even more vex, and then something else will happen, until when I finally look up, it's cause I'm ready to take the cutlass to somebody backside".

"Oh my days Granny!" Wayne laughed aloud. "You're killing me here!" he added before testing the validity of her theory in his own life. After a moment he nodded his head in agreement, seeing the pattern of his thoughts and his life in her words. "It's true" he agreed. "Yuh telling me! Boy I learned that the hard way. I wasted countless time feeling vex and looking for revenge, I spent time on that same merry go round you on right now, keeping myself stuck in bacchanal, going from one drama to the next! One day I finally just got tired. I realised that I was the one keeping the bacchanal in my life, by giving it my attention, my thoughts, my time, my emotions. So I chose to just stop. I stopped giving it my energy and fuelling it, and you know what happen?" Before Wayne could shake his head, his grandmother answered her question. "It just fizzled out! Dried up and evaporated! It stopped being a regular feature in my life. It still shows up every now and then, but when it does, it's stay is very brief because I don't energise it, I deliberately limit how much time I allow my mind to focus on it! At first it was a lil hard, because my mind wanted to react how it normally did eh, you know, get vex and ras somebody, but I stuck with it, I believed and now I know for sure, believing is seeing! You can definitely choose to be happy and you can definitely create the life you want. If you really want something different, regardless of what's going on in your life, give your attention to what you want more than what you don't want, believe in what you want over what you see, and it will be.

He listened intently, subconsciously feeling the truth in his grandmother's words. "You could sum it up like this. When anything, whatever variety, good or bad, is happening in your life, God is asking you if you want more of it. You dwelling on it, whatever it is, is saying yes please, give me more. You taking your mind off of it, is saying no thanks. And dwelling on something else, is saying I want this instead." Wayne followed the formula in his grandmother's words until his eyebrows knitted, and Isobel laughed. "Actually granny, that's the opposite of what we do, but I feel like it's right." "Test it, that's how people get what they get baby, whether it's good or bad...it's your attention to a thing that brings it into your life...so you see, you are in control of what happens to you, it's not 'God's will' as people like to believe!" Isobel replied earnestly. "You have power over your life, use it, don't just give it up. So, if you believe it before you see it, and remember all a belief is, is a repeated thought, you can make your life, exactly how you want it." She paused to wipe the sweat from her forehead and dry her hands on her dress's hem. "Ok, last load." She grinned as she passed the bucket of clothes to Wayne, looking to see if her words registered. Satisfied, she left him to dwell on them, breathing a hopeful sigh of relief.

Wayne finished hanging the clothes and lay down on the hammock, dangling his feet over the side. Isobel's words were so simple, and yet they were the opposite of what he normally did. He puzzled over it, not understanding why he'd never heard it before, yet in the deepest part of him, her words rang true. At least now he understood why his prayers were hardly ever answered. "Wow!" was all he could think as he dozed off. Hours later, a mosquito buzzed past his ear, landing smoothly on his forehead.

Turning to itch the irritated spot, he half opened his eyes in time to see his uncle Terrence jumping down from the climbing slates of the coconut tree. He rubbed his eyes open, stretched and sat up. "Eh eh!, you wake up!" Terrence grinned, chopping the top off of a coconut before handing it to his nephew. "Thanks man" Wayne eagerly replied, retrieving the heavy nut.

The coconut water was sweet and cool and Terrence deftly chopped the husks in two, revealing the soft jelly inside. Wayne scooped it out with the coconut 'spoon', repeating the process with another nut before unbuttoning his shorts and laying back in the hammock. "Ok you ready?" his uncle asked, swallowing a last spoonful of jelly. "For what?" Wayne asked quizzically hoping whatever it was didn't involve manual labour. "To kill the pig!" Terrence answered pointing at the post and hoist securely holding the animal. Wayne looked over to the orange grove following his uncle's finger. He made out his grandmother placing a pan under the head of a pig. "Oh shit, ok let's go." He jumped off the hammock and stepped into the old garden boots Papee had given him. Terrence handed him a knife with a ten inch blade and a bandana. "What's this?" Wayne asked, wondering if he was going to help kill it. "Well, that's what you're thinking about doing back in London right, here's your chance to feel what you're going to go through".

Panic surged through his being in the moments they took to reach the post. Terrence covered his face from the nose down, and gestured for Wayne to do the same. The pig had been cleaned and gleamed in the sunlight as Terrence and Papee stood on either side looking at Wayne. Terrance ran his thumb across the pig's throat and waited for Wayne to perform the deed. Wayne's heart raced, shooting from a distance with a gun was one thing, entirely different from doing it so up close. He walked up to the animal avoiding looking into it's eyes. It was a big pig, and he wondered if it knew how close to death it was. He ran his hand down its side and felt it's heart beating. Lifting the knife, he placed it against the pig's throat. "Do it quickly boy, you will have the pig in distress!" Isobel urged. Wayne drew the knife across the surface of it's throat but barely cut the skin. The pig wriggled in it's harness, emitting shrill squeals that caused his stomach to heave, threatening to return the coconut jelly. "Wha, you can't do it or what!?" Terrence teased, secretly glad it wasn't easy for his nephew. "I'll do it, give meh the knife" he added. "It's alright Uncs!" Wayne returned, trying to sound nonchalant. He took a deep breath and pressing as firmly as he could this time, he drew the knife across the pigs throat. Blood sprayed then poured out into the pan Isobel adjusted to catch the flow. Feeling suddenly weakened, he sat down, staring at the life and blood draining out of the animal. Seconds later, he got up and darted into the foliage, releasing the jelly that made its way back up to his mouth. Isobel, Papee and Terrence grinned as he returned with a flushed face and a weak smile. "You vomit boy?" Papee teased, "Don't mind dat and don't study Terrence, he went through de same ting went it was his first time and I was glad, it show me he don't take life for joke!" Isobel deftly removed the pan full of blood, poured the thick dark red liquid into a waiting pot, and replaced the pan to catch the remnants.

The trio returned to the house where Isobel set the blood to boil, mixing in sweet potatoes, oats, onions, breadcrumbs and seasoning in a big dutch pot. Papee brought four glasses and poured four drinks, one, more coke than rum and passed them amongst his family. "Yes Fadder, give thanks!" he exclaimed raising his glass to toast. They each swallowed their drink, finding a spot to relax. "So your grandmother tell meh you have some troubles boy!" Terrence revealed, hoping Wayne wouldn't mind them discussing him. "That's some deep shit you find yourself in there man! How yuh coping with that?" Wayne shrugged his shoulders, feeling a familiar pit return to his stomach. "I don't know Uncle, I just have to deal with it innit." Silence fell between the pair of them, each perusing the same issue, but from different perspectives.

"Did your grandmother tell you her formula?" Wayne nodded his head. "Well what I go tell yuh boy? I can only tell you what I know and how I live my life. The first thing is, I use the formula! In addition to that, you have to watch the friends you keep, the ones you see regularly, because where their focus is, is where yours will be. That's why they say, show me your friends, and I'll tell you who you are. The next thing is, you have to know where yuh going. Get a book and write down where you want to be in five years' time and in ten years' time. Figure out why you want it, and write that down too, and think about that everyday too. Work out what you need to do now, to put you on that road. Do something every day towards it, even if that means just imagining it. Imagine it, like you already doing it or you already have it. As you start thinking about these things every day, after a while, you will see things showing up in your life to guide you to that goal, then you'll start making the choices to keep you on that road automatically. You have to make your life the way you want it, it doesn't matter what the situation is. That's why, just the way you watch the friends you keep, you have to watch the thoughts you keep too, especially the ones you think regularly, because those will become the things that show up in your life. Yuh understand?" Terrence paused intently, hoping he'd explained himself clearly.

"Kinda..." Wayne answered feeling a familiarity in his uncle's words. "Ok, do you understand that it's your regular thoughts or beliefs about yourself that cause you to make the choices that you do, to take the actions you do?" Wayne pondered the question. He knew his priorities and choices as a Millitant had changed his thinking from who he was before, he saw the world differently when he was with them, he felt different with them. But he felt empowered, and it felt good. "Yea I guess so" he replied slowly, not sure where his uncle's train of thought was heading. "Ok, so what do you think these Millitants think or believe about themselves, deep down, you know, when they're alone and they're not trying to impress anybody?" Wayne grinned, "That they're bad man! Dons! On top the pecking order, the bosses!" he grinned, sure of his reply and of himself. It was Terence's turn to grin. "On top of the pecking order!" his uncle exclaimed "I like how you put that! But what exactly are they the bosses of, what pecking order is it that they are on top of?" he continued, removing his grin, replacing it with solemn sincerity as he looked earnestly into his nephew's eyes. Wayne kissed his teeth, suddenly irritated by his uncle's line of questioning. "Ok ok, don't get vex with me nephew, I'm just trying to show you a motion, because if they were as you say, surely there would be obvious signs right? Plans, ideas, a trail leading to their rank? You know, academic attainment, business success, banking experience, respect from the masses, should I go on? But the truth is, and this is just from what you've told me, I can tell by the shit you're in right now, that they don't think much of themselves. I can say that confidently because if they really thought they were bosses and on top the pecking order, they would be preparing for their future, laying down goals, they would be hopeful, and expectant of the future. They wouldn't be taking such high risks for such small rewards. They would know their own value, and what they're worth. They'd want to invest in themselves and their futures, doing the ground work, laying foundations; if they felt they had one, and that it was bright!

Terence buttered a piece of bake and Wayne paused to digest his words. He'd never really thought about it like that and it momentarily stunned him. "You are the owner of your life boy. Think about it, think about your friends, your thoughts, your dreams. If you're truly happy with that then cool, but if you're not, then instead of following it through, change it! You can figure something out, you can fix it if you believe you can, if you believe you can't, then you won't. You feel me, it really is as simple as that! How you choose to use your time and your mind, that's what life comes down to, in my experience anyway!" Terrence grinned at his nephew, squeezing his shoulder as he handed him a slice of the hot buttered coconut bake. "So you see, choose what you consistently think about. Choose who you consistently hang about. Have a plan. Use the formula. Practise it and you will see the difference. Don't be so concerned about what your friends are doing or how they see you. Be more concerned about your perception of yourself and your plan, because if you think you could only do this and only go there, you will be correct and that's what you will generate in your life. Likewise, if you make a plan, have big goals and know yourself, you will also be correct, and that's what you'll generate." His uncle's words hit home to Wayne as clearly as chalk on a blackboard. Simple as it was though, he didn't really have a plan nor had he thought of his future.

"So when you going back?" Terence asked his nephew. "Three days." Wayne answered sombrely. "I wish you guys could come with me man!" Isobel looked at her husband and laughed. "Boy, you cyah ask me to leave here, for what, leave my land for a microwave and a inside toilet...you making joke yes?" Papee grinned refilling his glass. "Just to see it init." Wayne answered, thinking it strange that he wouldn't want to. "You know why I love de bush?" Papee continued laying back in a hammock. Wayne shook his head, "The peace...a man could think here, he could get to know himself and as for de hard work, dat is exercise for the body man..." he teased in his version of an english accent, striking his favourite pose. "How you think I looking so good? I tend to my land, and my land tend to me. That mouthful of fresh air you just take come from those fig tree dey, orange, pommeseterre, plum, look over so, grapefruit, cedar, mango, pommerac all dem big ass tree in de bush over so. They are what gives you that mouthful of high grade air you just put in your body!" The trees need my carbon dioxide and I need their oxygen, so where I going? I need de tree, and de tree need me!" Papee teased sipping his drink and raising his glass for a toast.

At that moment Wayne finally understood his grandparents and their love of the country. It was ok that they didn't have a microwave or an inside toilet, it didn't make them any less important or happy or alive, and he began to understand himself. He didn't need the things nor the people he thought he did, he just needed to know himself, to have a plan so he would know when he wasn't on it. The remainder of the evening passed jovially and Wayne slept easily, thinking maybe all wasn't lost after all.

∞

He woke to a silent house and lay on his back staring at a cobweb in the corner of the ceiling. It was two days before he was due to go back and all that he'd been able to push to the back of his mind or rationalise over the past days were suddenly at the fore. In two days he would be back on the frontline, the peace of mind he'd internalised from the words of his elders disappeared, leaving him irritated that he was stupid enough to think that they could help. This was fucking Tamana, he might as well have called it Lala Land for how different from the reality of London it was. He sat up, trying to stop the barrage of thoughts deepening the frown between his eyebrows. The more he tried though, the more consuming they became until it was all he could do, to prevent himself punching a hole through his grandparents' wall.

By ten o'clock, Isobel and Papee returned from their days work on the land, dragging two crocus bags full of cocoa pods behind them. Wayne stayed in his room as he heard the noises of their return, hoping they wouldn't come to find him. He wasn't in the mood for their joviality, and didn't want them to see his anger. Half an hour later, the building heat in his room, forced him to retreat to the breezy shade of the back of the house, and their company. As he slouched down the back steps, Isobel took one look at his face and knew something was wrong. Judging by the crimpling of his mouth, she knew he was thinking of Black Ice and his vengeance. After their morning greeting, she gestured to his breakfast under the cheesecloth on the table. "So you looking forward to the fete with Semp and de boys tonight?" she asked enthusiastically. "No, not really" he replied shortly, I ain't really feeling to go nowhere granny." He answered sombrely, and with a tone that did not encourage further discussion. Isobel disregarded it and continued, "Why? just go and enjoy yourself nah boy?" she encouraged, knowing what he needed was a distraction from his thoughts. Wayne kissed his teeth, "Granny, when I go back, it's all about the street, man is gonna be on my case straight away! There's no point in me being over here pretending everything will be ok, cause it won't!" Isobel bit her lip. "Yeh ok but worrying about it isn't helping either, it's just preventing the solution from coming to you, and making the problem grow bigger and bigger." "Granny, look, you don't know what you're talking about!" he replied tersely before getting up and walking through the house to the front porch. Isobel followed on his heels.

"You can't keep dwelling on it sweetheart, you'll keep it in your vibration and if you keep it in your vibration, you'll keep it in your life!" "Aaaarrrrggghhhhhh!" Wayne exhaled angrily leaning over the porch wall with his head in his hands. "Look, I hear what you're saying, I just don't know how it's going to work when the shit hits the fan. I have to hit the ground running granny, there's no time to get your mind right over there, it's just on, twenty-four-seven" he continued trying to control his rising irritation. "But that's just it see, you have to have time by yourself, make time, time to stop thinking, to cleanse your mind, so you can understand who it is you are and what it is you want otherwise you'll think you want what the people around you want and dat might not be the right choice for you! Look, let's do something now, my fadder always said, 'experience is the greatest teacher'.

Isobel sat on her rocker in front of Wayne. "Sit down and close your eyes..." "Granny..." "Just do it, humour me if you will...keeping your eyes closed, look upwards. Inhale deeply, hold it for three seconds...exhale and hold for three seconds. Keep your attention on your breathing, as thoughts come in your mind don't fight them, just return your attention to the air filling and emptying your lungs. Be aware of how your entire body is feeling as you breathe in and out and how it feels in between your breaths. If there's any uncomfortable sensations anywhere in your body, put your attention on them, just feel them, don't analyse them, or judge them, and continue inhaling and exhaling. Remember the point of meditation is to silence your thoughts, to quieten your mind, to create gaps so God can work her magic!" Isobel continued eager that her grandson experience the relief only a higher consciousness could bring. Wayne felt too self-conscious to relax, and at first he couldn't stop his thoughts or stop opening his eyes every few seconds to check he wasn't being observed. "As soon as you realise you're having a thought, just return your attention to your breathing." Isobel peeped at his face. His eyebrows were still tensed so she knew he hadn't yet managed to stop his thoughts. She repeated the process for ten minutes before his face relaxed and another ten before she was sure there were longer and longer gaps of nothing between his thoughts.

"Ok, open up, how you feeling now?" she asked, hoping he was able to create enough 'no thought' gaps to make a difference. Wayne stretched and looked around. To his absolute surprise, he felt relaxed and at ease. "Woa! yeh, I actually feeling better now granny!" he nodded smiling. "Good, your perspective has shifted a little; so when stress comes up again, and it will, but unless you know the answer to the issue, just say ok. Then deliberately look for something else to think about, and if you can't conquer that, stop thinking altogether, just meditate, stop your thoughts, and it will pass. Not only will it pass, but as you practise meditation every day, you will align yourself with your spirit, with God and you will be inspired to certain steps to easily deal with anything in your life.

Wayne looked at his grandmother, overwhelmed with appreciation for her wisdom "I real love you yuh know granny!" Isobel smiled, "like cook food ent!" she grinned immersing herself in the look of adoration he bestowed on her. "I want you to meditate every day from now on, do it every morning and in a few days your mind will start clearing and you'll see the difference, less struggle and more flow, I guarantee it!

He got up and hugged her. "I wish I could put you and gramps in my suitcase and bring you back with me." Isobel grinned picturing herself and Papee squeezed together in a suitcase for a nine hour flight, "and what you will do with a old ass like me up there?" she laughed out loud with her hands on her hips. "You don't need me babes, you just need to believe in yourself and everything that's not up to speed with that, will just melt away. I can't do it for you, you have to do it for yourself." "I hear you granny, but it would just be so much easier if you were with me." "I hear you too, but I know you could do it! Wayne nodded his head in agreement more in acknowledgement of the fact that they weren't coming than in him being able to persevere in their absence. "Now go and help your grandfather dance de cocoa, and think about going for de lime with Semp, it might do you good." He hugged his grandmother and walked down to the cocoa house. Isobel watched him walk away and prayed that he would heed her words.

The succulent white cocoa seeds, put to sweat, and covered with banana leaves since his arrival, were now brown and spread out to dry on the rolling floor of the cocoa house, allowing the gum to dry up and easily fall away. Wayne found his grandfather with his trouser legs rolled up, gingerly manoeuvring back and forth on the beans, holding the overhead wooden beams for support. "Want some help gramps?" he asked, hoping the old man didn't fall. He climbed up the three concrete steps to the doorway of the mechanised structure, took off his slippers and washed his feet with the bucket of water on the top step. After half an hour of 'dancing the cocoa' beans, polishing them with coconut oil in the process, the pair were sweaty and aching. Papee kissed his teeth, and wiped his forehead with the bandana always kept in his back pocket. "Boy that's it dere yes! I tired!" he exhaled heavily, "you want to take a spring bath?" Wayne could think of nothing better and eagerly nodded his head as he made his way out of the cocoa house. Grabbing his cutlass, Papee joined his grandson already standing in the cool of the forest's edge. "Let's pass this way and get some coconut nuh, my belly rumbling, your grandmother trying to prove a point, and say she ain't making no bake, so I had to eat de shop bread!" Wayne laughed. "I not eating no damn shop bread, but I not telling she that cause she too damn stubborn, but I not going back hungry either!" he added adamantly "I feel you gramps, but I know you know granny don't muck about when she's proving a point!" The pair laughed. "I know, but where you think she get that from?" Papee grinned winking at Wayne, "...obviously don't tell her I said that though, it's good to let a woman feel like their name is boss every once in a while, it keeps the engine running smooth!" Both Papee and Wayne laughed aloud in the silence of the bush, sending birds flying from tree tops, squawking irately at their uninvited visitors.

They arrived at the spring and stripped down to their boxers before jumping into the pool of emerald water. Papee emerged, cupping handfuls of the cool liquid and dousing his head. "Oh yes fadder!" he exclaimed before swimming over to the heavily laden mango tree over hanging the other side of the spring. Wayne floated on his back watching his grandfather return with two armfuls of fruits which he let float in the water between them. "So how yuh feeling about life now boy, you getting any respite from your troubles?" Wayne laughed, "Kinda I just trying to figure things out you know!" "Yeah, that's a hard nut you have there to crack boy! I don't even know what I would have done had I been in your shoes! I tell you this though, and I didn't learn this till I was in my thirties I think, but you see hope, hope moves mountains when you don't know where to even begin. Hope is what opens doors, or allows you to even see doors and 'way out' signs. When you have no hope, that's when you let struggle, pain and lack into your life, that's when you really lose your control, your power. You stop looking for doors or 'way out' signs, because you don't think there are any...so there aren't any. Without a way out, you start to contract, and your life begins to stagnate, oscillating just within the confines of your limited hopeless beliefs. And as you live it, and dwell in it, your thoughts become more and more hopeless, creating more hopelessness. But you see hope, hope is an interruption and a disruption to any problem you could have. Know it will get better and it will, don't have hope and it will get worse!" Papee sucked the flesh of the ripened fruit and relaxed his body on the surface of the water to float. "Keep that in mind when you can't figure your way out." "O.k I will Gramps, thanks!" Wayne answered relaxed, appreciating the empowerment of his grandfather's words in the security of his company.

∞

By 10.30pm Semp's brother pulled his truck into the driveway, softly tooting his horn to alert Wayne of their arrival without disturbing his grandparents. Wayne splashed on a little of his Calvin Klein cologne and smoothed the straggly hairs in his eyebrows. Lacing up his Converse, he closed the door quietly behind him and gingerly walked up to the truck avoiding kicking up the red dust on to his new white Nikes. Robin grinned and immediately grabbed him, putting him in a head lock. "Boy, you get pretty dread, don't think you too pretty for dis eh!" Wayne struggled to break free to no avail. "Boy you crimpling up my jersey boy!" he shouted trying to drop Robin with his left foot. "Oh gosh leave de boy! Come leh we go nah!" came a female voice from inside the cab of the truck. Robin released his grip, allowing Wayne to break free, slapping the back of the bigger boy's head as he escaped. Robin kissed his teeth, pretending to be vexed before extending his fist and then embracing his friend. "Good to see you horse." "For real dog!" Wayne returned.

"Woa, Dapper Dan!" Semp exclaimed watching Wayne walk towards them. Wayne grinned, striking a pose. "Best watch your gyal..." he exclaimed as he jumped on to the open bed of the truck. "Boy, you couldn't get my tings...you could only wish for something like she, but don't worry, I go find something for you to hold on...Marissa coming or wha?", Semp asked the group of boys seated around him, eyeing Wayne for signs of familiarity. Wayne kissed his teeth and shouldered his friend before greeting the other occupants. "Boy don't play in your ass eh, you can't be talking bout King sister...boy fuck you nah boy! he added, remembering the overweight girl with the moustache from his primary school.

The night was cool and clear as they resumed their journey on the potholed road. Each hole caused the boys to bump up and down on the metal ridges of the truck's tray. "Dis is when I'm happy being fat cause I kno all yuh boney asses getting a good scrapping right now" a plump boy declared victoriously. Wayne and the rest of the boys couldn't help but laugh as the left front wheel went into a sudden drop. It sent them each about eight inches in the air, landing with a bounce on the ridged iron floor. He winced, shifting his weight to one bottom cheek. Semp banged the top of the drivers cab to get his brother's attention. "A boy, my ass can't take dat pressure dread, slow down nuh!" he implored. Laughter erupted from the front of the truck as instead, it speeded up. Semp kissed his teeth, "Boy, you is a cunt boy!" he shouted as he tried to hang on to the side bar. "Leave him, we reaching just now and I go take dem gyal he trying to impress!" he continued, picking a dot of fluff from his t-shirt. This time the back erupted in laughter. "Take which gyal, boy you's a virgin still dread, who gyal you could take!" Heads exclaimed kissing his teeth. "A fuck you nah boy! Virgin which part?!" Semp continued indignantly. "Don't worry boy, he only buss he gun last month!" Fingers interrupted eagerly. More laughter erupted from the truck as the boys wrestled each other to the floor. Wayne thought about Ellie, he hadn't in a while, but driving under the open night sky, he wondered if she saw the moon he was looking at.

Before long they reached the fete and the boys jumped down, straightening baggy t-shirts, and dusting off three quarter length shorts before scanning the crowd. "Ok, we setting up here" Robin advised, pointing to a spot under a huge tamarind tree. He supervised the boys as they set up a generator, six speakers, amps, and decks before making his way to the other side of the field, signalling Fingers and Heads to follow him. Wayne, Semp and the rest of the boys surveyed the crowd, looking for signs of possible entertainment amongst the girls in attendance. He felt alive and he was aware of it. Not sure why, he smiled to himself and stretched, truly appreciating the once familiar feeling. Heads and Fingers returned five minutes later, struggling with an oversized aluminium basin, packed with ice and full of beers. "Now that's what I'm talking about!" Semp grinned, pulling out a 5ml bottle of forty percent proof puncheon rum from his pocket. They each reached in for a drink, toasting the sound man skills of Amazon as their mic man opened the set.

"Listen I regret how we get away de other day dread, for real" Wayne said momentarily reminded of his actions the last time they met. He respected his friend too much to just let it slide. He was wrong and he felt no way to say it. Semp kissed his teeth. "Boy you think I studying you? Well actually I have been, but I not studying it like dat, if I was in your shoes who knows, I might have been the same. Just cool dread!" his friend grinned, extending his arm and slapping Wayne on his shoulder. "You's still my dawgie, don't worry!" Wayne grinned, glad his friend made it that easy for him. "Look, it's only natural that people get affected by the shit we come into contact with; our surroundings, our friends, our school, the people, the weather, you follow me?" Wayne nodded his head. "Ok good, so if I living there, and all I hear about, see about or feel about every day is, fucking up my vibes, how I go feel after a day of living in that, much less a week, a month, a year, forever? So I think I understand how you feeling, but seriously, I don't understand why you going back?"

Wayne looked at his friend. It hadn't crossed his mind to stay. "I being real, why go back horse?" Semp extended his arm and encircled the forest that cocooned them. "I get what I need right here, that's why I staying right here. Do you get what you need over there? It don't seem like it to me." Wayne looked at his friend and bowed his head, 'why should I go?... could I stay?' he thought the words aloud, but didn't have an answer. Semp paused, opening the cooler for some fresh ice. "I still want to go doh!" Beenie grinned, touching Wayne's extended fist before side stepping Semp's extended arm and open palm. "Yuh mudder cun..." was all Semp could say as Beenie and Heads pushed him to the ground, sitting on his chest. The rest of the boys raucously voiced their agreement and laughter rang out, absorbed by the heavy base coming from the speakers.

"So what's the females saying?" Beenie asked returning to the upturned beer crate next to Wayne. Semp kissed his teeth. "Boy I could put a fresh pot of pussy on your lap and you wouldn't know what to do with it!" "So yuh feel!" Beenie replied, positioning himself horizontally on the crate before gyrating on it. "Boy, go back to school eh!" Heads shouted, snatching the crate and placing it in a variety of positions, gyrating his hips all the while. Wayne couldn't help but laugh. "Cunt yes!" Semp laughed wondering if Wayne had popped his cherry. "Come we go get some food nah?" he gestured to Wayne, motioning his intention to the rest of his boys. Within minutes they each held on to paper plates of curry goat, rice and green salad. Silence hung easily in the air as they ate the succulent, well seasoned meat, refilling their plates before returning to their spot near the giant tamarind tree.

"Ok go back I guess but all I want to say, is that revenge shit, could never be good, you should forget dat!" Semp stated flatly as he handed Wayne a Stag beer. "What, you mad boy, dats de first scene dat have to get handled!" Wayne replied pulling a face to reinforce his seriousness. "Mama always told me, looking for revenge is like you drinking poison and expecting your enemy to die from it." Wayne kissed his teeth, "so...what, I should just let it ride...is dat what you're telling me?" he continued beginning to feel slight irritation. "Look, fuckery is fuckery, it don't matter who dishes it out, what you put out is what you going to take in. It's more of a percentage fuck up thing!" Wayne laughed, spitting out the sip of Puncheon burning past his lips. "What are you talking about?" he replied looking totally confused. "Horse, if you fuck up people ten percent of de time, than by all certainty, you will be fucked up ten percent of the time!" Semp continued searching the bucket for a Guinness. "Yeh, so if you bless up a boy, you bound to get blessed." Wayne agreed. "Ok then, so why fuck up your life trying to get somebody back, it's unnecessary, and it's dumb, because your jeopardising yourself by doing something that's going to get done anyway...yuh feel meh? What you put out there is what comes back, one way or the other, it coming back in your ass!" Semp paused, opening his Guinness with his teeth. "Ah you!" Wayne grinned jumping up in the air, "I see where you're coming from!...alright!, alright!" he exclaimed as if a lightbulb had illuminated his mind. "...but I want them to know it's me though."

Semp kissed his teeth. "What they think is that important to you?...whey big boy!...wha happen to you dread, you used to be a leader not a follower!" he sighed, "You real change boy." Wayne kissed his teeth. "Yuh think?" he answered, knowing full well that his friend was right. "It's not like here man. You have to live it to understand it, I can't explain it, that's just how it is there. It's kill or be killed and you have to have your soldiers. It's not about grades or your goals or anything like that Semp, it's about what you're wearing, how much money you're spending and how bad you could be, that's it!" Wayne dug his hands into his pockets and looked around. Semp tried to put himself in his friend's shoes, to understand his perspective.

"Maybe I wasn't so lucky to go to England. Maybe I wasn't lucky at all...look what I gave up and look what I got!" Wayne exhaled and looked at his friend. "I feel yuh dog...that's why I feel you should just stay!" Semp replied. "Yeah, I hear that, but I can't leave my moms...I dunno...Jah!" Wayne shouted with his head back and hands clasped on top it. "Don't worry horse, we'll figure it out", Semp assured his friend. "Come we go take a wine on a tick ting!" The boys agreed, each ready with a signature move as they made their way to the gathering of gyrating bodies. The dance went on till 6am. Wayne was dropped home, and after a truck load of fist bounces, he staggered to the front door, high and happy.

He slept heavily, waking only when Isobel roused him for something to eat at five o'clock that evening. "Morning granny!" he announced chirpily making his way to the toilet. "Morning? Child, young people not supposed to be sleeping all day!" Wayne laughed, "Oh gosh granny, in England, no-one gets up before twelve o'clock you know!" "Twelve o'clock!...by that time I finish my day's work, bathe and cooking food!...anyhow you're not in England now, and I think you going with your grandfather tonight." Papee emerged with two shot guns, handing one to Wayne before returning with cloths, what looked to Wayne like long cotton buds, and a small can of oil. Wayne perked up immediately. He'd always wanted to hunt with his grandfather, but had always been too young. "We leaving at eight eh, be ready!" Papee announced sitting next to him. Wayne grinned like a Cheshire cat, his sleepiness suddenly replaced with an uncontrollable urge to hop, skip and wine.

"My God granddad....I just can't believe it, you know how long I been waiting for a chance to do this with you!" Papee grinned and proceeded to take his weapon apart and gestured to Wayne to do the same. It was an old well worn, sawn off rifle, but to Wayne, it may as well have been a brand new Glock. Still smiling from ear to ear, he gingerly dismantled the barrel, butt and arm rest before meticulously cleaning, oiling and polishing it. The rifle wasn't loaded but he aimed at a grapefruit and pulled back the hammer pretending to shoot. Papee laughed. "Just watch where you aiming dat tonight eh, as a matter of fact, you walking in front of me!" Wayne laughed, "don't worry granddad!" He gave him a pair of old pants, a long sleeve jersey and a well-worn khaki hat. Wayne put them on straight away. "What we hunting?" he asked his grandfather and in the same breath, "how am I looking?' he asked his grandmother. They both laughed, happy to see their grandson in a mood befitting someone of his age. "Just mind yourself out there, and keep alert!" she demanded. Papee grinned, "Don't worry woman, you think I will let something happen to your grandchild, no sah!, I love my balls too much!" Isobel kissed her teeth. "Remember dat eh!" she returned teasingly.

By 8 o'clock the hunting party were gathered in Romero's front yard, the gateway for easy access to the night's chosen hunting grounds. "Eh eh, small man making de trip tonight!" Wayne recognised the voice of his old principal and scanned the gathering. "Hi Sir", he announced as he found the familiar face of Mr Ayoung. At the same time, John and a handful of other men joined the group, each louder than the last, and each with a bet on who was bringing back what, from the night's escapade. The night was clear with a big beautiful full moon. Stars twinkled brightly in the vastness of the dark blue sky. Wayne felt alive, eager to get the night under way but his elders had different ideas. First was a toast to the success of the night's ventures. Expecting to leave any minute, Wayne kept hold of his supplies until after fifteen minutes, he realised departure, far from imminent, rested at the bottom of the bottle of White Oak. An hour later, Papee finally stood, making the call for the hunt to begin.

The bush was pitch black as they began the three mile hike to the camp. After a few minutes, they left behind the last remnants of electricity and were completely consumed in darkness. Wayne could barely make out the outline of his hand as he stretched it out in front of his face, keen to ward off anything, plant or animal, that may take him by surprise. The night dwellers filled the air with their sounds and calls, encouraging him to hug his weapon tighter and be thankful for the thick socks his grandmother gave him to stuff his trouser legs into. The group walked steadily and silently, and as promised, soon enough his eyes adjusted to the dark and the light of the full moon.

Before they reached the camp, one of the dogs, Simba, picked up a scent and darted off into the bush, with Papee, John, Chester and Wayne giving chase after her, listening earnestly until they heard her barks signalling she had an animal trapped. Ten minutes later, they arrived in a small clearing with a bed of fallen leaves. Simba was focused on a bamboo patch, barking furiously at it's centre. "Alright boy, alright boy, good boy" Papee repeated softly, appeasing his dog into submission so he could inspect the patch. They each aimed their guns, lighting up the base of the bamboo clumps with the torches securely fastened to their barrels. The roots were thick and dense, making it difficult to see anything. "I'll smoke it out, but this one is Wayne own." Papee confirmed, gathering a fistful of dry leaves. Wayne's heart was already racing. Adrenaline rushed in waves through his body, causing his arms to tremble as he held his weapon aimed at the roots.

Seconds later Simba found a route in, and scrambled amongst the roots in search of the animal. "Cock your gun, get ready, I looking for it to come out over there so." Papee shouted pointing to the other side of the clump. Burning a root, he fanned it until the flame died and placed it as far into the clump of twisted roots as he could reach. The men positioned themselves and waited. Seconds later, a pair of eyes shone brightly under the foliage as Wayne pointed the nozzle in it's direction. They couldn't yet decipher what animal it was, manicou, agouti, tapir or lappe. Suddenly, it moved it's position and Wayne had a clear shot, it was an agouti. "Don't stick! Don't stick! Leggo shot!" Papee urged, keeping his eyes on the roots. Wayne stood immobilized, wanting to pull the trigger, but seemingly mesmerized in the eyes of the animal. Moments later, released from his trance, he pulled the trigger releasing a casing of buck shots in a thunderous clap, throwing him backwards to the ground. Papee and John, both cocked and ready, looked at each other and grinned but kept their aim. Seconds later Lover froze, silently sniffing the body of the lifeless animal. Wayne got up holding his face, and trembling with exhilaration. This time Papee and John laughed aloud, signalling for him to collect the agouti. Wayne was still shaking. His legs felt wobbly and his body coursed with adrenaline. "Yes boss, yuh did it, how yuh feeling?" his grandfather asked, sizing up the dead animal under the light of his torch. "I good." Wayne answered, not really sure if he was. He felt euphoric but somehow filled with dread. His mind was blank, he either felt really good or really bad but in that moment, he couldn't differentiate. He hardly noticed the journey as they returned to camp.

∞

After a belly full of wild meat and dasheen, the men opened another bottle of rum and began their second favourite pastime, old talking, easily passing the night away in a fervour of animated discussion. Wayne sat against a wooden beam on the hardened dirt floor forcing the food into his mouth and trying to breathe as his grandmother had shown him. To his surprise and irritation, the discussion turned to his trip to the village shop. Angst consumed him as he awaited their judgement, and he readied himself for the attack. It wasn't necessary. Tears came to his eyes as his grandfather immediately rose to his defence, explaining the gravity of his grandson's situation. The group paused, exhaled and fell silent as each pondered the depths of their behaviour under times of stress. "I always hated that phrase 'when in Rome, you must do as the Romans do!" Mr Ayoung spoke, breaking the pause. Wayne squirmed at the prospect of his teacher's lectures, equally aware of his duty to listen. "I do because it could mean in certain situations you can give up yourself...like Third World, I always resented that title!" he continued throwing his arms downward to emphasise his point before calling for more ice.

"I don't understand Sir" Wayne continued, suddenly aware that he'd missed the old man. "And I not too sure mehself!" teased his uncle Earl, returning the cup after chipping off a piece of ice from the block. "Ok, sit down let me school you then, it's been a while since you have been in my classroom but the key rules remain..." "Close your mouth, open your ears and open your mind...then open your mouth!" Wayne interrupted, surprised at his own recollection. "Aye ya yai hear my boy, so you didn't forget everything then!" his old principal exclaimed proudly, tapping the back of Wayne's head as he sat down.

"We have been labelled as a Third World country, whilst our labellers, have taken on the title First World country, so already you should be able to see that this game is about competition, exclusion and supremacy. According to them, they are first and we are last, their way is good, our way is bad, or at least not as good as theirs. Therefore, they are the teachers and we are the students, and so if something is not sanctioned and authenticated by them, it is not valid or worthy.

You following me?" Mr Ayoung enquired, pausing to ensure the group understood his words. Wayne quietly nodded his head, digesting what he had just heard. He'd never given that perspective any thought but was intrigued with the innate resonance his teacher's words provided. "What then, do you think the average citizen of the First World will think about the average citizen of the Third World coming to their land? and conversely, how does the Third World citizen feel about themselves when in a First World land. I don't know about you, but the phrase 'less than' comes to my mind. And so you see, that will be the route that is assigned to you, and so if you are unaware of yourself or have not set your focus or made a plan, you will take on that which has been assigned to you, 'less than', because that will be all your mind will have access to.

Here's an example for you. How is the son of God represented?...a blue eyed white man...not so?" Wayne nodded in agreement. "And so bearing in mind what you have been taught of geography in my classroom; when you think of the climate, and indigenous peoples of Bethlehem, Jerusalem or any place in that part of the world, how then is it possible, for Jesus to be this blonde haired, blue eyed man?" Wayne laughed and the group raised their voices in agreement. So from the get go, this lets us know, there is an issue here, and that you must not allow these people to decide who you are, because they only have their best interest at heart. Therefore, it is imperative that a man knows the greatness of who he is, so that he knows the realms of that which he can become, and consequently, cannot become something that has been caged, curtailed, limited or pre-defined."

The silenced gathering erupted in acknowledgement of the wisdom in the teacher's words. "That definitely calls for something sweet, eh Teach?" Earl smiled slapping his back as he passed over the White Oak bottle. "You understand what dis man telling you boy, take it in because none of us are coming on that plane with you, we won't be there to guide you or to nurture you!" Earl opened his arms to engulf the gathering in the old wooden structure. "You have to keep it up here", he pointed to his temple, "and in here" he continued slapping his chest before engulfing Wayne in a bear hug. "I love yuh, yuh know dat right?" Earl asked as he squeezed his nephew. "Yes Uncle! I love you too!" Wayne replied grinning, feeling awkward and comfortable at the same time.

"So you see, embracing the limited route that is being given to you, can cause you to lose yourself, lose your dreams and lose your focus as you become the 'thing' that your surroundings have allowed you to become. Then you complain about what has been done to you, when it is you that has embraced their ideas, models and perceptions of you and lost your own. You see your mind is constantly thinking about things which eventually make up your life. You will notice if you take a moment to look at yourself, that your life is a picture of the things you think about the most. So if you are in a situation that is not necessarily nurturing towards you, you will be thinking about what you are living and so you will feel, and so vibrate and so receive, what you are thinking." The puzzled look on Wayne's face made Mr Ayoung laugh. "You with me or I lose yuh?

Let's put it this way...you cannot receive what is being broadcast on 104.2 FM, when you have your radio set to 90.9FM. You can't then want to get vex with the radio, stamp your feet, fling it against de back wall or complain about de shop where you buy it from. What I'm saying is, you can keep things out of your life and you can bring things into your life. What you keep in, and what you leave out depends on what you think about the most. So when you are on their route for you, and you are confronted by their offerings, remember what YOUR plans are and where YOUR focus should be. That's why the rich get richer and the poor get poorer. Every day, from the moment they awake, the poor man thinks about the bills they have, and how much they can't afford. The rich man on the other hand, thinks about what they are buying next and how to make more money. So you see, they are both thinking about money; the poor man thinks about the lack of money and so receives that, whilst the rich man thinks about more money and so he receives that.

And as a young man, you want to fit in right!...I know this, it's extremely difficult to be on the outside looking in! You're damned if you do and damned if you don't, I know...for I was young once too yuh know!" The gathering laughed, each one reminiscing for a brief moment of the days of their youth. "Don't watch this crispy beard, and wrinkly skin, and out-a-timing clothes and think I don't know yuh know!" "I know, I know!" Wayne responded laughing. "And doh laugh too hard either, because this is also what is waiting for you...if yuh lucky!" "Aye-ya-yi!" Papee exclaimed. "But all joke aside, I know it's easy to get caught up in the mind set of your surroundings, but if you pause and bring to mind your plan, your focus, you will be reminded that the currency they are trading in, is only valuable amongst themselves and others of similar trajectory, but crucially, you must remember, the world is so so much bigger than them boy!" Wayne exhaled and stretched his legs. He understood his teacher's words but it wasn't as easy as that, he was only a child, how could he stand up to a way of life whose purpose seemed entirely to distract him from his goals, his manhood. Mr Ayoung could see his resistance and indeed, expected it.

"It's not hard, I know it seems that way when all you could think about is your trouble, but stop for a minute, put your focus back on your goals, ask yourself, where do you see yourself in three years or five years' time?" Wayne churned the question over in his mind remembering the moment it was first put to him by his uncle. As simple as it was, he still didn't have an answer. Mr Ayoung laughed. "This is what I'm talking about, this is why what everybody else doing becomes what you doing!" the silver haired teacher explained. "To be happy I guess" Wayne answered finally. "Ok, so what does happy look like to you?" Wayne smiled, "I dunno..., a car, clothes, working..." "Ok, so what kind of car, what kind of clothes?...what kind of job?" Wayne grinned. "I dunno, nice ones innit..." he replied sheepishly. "Well how nice, are you going to need a job that pays five dollars an hour, fifteen dollars an hour, fifty dollars an hour or five hundred dollars an hour?" his principal continued. "Five hundred dollars!" Wayne replied "Finally, a sure reply! So there's the answer, it's immediate, and so if that is the case, shouldn't you be focusing on plans to achieve that instead of plans to take you in the opposite direction! You can't say you want this but put your energies into that! My point is simple, perhaps their way is the wrong way for you." Wayne nodded his head in agreement. "So then don't lose yourself following them...use your mind to get you where you want to be!"

By the time Mr Ayoung stopped for a pee, Wayne felt relief in the formation of a new perspective. It was London, not him! He had been sold a lie, been fooled into thinking he was going to have a better life. He exhaled audibly, it felt good to have something other than himself to blame for his predicament. "Look like you getting schooled again boy!" Papee joked, slapping his grandson's upturned knee as he sat beside him. "You alright?" "Yeah I cool gramps, I'm listening to Mr Ayoung, he's making sense. I don't know, if mum made a mistake carrying me to London..." Papee kissed his teeth. "Eh Eh!, don't blame your mother, she was trying so hard to give you a better life, to have what she didn't have, and in trying to get that, she just overlooked what she did have right here that's all...she's your mother yes, but she's also human too!" Wayne said nothing. "I just know if I stayed here, my life would have been so different, just normal, London just ain't a good place for people like me."

Wayne exhaled and stretched out on his crocus bag, gazing up at the clear night sky. He pictured all the things in the way of him focusing on his goal, and in a few moments, he felt a familiar anguish settling under his heart. Papee sipped his drink, listening to the night's sounds beyond the camp. "You alright boy!" he asked observing the despondent look on his grandson's face. Wayne lifted the corner of his mouth and shrugged. "How can I, when I live where and how I live, not get caught up? How can I achieve my dreams, everything around me is a nightmare...I don't even know my dreams!" His grandfather swallowed the last mouthful in his glass. "Boy just stay here then. You went, you see it, you didn't like it and you come back! Nothing wrong with that!" "That place sound like it would suck your spirit out!" John added refilling Papee's cup, "sound like when me and Carina just get married, and we had to live by she father house! Man, dem people was evil yuh know, just waiting for me to put a foot wrong and setting trap cause they waiting too long!" The gathering laughed in agreement, each acknowledging their experience of feeling unwanted.

Wayne's relief at not being the cause of his predicament or at least that it was understandable, was short lived. Mr Ayoung returned. He'd heard the entire conversation and wasn't about to let Wayne take the easy way out. "Don't blame London! Negative and positive are everywhere! You've nothing and no-one to blame but yourself!" Wayne's heart dropped into his belly and he bowed his head. "You either chose it intentionally, or you chose it by default, by getting caught up in the fears of the ignorant, because you didn't have goals or you didn't choose to focus on them. Whatever it was, it was your choice, so it's your fault. It's that simple I'm afraid."

The camp fell silent at the teacher's words. The sounds of the night dwellers, usually a dull hum in the background suddenly seemed to deafen in their intensity as eyes fell from Wayne and his teacher to the ground. "Yes, we understand, it's not what you were expecting. And we see that you are not in a nurturing environment. But true power, and the mark of a man I think, is to know himself through all of this, to keep his focus despite what's happening around him, to be confident enough to listen to his own gut, to focus on his goal and not the goal being offered to him! To focus on his potential for excellence, focus on the success of his fore fathers who came before him and accomplished huge feats, opening doors regardless of what was holding them closed! Do you really understand your potential? Your ability to create, your resilience, your innate intelligence? Do you understand your natural born greatness? I'm not sure you do, otherwise you wouldn't sell yourself so short. Mr Ayoung paused and raised his glass. As a black man, do you know it's your kind that invented the alphabet!...the wheel!...mathematics! That's the stock you come from, that's the capability you have!

Do you think all these magnificent black men didn't go through, in their time, much more than what you feel you have to go through now?...and they made it right! You think Jesse Jackson or Olaudah Equiano or Dr King let adversity stop them? They didn't say, 'oh but the white man doh like meh' or 'the teacher don't like meh' or 'I have to join a gang', or 'de boss man not hiring meh....no! not at all! Instead, they said 'fuck that!' or words to that effect, excuse my language eh, but it was called for. Mr Ayoung grinned. Pardoned by the crowd he continued. "No sah! They held firmly to their own ideas of who they knew they were, kept their focus in the forefront of their minds, and so achieved their intentions. They didn't wait for racism or discrimination to stop and they didn't need to be nurtured by the society they lived in! And so young man, don't go back there thinking their way is better than yours, or that you have to embrace the lifestyle that is being offered to you..." "Be man enough to make your own mark!" John added. "Exactly!" Mr Ayoung agreed.

∞

Papee and Isobel busied themselves with chores as Wayne finished packing and dressed for his journey back to London. He surveyed his room and exhaled before making his way to his grandparents in the back. They were all unusually quiet, each wrapped in their own thoughts about his impending return. Wayne was ready to go, he was going to miss Tamana, and everyone in it, but he'd been missing his mother since he left her. His thinking had changed since his arrival and he felt confident in his decision to return. The prospect of seeing the THM or Black Ice no longer filled him with dread. He'd formulated his plan and they weren't included in it. Somehow, their priority position had been dislodged, but he knew, only time would tell if his new perspective would override the will of the street, of Black Ice and of his boy Marcus.

"How yuh feeling...you ready to go?" Papee asked his grandson as he stripped the hard purple skin from a thick stick of sugar cane. "As much as I'll ever be", Wayne grinned. "Nah for real, I think I have a better understanding of myself and I guess how life should work, so yeah, I'm good..." His grandfather nodded his head and smiled. "You are the same as a plant." Papee reached over the back of the wooden bench and retrieved a tray holding a dozen saplings in small black plastic containers. Passing one to Wayne he explained his statement. "If I don't tend to it, it will grow anyhow-anyhow, if at all! If I want to pick fruits from it, I have to weed and hoe. Only then do I plant it. While it growing, I still have to keep my attention on it. I have to make sure it have enough water and sun, that it ain't ketch no blight, no insect terrorising it, nobody trampling on it, no weed suffocating it. If I don't tend to it, it will struggle to survive. More than likely weeds will over-take it, blight will play mas on it, it won't get a fair portion of water or light and soon enough it will dry up. It may still grow but I'm not so sure about the fruit it will provide" Pappee sat in the hammock next to Wayne with his cutlass and finished skinning his stick of cane.

"But I could still bring it back though, with a little time, love and patience, it could fix back and grow big and strong like de starch tree." His grandfather pointed to the starch mango tree to the left of the front balcony. "Now, the birds sit in it and sing to me every morning, it blocking the sun from de porch so I could get shade in the afternoon, and every couple of months I does get the sweetest starch mango boy, well you know!" Papee grinned kissing his fingertips. "And all that is because I tended to it when it was young, just like you have to tend to what's going on in here," Papee knocked the side of his head, "...and in here!" knocking his chest. "It's the same with we humans, what you put in, is what you get out. Take time to know yourself, learn who and what you are, what tools you have, what strengths and what weaknesses you have, keep your peace of mind...value and treasure peace of mind above all else! Make a plan, then move in the direction of your plan. Just set your mind to it, don't be distracted by the distractions that are in your life, and you will reach it! I have utmost faith in you, God has faith in you...now you need to have faith in yourself" he concluded earnestly. "I hear you gramps!" Wayne answered feeling suddenly invincible. Papee passed him a stick of the peeled cane, and the pair lay back in their hammocks listening to a chorus of mid-day birds. Soon enough, Isobel joined them, preferring instead, the familiarity of her rocking chair in the cool spot at the end of the hammocks, they each sucked and chewed the sweet fibres, discarding the remains on a well placed crocus bag.

"You know what I was thinking granny?" Wayne asked as she sat down. "No what? pass me some of de cane." Isobel replied stretching over to retrieve a stick from her husband. "That it's the normal way of life for us over there. Feeling that anxiety, feeling that imminent danger sensation, living under that stress and that angst, every day like it's normal. We take it, we accept it and internalise it and act from it like it's nothing, like it's normal. Look how easily I got used to it, became it. I completely forgot how it feels to feel how I'm feeling now, stressless, untense, relaxed, I feel like I can breathe real deep. I haven't felt like that over there since I landed." Wayne exhaled, still holding their attention. "That's not good nuh, it sad, I feeling all kinda how that you going back there." Isobel returned. Papee picked up one of her legs and placed her foot on his hammock, rubbing it's arch as Semp called out from the front of the house.

"Ooii" Wayne returned, alerting him to their presence at the back. "Good day, good day! So yuh leaving we again horse?!" he announced finding a seat on the wooden bench. "Boy I have to go back, but don't worry, this time I going with my eyes open." Semp grinned and touched Wayne's closed fist. "I have to go dread, I have to let my boys know shit don't have to be like this, we can live different yuh know. Trust me when I say it don't feel good living like that. We don't even realise we don't feel good, because that's how we're accustomed to feeling...every day. We've forgotten what it's like to feel how I feel now. I have to do this, or my trip to England was a waste!" Papee looked at Isobel as Wayne spoke to his friend. "Sound like he have it...what you think?" Isobel returned his grin, assured that her grandson might be on the right path after all. Silence hung easily over them as tears rolled silently down Wayne's face. "Is cry you crying there?" Semp asked ready to release a few himself. "What yuh crying for, what happen you going and miss meh or wha?" his friend teased animatedly. Wayne grinned wiping the corner of his eyes. "I will miss all you guys man, I wish you all were coming with me, you know, just to hold me down when shit explodes!" Semp nodded his head in agreement. "Boy if you know you, you will be alright where ever you are. It's not about what or who is around you, it's about what you're carrying in your mind so it doesn't matter where we are, it only matters where your energy and focus are yuh feel me?" "Aye ya yi toast to that one papa!" Isobel exclaimed blowing a kiss to both boys at once.

Hours later and standing in front the international departure gate at Piarco airport, Isobel felt unusually helpless. She embraced her grandson, hugging him harder than he thought she could, all the while, her heart ached with yearning and hope for his future. Composing herself so as not to be overwhelmed by her emotions, she looked squarely into his eyes, hoping she didn't see signs that he felt the same. He too was consumed by his emotions, he didn't want to leave his grandparents and he knew what awaited his return but to her relief, his eyes were bright and his body relaxed. She couldn't remove her smile as she spoke to the empowered young man in front of her. "Well Papee, what should we say to this child?" she asked beaming widely. Wayne jovially kissed his teeth, reddening under their obvious gaze. "We love you and are very proud of you." Isobel began, "we know what you're facing and we believe in you. We're a phone call away." Wayne embraced his grandfather, already missing him. "Keep your mind ON what you want in your life and OFF of what you don't want. Spending time worrying about something when it's not within your control, just makes it bigger, like digging a deeper hole. But spending your time and energy appreciating the things you do like, or that are going well makes those things bigger instead, and brings to you even more to appreciate. Promise me you won't forget that.

Remember it's your perspective of a situation that makes you powerless or powerful. It doesn't matter what everybody else is doing, or who hates you or who's not supporting or nurturing you or even what's been done to you. All that matters is do you want it in your life or not, and if you don't, then don't let that be your focus, don't put your attention on it, don't feed it with your energy. Focusing on the unwanted disempowers you and keeps you small, disconnecting you from the power you share with spirit.

Remember your spirit, that's your true friend and counsel. Stay connected. If you don't know what to do or you are unhappy, or you're struggling, then you're not connected. Breathe. Meditate. Appreciate. Do whatever you can to connect. Listen to your emotions. Plan and focus on what you choose to become. Create the life you choose, you were born with the tools to do that, learn them, cherish them and above all, use them.

These boys, your teachers, the police...what and how they choose to be does not have to affect you unless you use your time thinking about them.

Don't carry hate or seek revenge; not only because it's like you drinking poison and hoping they would die from it, but because they are no better or worse than you. They are just experiencing what their focus has produced in their lives, not realising they have the power to connect and end their struggle, so they will just keep going round and around the merry-go-round, feeling powerless over themselves. That's why they only offer pain, because that's all they have access to. You have knowledge now, and knowledge is the only power you need, not brute strength. Don't use what's happened to you to fuel your anger, use it as fuel to overs it, to be more. And too, with power comes responsibility. So when you think of them, don't dwell on what they're doing, notice it yes, but don't feed it with your focus, unless it's something you want in your life. I know they've caused you to experience hell, but they are no better or worse than you, they're just experiencing different perspectives, so honour and respect the spirit that they are, and that you share.

It will be tough at first, but the more you get to know yours, is the more you will value and respect theirs. That is the salvation of your perception and when you know better, you do better." She kissed him, and stuffed a bundle of pound notes in his pocket. "Now go on, you know I don't like dragging out good byes."

∞

Hot Baths

Come to the edge he said - no they said, come to the edge he said, no they said, we're afraid they said - come to the edge he said - they came - he pushed them - they flew. Guilliame Apollinaire

It was a grey drizzly morning offering cloud filled skies, as the pilot announced the impending descent. Wayne buckled his seat belt and exhaled. He could see the plane's wheels and landing gear untuck from their position under it's wings. He put on his headset and looked out the window wondering when next he would see his grandparents and swearing to himself, things would be different. As the landing strip came into view, the frown, which disappeared unnoticed during his time in Tamana, returned easily, deeply etched between his eyebrows, also unnoticed.

Ivy held her breath as she eagerly scanned the faces appearing through the double doors. She hadn't spoken to him since the day he left. She remembered their argument vividly, and her gut wrenched in anticipation. She missed her son and was unsure if he'd missed her. Wayne saw her first, grinning uncontrollably as he made his way to her. He seemed bigger and lighter at the same time. He embraced his mother, lifting her up off of her feet. "Mom! I missed you man, I'm sorry mum, for real, I been a cunt...but...I'm gonna do better, I promise you!" Tears flowed eagerly down

Ivy's face only this time, they were of hope and joy as she walked out of the terminal with her arm around her son.

The pair made their way to the underground taking the train back to Victoria to catch the bus back to Hackney. But by the time they arrived at their destination, Ivy could see the change in him as soon as they got off the bus. The relaxed, approachable, happy boy that walked out of the airport only a couple of hours ago had gone, and been replaced with an exaggerated walk, and an attitude and expression to match. It aged him, she thought silently, as she too held her breath as they made their way onto the estate. Wayne felt everyone's eyes on him as he pulled the suitcase behind him. The wheels made an exaggerated noise, as if sounding the alarm of his return, until he finally lifted the heavy case and carried it to his front door. He opened his gate and walked through, breathing a sigh of relief. He wasn't ready to jump in the deep end just yet.

"Oi oi!" came a voice from behind them, stopping him in his tracks just as he crossed the threshold into the safety of his home. Wayne turned and saw Babs walking briskly up to him. "So you come back then!" Wayne smiled and extended his fist. "What, you thought I wasn't?" he replied lifting the suitcase through the door. "Well, you kinda went awol right in the middle of shit, mans needed you here, you should of known that bruv!" Babs continued with a smile Wayne knew was anything but friendly. Wayne kissed his teeth, "Look man, I just got off the plane, let me put my shit down and I'll be out innit!" he replied sternly, stepping into the hallway. "I can wait." Babs returned, eager to present him to the boys. Isobel called for him. "I said I'll see you later" Wayne continued with a coolness that belied the turmoil waging war in his body. He closed the door as Babs kissed his teeth, mumbling something Wayne couldn't decipher.

Ivy and her son talked until evening was upon them. At the end, knowing the full extent of his life outside their home, she cried for him. She was stunned, it was almost as if they lived in separate places. Yes she knew about the gangs and the killings, she saw the signs and dried flowers wherever she went, but it never occurred to her that her beautiful boy was a part of it. "What are you going to do?" Ivy asked, earnestly hoping his response would be something she wanted to hear. He looked like the fourteen year old boy who first arrived almost three years ago, as he searched for an answer. Finally he exhaled and spoke. "I don't know mum, honestly I really don't, I know I'm not a murderer, but at the same time I ain't no pussy neither. But I know I don't want to live that kind of life anymore...it's just not for me." Ivy exhaled, overwhelmed by the words coming from her son's mouth. "Look, I'm supposed to be at work in an hour, Andy might be home in a few hours, but I could stay with you if you need me?" "Nah, don't be silly mum, I'm a big boy now, badman don't need mummy protection yuh know!" he replied grinning. "You're not going out are you? I think you should stay in ok." Ivy replied looking straight into his eyes. "Everything's going to be alright mummy, I promise you, hurry up or you're going to be late." he answered lovingly, embracing her until she had to beg to be let go.

After she left, Wayne went to his room. Leaving his light off, he lay across his bed staring up at the shadow of the street lamp on his ceiling. His mind raced with images, scenarios and conversations, real and imagined. He strained his ears to listen for any voices in the swing park outside but heard nothing. He got up and walked to the side of his window, gingerly cracking the curtain to peer outside. It was empty and he breathed a sigh of relief before throwing himself back across his bed. Moments later he was asleep. He was awoken a while later by the sound of heavy banging on his letter box. He sat up with a start, heart racing as the knocking continued with increasing fervour. He tiptoed as silently as he could into his mother's room, and standing in the shadow, looked out the window, but he couldn't see anyone. As he tiptoed down the next flight of stairs though, raised voices revealed their identities.

It was Marcus and Babs. Wayne's heart somersaulted in his chest as panic took over his being. He sat silently on the bottom step hugging his knees as the letter box continued it's barrage against the door. "I'm sure he's home you know!" he heard Babs say after two full minutes of knocking. Marcus kissed his teeth. "And this is the man my brethren lost his life for!" Marcus replied kissing his teeth again. "I knew it, I told Cs he was a pussy and look now!" Babs knocked once more with enough force that Wayne was sure was going to break it. "I ain't got time for this shit man, come we go innit...pussy fe dead!" Marcus exclaimed loudly kissing his teeth. Wayne stayed on the bottom step until he was sure they were gone before heading back to his bedroom. He paced the small space left unoccupied by his bedroom furnishings, feeling increasingly powerless and caged. Thoughts and images of the past months assaulted his mind uncontrollably, until finally, in an effort to retain control he lashed out, sending his clenched fist through the plywood bedroom door.

At the same moment, a female voice called to him through his window. Wayne froze, it was only then he realised the uncomfortable pit, gone since his time in Trinidad, returned to the space in his belly, and expanded to consume his chest, neck and head. Bending down so as not to cast a shadow with the street light, he moved to the side of the window and looked out. His breath threatened to move the curtain and he dropped back. It was Ellie and some other girls. He looked at her and his heart, already beating like he'd run a race, almost stopped as he held his breath. She looked drunk, they all did. Instead of answering her, Wayne returned to his bed and lay down. He pictured his grandmother and tried to remember the words that provided such solace, guidance and hope, but his mind couldn't focus on anything but Ellie and the revenge he was destined to take.

Laughter came through his closed window as he lay on his back trying to imagine what had been happening in his absence. He tried to meditate, but couldn't stop thoughts enveloping his mind, he tried to imagine how he wanted things to be, but it just irritated him. His effort at relief would only muster a few deep breaths, but he concentrated on them, until a hundred breaths later, he finally closed his eyes for sleep. He dreamed of Cavell. His friend stood at the top of a block of flats, dangerously close to the edge. Wayne stood at the bottom, sure Cavell was going to fall, even more sure that he would catch him if he did. The fall, initially about twenty feet, kept growing and Cavell kept being blown back and forth in the wind. Wayne ran back and forth in front the building, trying to stand just where his friend would land but couldn't keep up. As Cavell drew closer, he heard his screams and ran even faster, determined to catch him. In the last moment, the dream slowed it's motion. Cavell turned his body to look into Wayne's eyes and in the second of impact, he grinned.

Wayne woke abruptly, sitting up as he tried to calm himself down. His room was cold but his body was wet with sweat. He recalled his dream vividly, aching that he hadn't caught his friend and wondering why he grinned at him. Before he could figure it out, the sound of pebbles on his window pane interrupted his reverie. He knew immediately it was the THM and sat on the floor underneath the window. "A!, lickle bitch!...pussy hole!" Babs shouted into the silence of the night. "Little pig, little pig, can we come in?" rang another voice Wayne couldn't make out. Laughter rang through the quiet of the estate as he sat with his head in his hands, waiting for them to get fed up and go. "Oi Wayne! Stop fucking about and come down will ya, I'm fucking freezing out here!" Diggy shouted. "I don't think he's in" he heard a girl say. Babs kissed his teeth. "He's fucking in, he's just too pussy to come out and handle his business like a man...bitch arse nigga!" After a few minutes the voices died down and Wayne stood up, peeping through the crack at the side of the curtain. He couldn't make out who was who, but faces and heads, covered with hats, hoodies and scarves were occupying the swing wall. Wayne dropped back to the floor, hoping they didn't see the movement in his curtain. He didn't know what to do, his mind raced in circles with no reprieve in sight. He knew he didn't want to do what they wanted him to do, he just didn't know how he was going to get out of doing it, and if he would survive it.

A brick crashed through the window pane, sending glass splintering over his head as it landed on his bedroom floor. "We're waiting yeah!" Marcus shouted as the cold night air rushed into his bedroom. Wayne dared not make a sound as he slid sideways away from the window in preparation for more, but none further came. The Millitants retreated noisily and as he heard them leave, he breathed a sigh of relief. He stood and looked through the net curtain just as Ellie turned for a last look at his window. Their eyes met for a split second before Wayne dropped back to his bed, embarrassed to have been seen by her of all people. She stared at the window for a few more seconds hoping to catch another glimpse, but he stayed out of sight holding his breath until he was sure she'd gone. She turned and ran to catch up with the group, annoyed he didn't acknowledge her, but saying nothing to them about it.

Wayne remained on his bed until long after they'd gone, consumed with fear of what was, and what would be. He finally got up in the darkened room, and made his way to the bathroom. Splinters dusted his forehead and he bent forward to wash them off under the shower. He looked at himself in the mirror and the taunts "bitch!, pussy!, dick head! swam round his thoughts, boiling his blood and fuelling his rage. 'Am I?' he asked himself silently, but no response came. Instead, tears of frustration now flowing in torrents, dropped off his face to the floor. He wished he'd gone outside and knocked Marcus out, and made Babs look like the cunt he was, but it was too late. They were gone.

Stopping himself from punching another hole in the door, Wayne turned on the light in his room, put a pillow case over the broken window and cleaned up the glass on the floor. Leaving the light on and half hoping they would return, he lay back on his bed and looked at the clock. It was 12.15am and he was wide awake and full of adrenaline. Still no clearer on his 'way out', he lay on the floor and did sit ups until he lost count, then turned over and did push ups until his arms burned, begging for relief. He turned on the shower and sat on the lip of the bathtub waiting for the water to warm up. His mind, though still full of thoughts, turned at a slower pace as he undressed and stepped under the shower. The hot water pounded the top of his head and soothed his body until he finally began to relax. "Talk to God child" he heard his grandmother's voice say, as clearly as if she was sitting on the toilet next to him. He opened his eyes with a start and looked around the small room. It was empty, but he heard the words in his mind again. Ignoring them, he resumed his shower, allowing the water to beat on his head, drowning out his thoughts. Half an hour later he emerged, bracing himself against the chill of his room, he lay on his bed and without conscious intention, began talking to God. It was 2am before his mind went quiet and Wayne finally drifted off to a heavy sleep.

∞

He awoke at 9am, unusually refreshed and with a clear plan of his next move. He smelt the aroma of fresh coconut bake wafting up from downstairs and knew his mother was home. Rubbing the sleep from his eyes, he stretched calmly, sitting on the floor to meditate before eagerly making his way to the kitchen, consciously aware of the absence of the pit in his stomach. Two hours later, the sun shone brightly and a cold wind whistled around him as Wayne searched for his friend's grave amongst the rows of headstones. As he searched for his name, he thought of the words he came to tell him and wondered what his response would be. At the end of the third row, two plots before the corner, he saw a small wooden cross with a name plaque lying on the ground next to it. It read "Cavell Jones 1992 – 2009". He was taken aback by it's stark appearance and for a while just stared blankly at the cross, wondering if Cavell was cold. The grave was covered in a bed of drying flowers, and they were covered in a melting blanket of snow, somehow unworthy of his boy beneath them. A sense of sadness and loss consumed him as the wind crept down the back of his hoody. "It's me fam...just come to show my respect and shit. I miss you man, no homo!" Wayne added grinning as he looked up to the sky. He took a deep breath and exhaled. "Listen yeah, I can't carry this on blood. It's not what I want to do, this weight is way too much for me and it's fucking with me...big time. I ain't about putting nobody to lie down next to you and I ain't ready for dat myself, you feel me?" Wayne paused, waiting for a response, looking for a sign that his decision was cool. None came.

He opened a 5ml bottle of Puncheon rum he'd brought back from his trip and spilled some on Cavell's grave before taking a swig. The undiluted liquid burned his chest, making him cough as he ingested it. "I love you bro, and I respect you for having my back, but I ain't playing this game no more. I just ain't doing it, it's pointless." Pulling out a pack of cigarettes, he sat on a discarded plastic bag on the grass next to his friend. He lit one and let it stand on the grave before taking another for himself. He inhaled, grinning at the grave, "sorry couldn't get no green, there's a shortage and shit, but here's to you my friend!"

Taking another sip from the puncheon and pouring some more out for Cavell, he told him about his time in Trinidad and the change in his perspective. "I miss you man...you were my big brother, I just can't believe you're gone...just like that, you're gone!" Wayne looked up at the sky and surveyed the cemetery. A hearse made it's way to the church followed by nine cars. He exhaled, the ground was hard, cold and unwelcoming, 'not a good day to be buried' he thought to himself. "And don't worry I'll keep an eye out for your mums and Keisha. I know you had my back, maximum respect for that...I know I could never repay you and I gotta tell you, no disrespect, I got mad love for you, but I'm not going to try. Wayne paused, half expecting to be struck with lightening for his audacity. "We gotta stop this blood, we got shit twisted...there's too much against us as it is, for us to be doing this to us, and it's pointless, none of us are winning! We're not living good, we're taking our own lives like we're so unnecessary, so cheap, so replaceable, so fucking dispensable!" Tears flowed once again down his face and Wayne laughed to himself, wondering if Cavell saw, and what kind of pussy he was calling him. He wiped them with the back of his jacket sleeve and exhaled.

"Look how we're living, everything's fucked up, and we embrace it like it's normal, but it's fucking not bruv! I feel like I'm on a merry go round and I just can't get off. And all I'm collecting along the way is fuckery! This is not how we're supposed to be feeling, it just ain't, and it's a long way from it!" Wayne exhaled and took another sip of the 'fire water', as a ladybug landed on his upturned knee. He looked at it and shook out his leg to get it off. It flew up, but moments later returned to the same spot. He flicked it again and it came back again. This time he paused, it returned to the same spot on his knee and he grinned. "Alright my friend, rest yourself." Wayne stared at the insect, wishing for a moment his life was as carefree.

"Looking over my shoulder every second in case a cunt try to step up. Living like we don't count, like we're worth nothing!...and we accept it blood!.. like it's true...we swallow it, breathe it...eat it, that's why it's so easy for us to take a life." Wayne dragged on his cigarette, blowing a puff of smoke at the ladybird. "We need guidance...I need guidance, we've spent our lives learning limitations which have led us to where we are now! We have to unlearn them...unlearn that we're just criminals, that we're not going to amount to much, unlearn that we can't have or do whatever we want, unlearn the hood trap, the limits we've accepted as our place in life.

Cs I feel so lost out here! I've forgotten who I am! In trying to beat a system that's locking us out, we've locked ourselves in! Somehow, somehow I'm getting out, and I'm bringing THM with me." By now Wayne's bottom was sodden from the melting snow and he was suddenly aware of how cold he felt. He got up and dusted off the ice stuck to his jeans, before looking at the remaining clear liquid in the Puncheon bottle. Smiling, he poured half on the wooden cross and drank the other half, groaning as yet again, it burned it's way to his stomach. "I'm sorry I didn't catch you man. I love you." He touched the dirt on his friend's grave and left the cemetery. Oblivious to Wayne, the ladybug moved to the shoulder of his jacket and accompanied him home.

The journey home past speedily as Wayne daydreamed of what was and what could be. He jumped off in Dalston, but instead of going to his front door, he made his way to the swing park at the back and sat down. The wind blew cold and sharp, but he didn't notice. He looked up at the broken window to his bedroom, and thought of Ellie. He missed her and hoped she'd missed him. He hadn't spoken to her since before he was shot, and he tried to remember their last conversation. "Fucking hell stranger!" Wayne turned his head to see Ade approaching from the back of the estate and grinned. "You going on like you don't know mans now!" Ade continued shouldering his friend. "What's gwarning bro?" he continued sitting on the tire swing next to him. "Bruv!" Wayne replied earnestly, glad to see him. They'd drifted apart over the summer and he wasn't sure how much Ade knew. "I been hearing the world a things blood, road is alive with drama about you lot! Wayne kissed his teeth. "Yeah it's true, but I ain't on that no more!" "Oh for real!" Ade answered surprised. "So what brought that on, I thought you was THM for life!" he continued grinning. Wayne kissed his teeth again. "Nah, shit's different now...I got plans and no time to waste blood!" he continued regaling Ade of his trip to Trinidad, his change of focus and his desire to share it with the THM. When he was finished Ade fell silent. "Sounds great...but I can't see any of them hearing what you have to say...can you?" he asked solemnly.

Wayne was glad his friend understood and nodded his head. "Well, I'll find out soon enough I guess" he replied staring at the space between the two swings. "So what you gonna do?" Ade asked, wondering how Wayne could take himself out of the game and still stay out of the ground. "I dunno blood, all I can do is keep waking up every day, try to do what my grandmother show me, try meditate, use my imagination on my plan, appreciate what going good, and deal with what each day brings." he answered exhaling. "Yeah but what about dem lot, word is, they're looking for you you know." Ade spoke looking seriously at Wayne. "I know, that's why I'm sitting out here, or did you think I just love freezing my dick off." Wayne replied smiling. Ade grinned, "Fuck me! Now that's da shit right there!...I'm in bruv!" he exclaimed jumping off his swing. "Nah, I ain't putting this on you blood!" Wayne grinned, inspired by his offer, despite his refusal. Ade kissed his teeth, "Yeah right, so you one gonna defend it yeah?" he continued animatedly extending his arms. "Listen, dem man ain't coming for joke you know bruv!" Wayne continued, resistant to his friend's pleas. "What you think I don't know this?" he kissed his teeth, "Look, I ain't got nothing to lose, I'm a dead man walking right now, but I'm gonna go out the right way...'on my terms' as your man say!" The boys grinned at each other and touched fists.

"Oi oi, de rat has come out of his hole!" The pair looked up, it was Babs and a few THM boys. Wayne's heart pounded in his chest, he was sure Ade could hear it but he didn't flinch and showed no fear as Babs came up in his face. "So what, you went out last night or what...had a date did you?" Babs enquired sniggering with the rest of the boys. Wayne didn't answer. "Did you get the present I left you?" Babs continued looking up at his bedroom window. "Oh that was you yeah?" Wayne replied holding Bab's stare. "You're a pussy fam!...but you know what, I got bigger fish to fry right now, I'll see you later though, for sure." Wayne replied, making a mental note. Ade watched the remaining boys crowd around them and stood up. One of the boys kissed his teeth. "Sit the fuck down you fucking bumpkin!" Chuckles momentarily erupted from the group. "Ohhh, it's Mr Goody Good Good!" Babs teased in a thick African accent. "What, you don't have no-body's arse to kiss today...fucking fool trying to be a grey man!" Passing his finger across Ade's cheek he continued, "That shit don't come off you know, no matter how polite you is or how much certificates you gets!" Ade stood his ground. "You're an idiot, true you don't even know!" he replied unflinchingly. "What!?" Babs replied, irritated by Ade's calm. "Yuh know what Babs, he ain't no sell out, what cause he learnt his lessons when you didn't, cause he spends less on his trainers than you do, cause he rock his Primark with pride..." Wayne looked at Ade and grinned. "You have to respect this dude cause he don't make his clothes...or his boys, speak for him. He stand up by himself, for himself. He's a bigger man than any of you lot, it's a shame I didn't figure that out sooner rather than later!" Ade struggled to mask his grin as he held out his fist to touch his friend. Babs kissed his teeth, "Yeah, yeah, fuck you and your mumbo jumbo yuh feel me!" he replied silently surprised at his younger's bravery. "Whatever man, if you want to feel I want to be a white man just because I'm taking myself and my future seriously and I'm not doing 'you', that's your business innit! I really don't give a shit, what you choose to do don't affect me, but let me school you for a minute. Firstly I rather save my money for a car than buy trainers every time Nike says they have something new. I rather spend these few years learning my school work so in ten years' time when you're making five pound per hour, I'll be making fifty pound...and riding in my Porsche...while you're at the bus stop...in the rain." Audible chuckles floated through the crowd. "Yuh feel me right...I know you do, you can't be that fucking dumb! You're always trying to go against what you think is the 'white man's' world in order to define your own world, but I don't have to be anti-white to be pro-black fam. I just am.

So yeah I am a full fledge AFRICAN black man and fucking proud of it! But I don't have to be ignorant and I don't have to be YOU fam. Yeh shit is set up against us making it that much harder for us to get in, but you're keeping yourself on the outside by not expecting more and acting like it's a good place to be. So Mr Babs, if anyone's a sell-out, you need to look at yourself first, cause you act the part that they created for you, Mr Lynch must be dancing in his fucking grave." Silence hung thickly in the air. "Who? What the fuck you talking about?!" Babs answered, annoyed that Ade was out-talking him, "Willie Lynch, 'how to breed a slave'...look it up!" Ade kissed his teeth and shook his head, "didn't YOUR mother ever tell YOU, ignorance is the root of all evil!"

"Cha, come we go, I ain't got time for these fools dread! Wayne you better step up fam, I'll see you soon innit!" Babs continued eyeing Ade up and down before backing out of the swing park. "When you're ready blood, you know where I be." Wayne replied calmly. As they retreated Ade breathed a sigh of relief. "Trust me when I say I was shitting bricks, I ain't cut out for this shit bro!" The pair laughed as they left the swing park. "Listen, do you want me to stay?" Ade asked earnestly. "Nah, I'm cool yuh know, I have to handle this on my own, but nough respect bruv, come check me tomorrow innit!" Wayne touched his friend and walked him to the bus stop before returning home. He felt good but he couldn't exhale just yet, he needed to see Ellie and Marcus.

The rest of the afternoon passed uneventfully, and he fell asleep in the front room. "Wake up Wayne, there's a young girl at the door to you." The voice startled him and he woke up with a jolt. Andy walked over to the couch and embraced him, welcoming him home, "It's good to have you back son." Wayne relaxed and grinned, "thanks...I missed you too." he answered earnestly. "Yeah right!" Andy replied pretending to punch him as he walked past. He hoped it was Ellie and jumped down the two flights of stairs, stopping only to wipe any sleep from his eyes before opening the door. It was, and his face lit up like a Xmas tree. He could tell by her grin she was happy to see him too, but shyly stood aloof awaiting his lead. He hugged her, lifting her off her feet until she begged to be put down. "I see you missed me then!" she said tapping the bulge in his crotch. Wayne grinned. "I thought you'd forgotten all about me babes, I been hearing all kinds a mad shit?" Ellie added straightening her shirt. "Never that! How's Tasha?", he asked wondering what shit Babs had spread around town. "She's not doing too good man, she's mostly better, her leg's still in the cast, but her spirit's fucked since Cavell passed. The only thing that puts a smile on her face, is knowing that cunt's days are numbered! I'm so glad you're back babes"

Ellie embraced him once more and their lips locked sending sparks of electricity through his entire being. Wayne pulled away from her and exhaled. "Hey, what's up babe, I ain't got bad breath have I?" she asked cupping her hand around her mouth to check. "Nah babes, it's nothing like that, but look, we gotta talk." he replied earnestly holding her hand and looking into her eyes. "What's up babes?" she asked concerned about the look on his face. He sat on the stoop and pulled her down to sit next to him, but he didn't know where to begin. "I saw you in your room last night you know, why didn't you answer me?" Wayne hung his head. "I've changed Elle." "What do you mean, changed, changed how?" Wayne turned to look at her but said nothing. "Don't tell me that alm's house I been hearing is true!?" she continued springing to her feet animatedly. "What alms house?" he asked holding on to her arm. "That you turn pussy!" Ellie replied exaggerating the word. Wayne kissed his teeth, "what, and you believe that yeah?" This time Ellie exhaled audibly and kissed her teeth. "It don't have to go down like dat, I ain't feeling it no more, I moved on to something else...we don't have to be living like this babes, there's so much more for us than this life for life crap...I can't fucking breathe!" Wayne answered, glad for the words to come out of his mouth.

Ellie looked at the ground and shook her head. "Look, you coming out or what? Them lot's waiting round the back?" Wayne sighed. "I want to talk to you man, come let's go upstairs for a minute." Ellie withdrew her hand and backed out to the gate. "Things haven't changed around here babes, you got whisked away to safety by your mummy, but we got left in the shit, we had to deal with it, we didn't have no knight in shining armour come to our rescue, we had to stay with it and we're still in it now! So don't come up in my face with no country shit about 'you've changed', and expect me to jump on your bandwagon, cause that shit don't fly round here, you know what the flex is, why you acting like you don't?"

Silence hung between them as Wayne searched for the words to relieve her, to let her know he had her back, when his actions made it appear that he didn't. Nothing came. "You know what Wayne, you know what I think, I think you're just a fucking coward!" Spitting on the floor in front of him, Ellie opened the gate and stepped outside, "I can't believe I loved you, I just feel fucking sorry for the time I wasted thinking you were the kind of man I wanted." She paused, waiting for him to look into her eyes but he didn't. He knew how she felt and he knew he was losing her, but he had bigger fish to fry.

He ran up to his bedroom and looked outside his window. Everyone was there, mingling on the swings, smoking, drinking and waiting. He saw Ellie huddled next to Marcus and their eyes met once again. This time, she alerted the gathering pointing a taunting finger up at the window. A flood of jealousy and betrayal washed over him, temporarily blinding and suffocating him until he had to sit down, forcing himself to calm down. The cacophony of voices grew in pitch and tempo as the crowd demanded he come to them. Wayne had every intention of going, but no intention of displaying weakness, and he stayed on his bed, taking deep breaths until the rhythm of his body returned to normal. "Life for a life blood, you know how we do, and it's your rounds!" Marcus shouted. "Time to pay the motherfucking piper!" Babs added, "...don't let daddy have to come and get you now!" Wayne blanked his mind, steadied himself and looked out the window. The crowd clapped and wolf whistled as he appeared, gesturing animatedly for him to come down. "I'm coming."

Moments later, he stood, surrounded on all sides by the boys who once had his back, and who now wanted his blood, as if he was the cause of every wrong they'd ever suffered. "So what's up? Mans is still walking on road without a care in the world yuh know!....what's up with that, you need to handle your business man!" Marcus began, circling him like a vulture on a wounded dog. Wayne kissed his teeth and eyeballed him until Marcus stood still. "Whose life you want me to take bro?...the man whose going to stop your granny from falling down? The person whose going to help your mom, teach your little brother, the man who could change the world, the person whose gonna mentor the next generation, the next Malcolm X or maybe the next Dr King...who do you want me to take out fam!? which fucking life shall I bring to an end!? And for what...?" Wayne breathed heavily as he stood in front of Marcus. "What do you mean who are you fucking taking out you cunt! Bucky innit, dick weed!" Marcus replied menacingly. "I ain't looking to do that." Wayne replied without losing eye contact. "What!...what da fuck is you saying you fucking muppet?!" "I said I ain't doing it, simple as. I'm looking to live my life in a different way. I hate that C's gone, believe dat!, but there's nothing I can do to bring him back, and I ain't about to do that to nobody." "You fucking asswipe!" Marcus replied shifting to centimetres from Wayne's face. Seething with rage he held his open palm millimetres from his temple, "You can turn the other cheek all fucking day long, but I beg you please, don't bring that shit here, cause I'm telling you blood, it's making me wonder what side of the fence you're on! And trust me when I say, that ain't a good spot for you to be in, cause you looking like a big pussy right now fam!" Wayne kissed his teeth and stood his ground. "It's not about turning the other cheek fool, it's about recognising the value of the life you're living, and of the life you want me to dash way!...I told you, I just see things differently now! We're not rubbish, your buying into the same shit your always vex with 'the man' for telling you blood!

Think about what you're doing blood, that's all I'm asking! You're acting ignorant, like you've bought into the idea hook line and sinker dread. Like my man Ade say, Wille Lynch wanted fatherless black children, uneducated black children so that we could remain dispensable. You are now helping him, you are now his foot soldier! Wake da fuck up Marcus! You're leading da boys astray!" The rest of the Millitants stood in silence, taken aback by Wayne's words. "That drama is over for me blood! I'm not gonna act the part created for me, I'm more than that, and I want more than that!"

The pupils of Marcus's eyes seemed to grow and darken as he looked at Wayne. "So the drama's over for you yeah? what just like that, you think you can switch it on and off like a fucking light bulb? So...what happens when you buck up on grief, what you gonna do then, cause you know say if you can't do for us we can't do for you right?!" Wayne shook his head but kept his eyes locked on Marcus. "And after I take out Bucky, then what, I know you don't think it's gonna be all hunky dory...whose gonna be next? Who...you Diggy, you Dollar or will it be you bad man?" Wayne continued softly cocking two fingers at Marcus's temple. "Or maybe you'll be after Dollar?...and how you gonna live whilst you're waiting your turn? What sleeping with one eye open? looking over your shoulder every minute, not planning for your future?" Wayne looked around at his squad, boys who just a few months ago swore friendship for life, now avoided eye contact. He hung his head, doubting in that split second that he was doing the right thing. Marcus pushed him hard on his shoulder. "So what's up...what's da play? Man ain't got all night yuh know!" Wayne stumbled backwards but steadied himself before he fell. Taking a deep breath, he positioned himself so he could eyeball Marcus and whisper into his ear. "Don't try to fuck with me Marcus, I got no problem crippling you." Wayne was shook. He could taste the fear at the back of his throat but he had no time to consider it. Marcus flung his head back and opened his mouth to laugh as if he'd just been told the best joke. "Hear dis fucking cretin!" he laughed. "Ah so you feel pussyhole?!" As he straightened his body he locked three fingers and held them up over Wayne's head.

Ellie saw the signal and her heart missed a beat. She knew what it meant, and didn't want to be around to see it. Before she could move, Marcus brought his elbow down, butting it into Wayne's throat before jabbing his closed fist across his temple. He stumbled and fell, coughing through the agony as his windpipe tried to recover from the crushing assault. He lay on the ground, clutching his throat and his head, as Marcus jumped from one leg to the other. "Shit man, I wasn't expecting it to be this easy...this ain't no fun man!" he laughed as he circled Wayne's foetal body. Wayne said nothing. Raising his fingers, Marcus gestured to his howling companions and in seconds Wayne was hidden beneath a canopy of flailing arms and legs. Ellie felt the air trap in her throat; breathless, she jumped off the swing wall, unnoticed by her companions. She made it to the corner before her legs gave way and she knelt down, allowing the vomit that waited at her throat since Marcus's first blow, to escape. She wiped her mouth with her jacket sleeve and looked behind her.

Everything seemed serene in the crisp night air until she focused in on the sounds of dull thuds, groans and frenzied voices. The remaining contents of her stomach forced it's way out and she wretched until her throat hurt and she struggled to catch her breath. Barely able to stand, Ellie forced herself to move off the estate, trying as hard as she could to delete the sight and sounds from her mind. She made it to the bus stop across the road and frantically awaited the bus, keeping one eye on the estate, praying her bus would come soon or at least before any THM emerged. By the time it did come, she tripped on the step in her eagerness to board. Unusually for her, she sat in the first corner seat at the bottom trying to hide herself amongst the other passengers. Noticing their stares, Ellie pulled on the strings of her hoodie, drawing it as tightly as she could to mask her face. She cried silently all the way home.

∞

Epilogue

Be the rider, not the horse. Gershon Hepner

Three weeks later, Ellie stood on Wayne's doorstep wondering if and how she should knock. It was the first time she'd been back to the estate since the night of the beat down, and it came back to her in vivid technicolour as she raised her hand to the letterbox. Anxious, nervous and scared, she heard the sound echo through the house. She was in two minds about running off when footsteps arrived at the front door, and it was too late as the door opened, and Wayne stood in front of her. On crutches and leaning against the doorframe was an unfamiliar familiar face. Ellie's pulse escalated as she took in the boy in front of her. In spite of his obvious injuries, he smiled widely when he saw her, and she grinned back like a Cheshire cat. At a loss for words, all she wanted to do was run into his arms, but guilt kept her feet rooted to the spot. He moved back from the door, creating space for her to enter and she grinned even wider. The pair, saying nothing but their grins, made their way to his room.

"I'm sorry Wayne" Ellie began, standing awkwardly in front his bedroom door. "Nothing to be sorry about babes!" he replied hoping on to his bed. "Come, sit down, it's good to see you man. How's Tasha?" he continued, pulling her closer to him on the bed. Ellie kissed her teeth and smiled at the same time. Her sister still blamed him for Cavell's death, and his refusal to seek revenge angered her beyond comprehension, refusing to speak to her if she contacted him, but Ellie didn't care. It was too late, she was in love. "She's alright, her cast is coming off tomorrow." She replied shying away from his eye contact. "Do you see them lot?" he asked, obviously interested in her reply. Ellie hung her head and picked a fingernail, "Nah, not since all that shit happened. So how you been, I'm kinda surprised you're still alive...happy though" she continued smiling widely.

Wayne grinned in agreement. "So what you gonna do now, have you seen them lot?" she asked timidly. He looked at her and exhaled. "You ever notlced the dude in the end house?" Ellie shook her head. He's just a couple years older than us, but you never see him hanging about on road or wearing anything that don't come from Primark!" Ellie laughed. "Nah for real though, he's always humble, going about his business, I'm not surprised you haven't noticed him. He told me he wants to be a doctor like his uncle, and so that's what he thinks about. He ain't got time for road drama so he don't think about it, he don't see himself there, he sees himself as a doctor.

His family and his peeps encourage him to see himself as a doctor, so the idea of becoming a doctor is familiar and comfortable, normal to him. That's why, despite coming from the ghetto, he believes he's gonna be a doctor and he's motivated towards it. He's in his third year now and he's on target to succeed.

The squad don't think like that dough. We wanna be on road, dress to impress, moving and shaking and getting respect. Ellie laughed out loud, feeling the truth in his words. "You follow me, we don't see ourselves as doctors, so we're not motivated to become doctors. I was too busy focusing on trying to be cool and fit in, that's what I was motivated to do. I didn't have a serious goal to take up my thinking time, so I wasn't headed anywhere and that's why it was so easy for me to get caught up in all that shit." Wayne paused and Ellie squeezed his hand. "I used to blame the manor, five-o, the gangs, white people, even my school, but I know now, they can only affect me if I keep their shit in my mind!

I want a f-a-b-u-l-o-u-s life, trust me babe, but I don't want to fuck anybody up getting to it, and I don't have to! I want to experience my life to the fullest, not just modelling round Hackney with THM and distressing a man for showing me screw face. There's so much more Ellie, that's a speck compared to what's out there, and I can't let that fuck up everything else for me...or take my life. Too fucking great to waste! Too fucking great to just fall by the wayside, you feel me!" Wayne grinned wanting her to understand him and most of all to know that he wasn't a coward.

I got big plans El. I know exactly where I want to be in five years' time and what I have to do to get there. I spend a little time everyday thinking about it, and why I want it. I don't worry about how I'm gonna do it, I just think about it till I can see it clearly in my mind. I meditate every day and its been weeding out the shit I've ingrained about who I thought I was and my place in life. It's been inspiring, guiding and calming me into what I need to focus on. Most of all I've been appreciating, from the fact that I'm still breathing, to my mum's saltfish and cassava, I am fucking grateful!" Wayne shouted jovially.

"Ellie everybody's supposed to have a good life, including us. It's not just for the rich, the pretty or the talented; it just depends on how we see our self, the thoughts we nurture and the habits we keep. Look, Jay-z made a habit of rapping, probably thought about it every day and now he's successful at it and he enjoys it and will always have a hit. A crack head made a habit of smoking crack, probably thought about every day and now he's also successful at it and will always come up with a rock. It's all about where you put your attention babes, where your focus is. I'm thinking about what kind of life I want to have, not how much I don't have or what dramas are going down. I'm thinking about all the experiences I want, regardless of what I see around me every day. I know now, there's nothing that's outside my reach, it's all about what I keep in my mind and how I see myself.

Ellie was mesmerized, noticing for the first time the light behind his deep brown eyes. His words inflamed her imagination. Inspiration and admiration coursed through her being, causing goose bumps to ripple across her skin. For the first time in a long time, Ellie felt eager for life.

To learn more about the topics discussed in this book, or to leave a comment, question or open a discussion, please go to Facebook: The Salvation of Perception

Printed in Great Britain
by Amazon